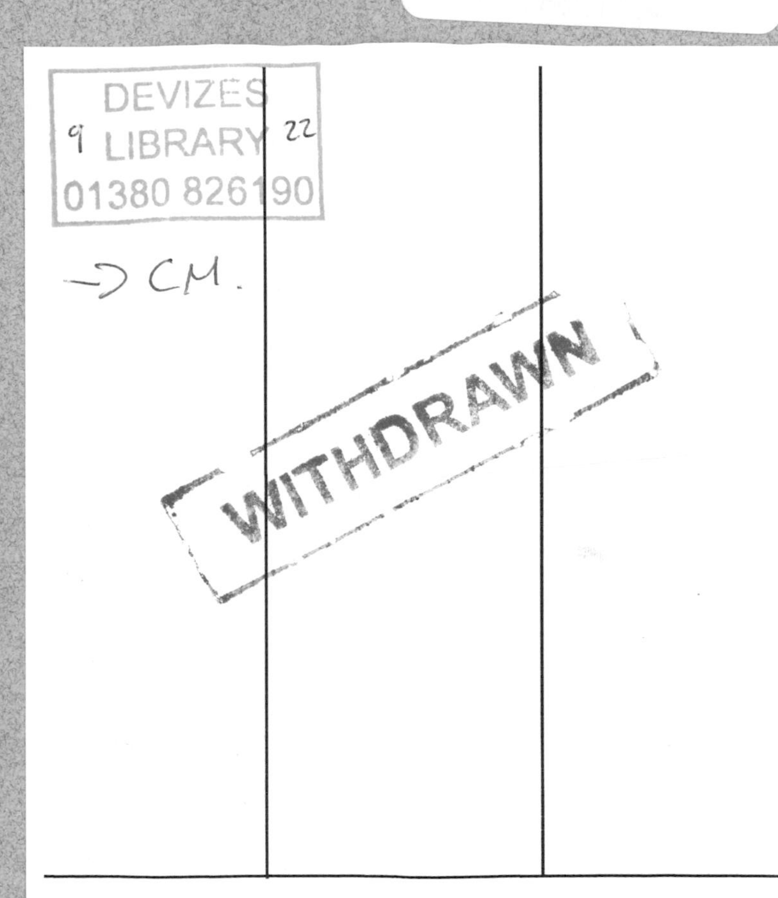
DEVIZES
9 LIBRARY 22
01380 826190
-> CM.
WITHDRAWN

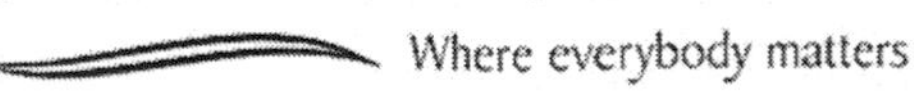
Where everybody matters

Undercurrent

By the same author

FICTION

Five Rivers Met on a Wooded Plain

Turning for Home

The Vanishing Hours

THEATRE

Visitors

Eventide

Echo's End

While We're Here

Nightfall

We Started to Sing

The Remains of the Day *(after Ishiguro)*

Blood Wedding *(after Lorca)*

The Wellspring *(with David Owen Norris)*

Undercurrent

Barney Norris

doubleday

TRANSWORLD PUBLISHERS
Penguin Random House, One Embassy Gardens,
8 Viaduct Gardens, London SW11 7BW
www.penguin.co.uk

Transworld is part of the Penguin Random House group of companies
whose addresses can be found at global.penguinrandomhouse.com

First published in Great Britain in 2022 by Doubleday
an imprint of Transworld Publishers

A CIP catalogue record for this book
is available from the British Library.

ISBN 9780857525734

Typeset in 11/15pt ITC Giovanni by Jouve (UK), Milton Keynes.
Printed and bound in Great Britain by Clays Ltd, Elcograf S.p.A.

The authorized representative in the EEA is Penguin Random House Ireland,
Morrison Chambers, 32 Nassau Street, Dublin D02 YH68.

Penguin Random House is committed to a sustainable
future for our business, our readers and our planet. This book
is made from Forest Stewardship Council® certified paper.

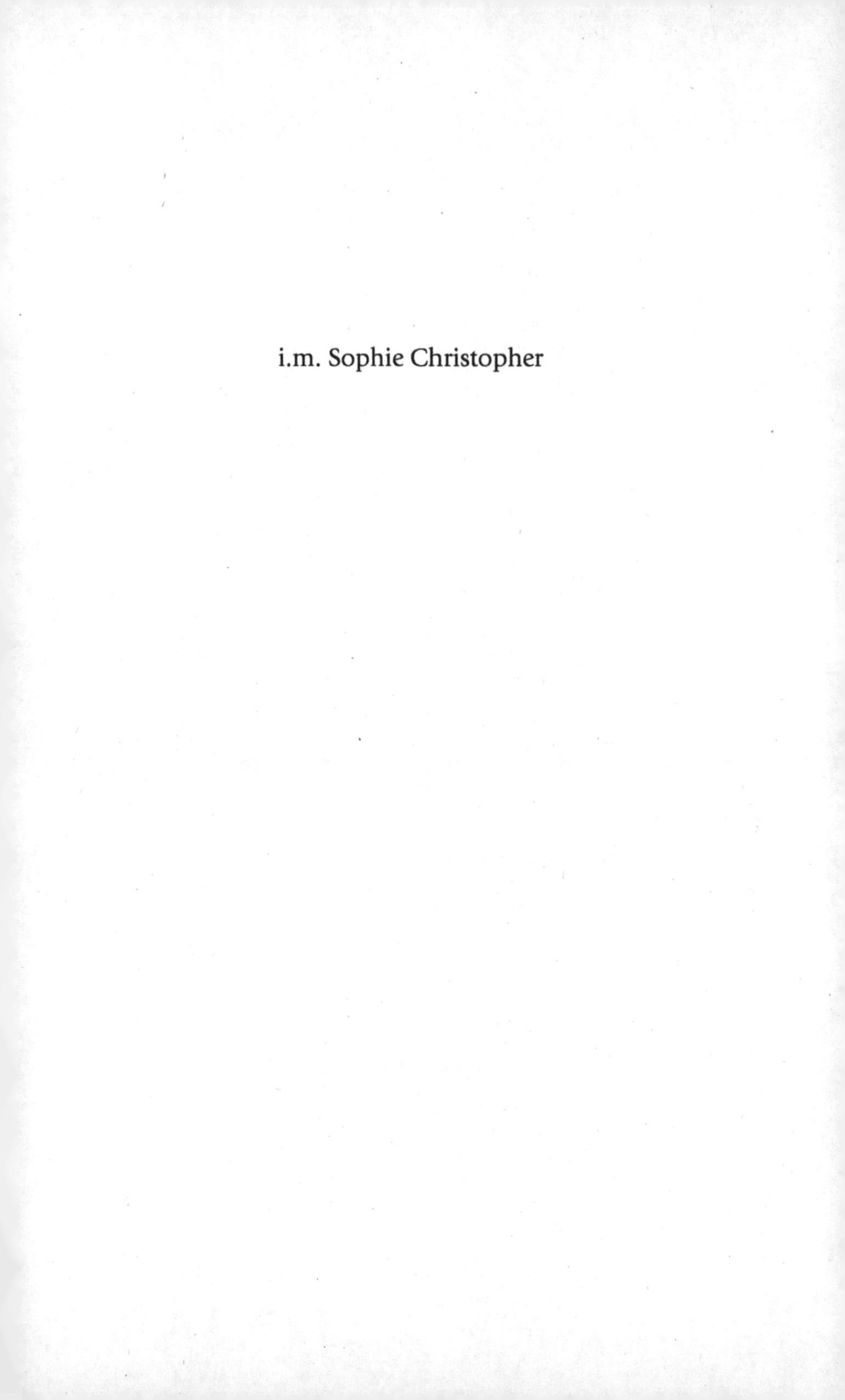

i.m. Sophie Christopher

Show me again the day
When from the sandy bay
We looked together upon the pestered sea! –
Yea, to such surging, swaying, sighing, swelling,
  shrinking,
Love lures life on.

Thomas Hardy, 'Lines to a Movement
in Mozart's E-Flat Symphony'

2019

A WEDDING IN APRIL. Most people wouldn't risk it, but there are discounts to be had, and Leah and Richard have been lucky: the weather's held off and the tents covering the tables and bar and the place where the band will play are unruffled by this still day. On the gravel drive outside the big house that's been rented for the reception, Juliet and I mill around among a hundred other guests, a mixture of friends and strangers, all bored and wanting to get through the photos so we can sit down to eat. We're at an age when weddings seem to happen every other weekend in summer, so even if an April wedding might be a change, the day still feels familiar in its rhythms: the ceremony, the drive to the reception, the photos, the speeches, the drinking, the food – pizzas or hog roast or cheese and biscuits, and cutting the cake – the band, the Airbnb at the end of the evening, drunk sex, a hangover the next morning, driving home to a takeaway in front of the TV.

On the regular occasions when Juliet and I arrive at these days, attending the weddings of friends and relations, enjoying some things, raising eyebrows at others, I often wonder how much she thinks about the day we'll get married, whenever that may be, if that day is going to come. The thought always preoccupies me at these times, but we never seem to talk about it, not in any depth. We'll critique the wedding favours on a table, perhaps, or note the cheap wine, maybe say we'd never serve anything like that ourselves, but the conversation never goes any further. I suppose we've both known ever since we moved in together that marriage would be the next logical step. So perhaps we are poised on the rim of that next chapter in our lives, and trying to work out when to jump.

It's been on my mind for a while that I should make the next move, buy a ring. I only ever want to do it once, though, so I'm taking this thought slowly, letting it creep up on me, letting it grow. I might as well marry beautifully. So I've been saving money, a little here and a little there, and trying to work out how to do it right. It's not the easiest thing to do if you're a copywriter, saving for a wedding. Not if you're paying rent in the city, and your girlfriend likes date night, and date night is always a hundred quid of dinner and wine and a taxi back home, and I suppose I've let thoughts of money slow me down, an excuse to put off getting on with life. Because we never talk about the idea of getting married, I have no clear hints to work on as to what kind of ring I ought to be buying, either, or where I ought to kneel down and propose. So I've let that slow me down too. More reasons to let time drift by, just letting it happen to me, rather than me doing very much with it. We just go from one wedding to another, as if we're glimpsing our own future, hidden in shards among other people's days.

'She keeps looking at you,' Juliet says. I turn to her.

'Who?'

'The photographer. Look, she's looking right at you – see?'

I turn and follow Juliet's gaze in time to see the young woman, standing on a stepladder preparing to take a photograph of everyone, suddenly look away from me and up to the sky as if she's worried about the weather or the light. I almost missed the moment, but as I watch the photographer stare fixedly into the blue, I can tell that Juliet is right. I turned, and the girl was looking right at me. She's attractive, about the same age as us, dark-haired, slender. She looks like a yoga instructor, and hasn't dressed up in wedding clothes. Instead of making her seem shabby, this somehow has the effect of making everyone around her in formal dresses or suits and ties look slightly ludicrous, as if they're wearing their parents' things. It always amazes me just how far into life the feeling persists that everyone you know is only really playing at being grown up. Here we are in our thirties, inheriting the earth maybe, and I still feel as if everyone I know is putting it on.

The girl on the stepladder doesn't look like that, though. She seems at ease, set apart from the crowd, and not just because she's standing above them. As I watch her, she looks back my way again, and smiles, then turns away to talk to one of the best men, who's trying to organise us.

'See?' Juliet asks me.

'I saw, yeah.'

'Who is she?'

'I have no idea.'

'Looks like you've pulled, then.'

I glance quickly at Juliet. Her neck is flushed, and I can see that she's unhappy. The idea that, of all the young men at this wedding, I might be the one the beautiful photographer fancies is patently ludicrous to me, but things like this make Juliet uncomfortable. I put my arm around her and kiss her on the cheek.

'I think it's more likely I've got something in my teeth,' I say.

The joke's not very good, but she smiles nonetheless and pushes me away from her. 'Either that or your flies are undone.'

Then the best man is shouting for our attention, so we turn back to face forwards, ready to be captured for ever as part of this group who were here on this day. Whatever becomes of us all, this happened, we had this much in common, all of us here. My eyes are drawn again to the beautiful young woman on the stepladder, and once again she is looking at me. Some men might be used to this kind of attention. Some might be comfortable with the idea they're attractive to other people. I'm not one of those people, and can't help wondering as we smile and throw hats and plastic cups into the air what the explanation for that look might be. I'm surrounded by beautiful people. It's not going to be that. How could it be?

When the big group photo has been taken, the bride and groom and their families and whoever else wander off with the photographer to be captured in smaller groups down by the river, and Juliet and I drift away from the drive and the front of the house to scrutinise the seating plan and find our way over to our table.

'Was it just that she caught *you* looking at *her*?' Juliet asks.

'Sorry?'

'She's very attractive. Perhaps you were looking at her, and she noticed.'

'Seriously?' Juliet looks at me, and there's an atmosphere

between us now, as unfair as that seems. 'I'm here with you at our friends' wedding. I'm not eyeing up the barmaids, I'm not eyeing up the photographer. Don't worry. It's all right.'

Juliet shrugs and looks away. 'I'd understand, is all I was going to say,' she says. 'Looking isn't buying.'

We find our table and sit down together, saying very little till some of our friends find us and sit down on either side. The thought of the photographer has fixed in my mind. I can only half concentrate on the conversations going on around me, because I'm wondering whether I could have seen her before somewhere, wondering why she was looking at me, and whether there'll be a moment this evening when we have an opportunity to meet and speak. It doesn't seem to me that this would be disloyal. Isn't it natural to be interested in someone who shows an interest in you? Isn't it natural to wonder what they're thinking? Under the table I reach out and take Juliet's hand, and she lets me hold it for a moment, then takes it away, and smiles at me, briefly resting the same hand on my arm just below my shoulder.

'Too hot,' she says. And I smile, but I know she's unhappy, because it isn't hot under the tents at all. It's neither my fault nor Juliet's, not really, but something strange has happened and I know we're not going to feel close to each other today. Whenever she encounters things that make her uncomfortable, Juliet's reaction is always to withdraw. I don't know whether I'm the same; perhaps I am. It means our unhappiness always makes us feel alone when it comes, because we're careful to hide it, not to share it with each other.

We all eat together, and then there are some awful speeches, actually quite memorably awful speeches because the groom has appointed four best men, all of whom perform a forfeit in the course of the hour they spend talking to us, which involves downing shots and the singing of songs. Then music starts up, and the guests dance while the tables are cleared and the cake is brought out to be cut. That being done, we all eat the cut cake, then start to get bored till the drink kicks in and a band begins playing and the evening flows more quickly after that.

After half an hour of dancing, once we've worked up a sweat, Juliet and I walk away from the party, down to the bottom of the grounds, past the swimming pool and the tennis court and the little walled garden, till we come to the lake that marks the edge of the park; beyond it, there are cattle cropping the grass in the next field. There's a pontoon jutting out from the side of the lake into the water, and tied to the end of the pontoon is a rowing boat no one's thought to store away while the wedding's going on. It seems to me that the presence of this boat might become dangerous as the night goes on, if anyone finds it once they've had a few drinks. Then I feel disappointed at myself for responding to the boat in that way; why think of the dangers when I could dream instead of launching out on this water?

It occurs to me that the situation Juliet and I find ourselves in gives us the opportunity to be one of three kinds of people. We could worry about the boat, and fret, go and find the people who live in the house, and tell them they ought to store it away; that would make us responsible, rational, grown-up, absolutely divorced from the kids we used to be. Or we could do nothing, which I suspect is what most people would do, just take in the pontoon and the boat at the end of it, perhaps even walk out to get a closer look down into the water for a moment, but then step back and walk away, leaving the boat lying silent in the water. Or, there is a third thing. Perhaps the most irresponsible thing. Perhaps the least sensible or adult or logical. Which would be to get into the boat and cast off and row round the little lake for a short while. Thinking these options through, it seems to me that this is the choice you'd make if you still wanted to be young; if you still wanted as much of life as you could get, all it could offer you; if you still thought the reason you were here was to seek adventure. I turn to Juliet, her face only half visible in the dark now we've walked away from the lights of the party. It's early still, the moon is not yet up.

'Shall we go out on the water?' I ask.

She laughs. 'Why?'

'Might be fun. They've left the boat out.'

'Not because they want people to use it.'

'No one could possibly see us out here, though; we'd be fine.'

'That's not the point, though, is it?'

'Come on. It'll be like Bridget Jones.'

'No it won't, it's dangerous. Let's go back, come on.'

'Just quickly, come on.'

'Ed, I don't want to. Let's go back,' she says. I shrug, admit defeat. But I don't want to go back with her just yet. This thought snags in me slightly. I wonder what it means. It's not the first time this idea has come to me in the last few months.

It occurs to me as we stand there by the lake in the dark, a moment that ought to mean something, that ought to be happy, a secret we ought to feel like we're sharing, that some kind of link seems to have unthreaded between us. I look at the woman I've been living with for six years and realise that sometime in the past year I stopped feeling like we were really together. And I realise I've known this for a while now. I just haven't quite acknowledged the feeling. I think of the way we've been falling asleep the last few months; both of us have started turning our backs to each other. I'd noticed it, been aware of it. I hadn't drawn any inference from it till this moment. But I've been waking up at the edge of the bed for some time now, and I realise suddenly that it has to mean something. We used to hold each other in different shapes. Now, unless there's sex, we sleep alone on different sides of our shared mattress. And what does that mean? Can you find your way back from that? I don't know exactly what we've stopped sharing. Unless it's love. Whatever love might be. I wonder whether it's something to do with weddings; we're not so young, after all, and things aren't so new between us. Was there a tide we missed a while back, when we should have done more than just live together? Should it have been the two of us in front of everyone, or is that a stupid thought? I look at Juliet and can't tell what's missing. But I think she knows it's not there, too. At least that's something we're sharing.

'I'll follow you in a minute,' I tell her.

'Why?'

'Don't worry. I'll catch you up.'

'What's your problem?'

'Nothing. I'll just catch you up in a minute, all right? I just want to stay out here in the quiet for a while.' She shrugs, and I can see that I've annoyed her. We're not in the same key today, somehow. I can see now that I made a mistake ever thinking she'd want to get in the boat with me. Juliet's life runs on train tracks, and isn't easily diverted; surprises don't delight her, she doesn't like trying new things, she likes comfort and security, as I suppose most people do. As I suppose I do, mostly. But something about the lake has caught my attention, some deep silence.

'Suit yourself.' Juliet walks away from me and goes off to dance with our friends, and I'm alone in the dark. I turn back to the pontoon and walk along it to the end. The night sky reflects off the still surface of the water. I watch it rippling gently under me. I have stopped being happy somewhere along the way. When did that happen? And what am I going to do about it?

I get into the boat and the ripples of its movement spread to the edge of the water. The oars are stored in the bottom of the boat. I take them out and fix them in the rowlocks before untying the rope attaching the boat to the pontoon and taking an oar in each hand. Leaning forwards to reach for the first stroke, I launch myself through a new element out into the night. The idea comes to me that it might be as easy as this to leave my old life and go looking for a new one. Letting go of one's unhappiness might be as simple as pushing away from a lakeside pontoon. Cutting through new water till you reach another world.

When I've done a circuit of the lake and tied the boat up again, I head back to the party, and skirt round the edge of the festivities, a little downcast, because somehow I feel as if I've done something wrong, though I don't know quite what. In the back of my mind the thought is keening faintly that when

I got back on to the pontoon after rowing, I stepped into a different world. Something intangible about this place is different – or rather, it could be if I chose it to be so. A band playing at a wedding always sounds to me like the saddest thing in the world. The noise of our lives passing. Or perhaps it's just that I never learned the trick of having fun, and moments like this remind me there are aspects of life I miss entirely.

I collapse on a sofa someone has put out in one of the dining tents furthest from the marquee where the band is playing and the guests are dancing. It must have been put there for the elderly to get away from all the noise, but for now everyone more advanced in years is dancing with their kids. That's where she comes and finds me, the photographer, the girl who kept looking at me earlier.

Through the open side of the tent I watch her approaching across the lawn, cutting through the guests, her eyes fixed on me all the time as she approaches. I watch her figure in the clothes she is wearing, wide linen trousers, silk shirt, her dark hair flowing down over her shoulders. She is wearing sandals and her feet are wet. She sits down on the sofa, then turns away from me, looking instead across the lawn at the band and the dancers visible through the marquee's open sides. I turn as well, following her gaze, looking out across the night.

'Hi.'

'Hello.'

'My name's Ed.'

She smiles at me. 'I'm Amy.'

'I thought I caught your eye earlier.'

'You did.'

'Do you know them?' I point to Richard and Leah, the bride and groom, who are dancing together to the band's cover of 'Teenage Dirtbag'.

'No, I'm just a wedding photographer. They found me online. I've got to know them since, but I don't *know* them.'

We watch the dancing for a moment before she speaks again. 'Do you like Laurie Lee?'

'Sorry?' Her question is so unexpected that for a moment I don't know who she means.

'Laurie Lee. Have you read him? *Cider with Rosie*.'

'Oh. Yes, I have. Yes, I do.'

'I want to tell you a story about him.'

I can't quite work out what's going on. It's impossibly surreal to me, that this girl wants to talk to me, but only about poets.

'Go on.'

She smiles, and leans towards me, so that she's looking past, lips close to my ear as she speaks. The words become secrets only for me, and I feel the heat of her breath on my cheek as she tells her story while Chinese lanterns are lit on the lawn before us and released into the clear night air.

'Not all of the stories about Laurie Lee are beautiful,' she says, 'because he liked women a *lot*, so a lot of stories about him have a very similar narrative. Benny Hill stories, if you know what I mean. But as well as chasing girls, Laurie Lee also liked to take his violin into pubs and play to people. And one night, in the crowd where he was playing, he noticed a very beautiful young woman. A girl really, no more than about eighteen. She was standing at the back of the audience gathered round him, and didn't seem to know anyone else there, and she looked at him very intently all the time he played. Of course, he wanted to play it cool, like he hadn't noticed. I quite like that about Laurie Lee; he still played the game that women might want to go to bed with him well into his seventies. So he kept going with the tunes, and then when the barman called time, he saw the girl who'd been watching him turn and walk out of the pub. And suddenly he was seized by this fierce feeling that he had to speak to her, and she was leaving before he'd had the chance. So he called after her. "Have we met before somewhere?" he asked. And she smiled. "We have," she said. "I'm your daughter."'

Amy shifts and crosses her legs, angling her body away from me as she leans back against the arm of the sofa, and I want to ask her why she's telling me this story, but I don't speak because I'm afraid that if I interrupt her she'll stop talking and the spell will be broken. She looks at me and carries on. 'Laurie Lee, you see, had had a daughter with the wife of another man years earlier. He'd known her while she was small, but then when she was five or six, he stopped talking to her mother and they lost touch. This was her. Her mother had never mentioned who her father really was, but she'd seen Laurie Lee on the TV one day and thought, "That man's my father." Apparently, people sometimes just know. I don't know why. Maybe she'd already heard stories, and knew her mum had known Laurie Lee, and something about him made sense to her. So she went to see him play the violin one evening. And they knew each other for the rest of his life. Can you imagine that? Wouldn't that be the strangest life? I don't think I'd ever get used to it. I thought of that story when I saw you today.'

I try to work out what she means.

'Why? Do I remind you of your father, or Laurie Lee?'

She smiles and says nothing to that, simply leaning further back into the sofa, comfortable now, relaxed.

'I'm talking too much,' she says.

'You're not.'

She smiles at this, as if she doesn't believe me. 'There was a point,' she says. 'But I've started on the wrong foot.'

'No, you haven't,' I say. 'What were you meaning to tell me?'

'You sure you want to hear?'

'Absolutely. Go on.'

She takes a breath, searches the night sky above her for the thread of the thought she's been unspooling. Then seems to find it again, and continues, this time looking up and not at me, as if the whole experience is suddenly painful, as if she's trying not to cry.

'Reunions don't always go as well as that, though,' she says. 'When I met my birth father, it was very different. I assumed it would be a good thing to do. But not many people will give up a child for adoption if they're in a good place. I went and saw him when I was eighteen, as soon as I was allowed to, basically. I thought it would help me understand who I was. My adoptive parents had told me all along that I had once been another couple's child, and that always nagged at me while I was growing up. I always thought it must mean there were things about myself I wouldn't be able to understand until I knew the whole story. I think that really affected me, growing up. I did all kinds of things I regret. It was an excuse, really. I told myself that justified pretty much whatever I wanted to do. It was stupid. I fucked up my A levels and it meant I didn't go to university. So when I turned eighteen, I thought it would be good to snap out of that. It would be good for this not to be a mystery any more, so that I could make whatever decision I needed to make about who I really was, and get on with whatever my life was going to be. So I got access to my birth certificate. I already knew my birth mother had died while she was having me, and that was basically why I'd been given away. But my birth father was still around, so I wrote to him, and he wrote back. My adoptive parents, my real parents, knew all about it; they were supportive. Cautious, of course, but they understood it was something I needed to do. So I went. He lived in a horrible little town by the sea, in this empty little flat in a council building, and he had no possessions, really, a couple of kitchen chairs and an old armchair and a fridge. He let me in and I wanted to recognise him like Laurie Lee's daughter recognised her father, but it wasn't like that. He was just a man I felt sorry for when I saw him. I didn't feel much connection at all. He was quite a tall man, and furtive, very distant; he didn't like making eye contact with me. When he saw me, he just cried. He just burst into tears.'

As I watch her, I see the memory of the day take over, see the tears start in her eyes. '"My God," he said. "My God, you look just like her." And I guessed he meant my mum. I didn't know what to say. I almost felt like I should apologise, because the way I looked had upset him.'

She pauses for a moment, breathing deeply.

I guess this must feel like someone walking on her grave.

The shiver of glimpsing the life she didn't have, the different person she might have been if she had been brought up by her birth parents. And how would that have changed them? What different lives would they have lived then? The possibilities become too many to take in at once. And the ghost lives that pass before your eyes in these moments are like very beautiful, very sad music. I find myself thinking of my own father, the last times we spent together before he died, and how keenly I wished things had been different then. I guess this young woman must be feeling something similar. Keenly aware of the lives she hadn't lived. She steels herself, goes on.

'I'd never thought of that before, you see. Because of course no one ever said I looked like my adoptive parents. So I'd never thought before about the way I walked round all the time actually looking like someone else. I still can't get my head round that, not really. My father invited me in and I sat down on one of the chairs. He put the kettle on, and apologised for the bareness of the house; he'd just been let out of prison and he was getting his life back together again, he said. He made me tea, and sat down in the other chair, and apologised for crying when he saw me, but he didn't even have a photo of my mum any more so it had come as a shock to see her again. That was the way he said it, "see her again". I was wondering all of a sudden whether he'd actually bought the chairs so that he could have me over, something about the way he sat down in them, something about the way they were positioned in the middle of the room with nothing to lean on, no table, not so much as a windowsill or anything, made me feel like they'd been specially set there, and he wasn't used to them. I felt so sorry for him then. This man was trying his best, he'd done what he could to be hospitable, and it was just crap, it wasn't nice at all, even though he'd tried. And I hadn't been gracious about it, I hadn't said anything about his flat being nice and clean or tried to make it OK between us. When it was very clean, actually; he must have hoovered and scrubbed all morning getting it ready for me to come round. And then I realised that this had been a terrible idea. I'm normally very careful about letting people into my life. Because once something's happened between two people, and it doesn't have to be a big thing – it could just be a coffee or a talk on a sofa in the middle of the night, or it could just be that you take the photos at their wedding – but once that's happened you have a kind of secret together. You've shared something no two other people have ever shared in exactly the same way. And that can last a whole life, it can bind you. But it was too late to back out of it by then. So I talked to him. I asked him about his life. And it was clear he'd been destroyed by the death of my mother. He gave me up for adoption. He had a job but he lost it, and then he assaulted a police officer one Saturday night – I got the impression he'd become quite a violent drunk – and was put away for a couple of years because of that. Then he'd come out of prison and got on with his life for a while, and actually things had been a bit better, he'd cut down the drink and the drugs and stayed in the one job, doing shelves at a branch of Tesco's, and he had an OK flat, better than the one we were sitting in now, he said. But then it went wrong again somehow. He beat someone up and went back to prison for another few years. I listened to him talking and it was just awful. I couldn't believe this was my dad.'

'I'm so sorry,' I say.

She shrugs and smiles. 'Yeah. It was hard. I envy Laurie Lee and his daughter.'

'Do you still keep in touch?'

'I do, yeah. I don't go and see him so much. But he's doing all right. Actually, he's doing better.'

'That's good.'

'I think it helped him to meet me, somehow. He'd never regretted giving me up for adoption, he said. Because it meant I'd had a better life, whereas he was sure he couldn't have offered me anything. But when he met me, I think that connected him with a part of his own life he'd lost when I left.'

'Did the same happen for you?'

'That's the sad thing. Absolutely not. I didn't learn anything about myself. Except that he said everyone had loved my mum, and she'd been very striking. That was nice, I suppose. And I realised what a complete idiot I'd been for the last few years, telling myself I could do anything I liked or as little as I liked, because I didn't really know who I was, so nothing really counted. That was always bollocks, it was always an excuse. Meeting him didn't make anything clearer. It actually made things stranger, I think.'

'Why stranger?'

'Just thinking of the other person I might have been. And having to confront how fortunate I'd been. And wondering where that other me was, and not being quite able to shake the thought that she existed in another ghost life somewhere else.'

'And can I ask you a question?'

'Go on.'

'Why are you telling me all this? I don't mean to sound rude. It's interesting. I'm interested. But I get the feeling there's a connection I haven't worked out yet.'

'Oh yeah,' she laughs, and her smile strikes me like an electric charge. 'Yeah, I should tell you about that.'

'I think you're about to say we've met before somewhere.'

'That's right. Can you remember where?'

'Not at all. I think I'd remember you if we'd met. I'm worried you might have the wrong person.'

She laughs then.

'I haven't,' she says. 'It just so happens that I looked you up not all that long ago. Just going down memory lane, you know? And I was looking at the photo list for this wedding yesterday and your name caught my eye and I thought it would be the weirdest coincidence if it was actually you. So I looked you up again last night, actually, then I saw you today and I knew it was you.'

'How do you know me, then?'

'Well, unless I've got this really wrong, I think you saved me from drowning when I was six years old.'

Memory rushes in. I look in amazement at her. I haven't thought of that day in a very long time. It comes back to me now like a dream after waking.

'That was you?'

'It was. I was thinking about it a couple of years ago. And I knew your name, because there was a little article about it in the local paper – do you remember?'

'I do. I've got the cutting somewhere.'

'So have I. I found it in a folder one day and I thought, "I wonder what became of him?" And I looked you up. So when I saw you in the crowd today, I knew it was you.'

A childhood holiday, ten years old. We'd gone to a town with a stretch of beach and a kind of swimming pool carved into the rock just below the high-tide line, I suppose because sometimes it got too choppy to swim in the sea. We'd been swimming in the pool quite a lot. The weather had been beautiful that whole week, and we'd spent a lot of time jumping into the pool then climbing out to dry off, lying on the rocks and looking out to sea. Then as the day waned and it got too cold, we'd walk back towards our holiday house along the beach or up over the rocks and the cliffs above it, and get chips from the little café by the car park, and eat them on the sand or in the car or once we got home. It might have been the most perfect holiday we ever had; my sister Rachel was only three years old, and I remember I loved those early years, following her progress as she learned to walk and talk, and seemed to turn into a proper person before my very eyes as if her life was some kind of magic trick. It was a lovely thing to be ten and have a sister whose wonder at everything could entertain you all day, but who would also go to bed early and leave you with time to play on your own, or go exploring round the garden or the now quiet rooms of the holiday home.

The day I saved Amy, though, Rachel had been playing up. This was probably the only reason the whole thing happened. We'd gone to the sea, and set up camp down on the sand because it was low tide and the beach stretched out for ever, but it was a hot day, and after an hour or so Rachel had begun to grizzle. We held out till lunch, eating the sandwiches we'd brought down with us in a picnic basket, followed by ice creams and cold drinks from the café by the beach, but by that time my sister was screaming, and Mum was losing patience and must have felt that all the other families on the beach were looking at us. So she decided to go back to the holiday house with my sister, in the hope that Rachel would be quieter if she could get out of the heat. Chris, my step-dad, offered to take my sister back instead, but I think Mum had had enough of the whole thing by then, the baking-hot sand and the time passing slowly as we all took turns to have a dip into the sea to cool ourselves off, so she said she'd go, and Chris could stay behind with me.

We helped her pack up and walked back with her as far as the café, then once we'd seen them off Chris suggested we move our camp, as the sun was beating down on the beach and we needed to look for some shade. He suggested we try the swimming pool in the rock. I wanted to go to the loos in the café first, so Chris said I should meet him by the pool when I was done.

As I came to the swimming pool, a movement in the water caught my eye. At the shaded end of the pool, out of the light and a little distance from any other swimmer, a child was swimming on her own. The end of the pool she was swimming in, being in shadow, was nearly empty; anyone who had got into the pool was trying to swim in the sun. No one seemed to be swimming with the child, who I could see now was a young girl, and who was splashing around a couple of feet from the edge of the pool without any armbands on. As I watched her, hardly concentrating on her because I was making my way round the pool and watching my step so I didn't fall in, it suddenly struck me that there was something uncoordinated and urgent about the way the girl was swimming. Even as I watched, I saw her head dip under the water. As I started to wonder whether she was really swimming at all, and might in fact be in some difficulty, my foot slipped on a slick patch of rock by the side of the pool, and I fell headfirst into the water, straight towards the girl I had been watching.

I realised before I hit the water what must have happened. The little girl had been walking round the pool like me, not looking properly at where she was going, just as I hadn't, and she had stepped on the same slick rock and fallen in. She wasn't swimming at all, and somehow no one had noticed she was missing, no one had seen her slip. As I plunged into the pool and salt water rushed into my nose and my eyes, I thrashed my arms and legs till I was the right way up in the water, and looked about, thinking I should call to someone who could help the girl, only to breathe in a lungful of seawater and find I couldn't speak. It was as I coughed this up that it occurred to me perhaps the person best placed to rescue the drowning child might actually be me. She was only a couple of strokes away, struggling underwater still – she must have been under for a few seconds now, and I worried she'd be breathing in water just as I had. So I swam over to the girl and grabbed her as best I could, manipulating her flailing limbs till her head came back up to the surface again, where she took a deep, desperate breath and started to scream. Now several adults looked over towards us, and I cried for help as best I could, finding that I was being pushed below the surface by the girl as she tried to scrabble away from danger. The next thing I knew, strong hands took hold of us both, and we were dragged forcibly through the resisting water and out on to the ledge around the pool. Chris had arrived by then, and rushed over to me where I sat and coughed up the last of the seawater I'd breathed in. The little girl's parents held their child, clearly in shock, a desperate panic setting in just as the emergency had passed because they'd only just discovered she'd been in danger.

I was accorded hero status for saving the child, who hadn't been able to swim, and shouldn't have taken off her armbands, and shouldn't have been walking on her own round the dark side of the pool without her parents, of course. One of the people who'd helped us both out of the water called the local paper to report the daring rescue, and I was both proud and embarrassed to see my name appear in print a couple of days later. The paper came out the day we were leaving to travel home, and Mum and Chris were triumphant, holding it up like a kind of trophy. This was too much for me, and I started to cry. They asked me why I wasn't pleased that I'd been recognised for my bravery in saving the little girl, and I said that I was, I was very pleased, but I thought I hadn't been honest as well, because I hadn't really saved her, I'd just fallen in and tried to save her but then discovered that I couldn't, and I didn't want to get in trouble for not telling the whole truth. This made Mum and Chris laugh, which confused me; but they told me there was no way that I could get in trouble, and when we got home, Mum gave me a rosette like the ones you get for horse-riding competitions, and said it was for bravery, and that I should keep it as a memento.

As for the girl I saved, I never spoke a word to her. She was quickly taken away by her parents, who were both terrified to discover how close she'd been to death, and mortified not to have noticed she was missing. Her name wasn't included in the article that mentioned me, as I suppose thinking back that the parents hadn't wanted social services reading what had happened, and I had forgotten all about her by the end of that summer, really. Years later, when I moved away from home, I had found the rosette Mum gave me, and remembered the day, and felt a little proud, I admit, because I realised that the situation might have been more dangerous than I realised. I kept the rosette because of that. But it was stored away in a box in the attic at Mum and Chris's farm, a buried memory; it wasn't like I took it out to look at all the time.

'That's extraordinary,' I say.

'I don't know,' Amy replies.

'Why?'

'Well, it just seems natural to me, somehow. It seems almost inevitable that we should meet again.'

Amy tells me she only dimly remembers the whole thing: a sense of panic, a sense she was going to die. She built up a picture of what happened through what other people had told her about it, her adoptive parents above all, who used the story to justify keeping her on a short lead for a while, and then, as time went by, made the story into something they could all laugh about. In their version, I was the hero who jumped in to save her. When I tell her I slipped just like she did, and my rescue attempt was more or less an accident, she's delighted. It seems wonderful to her to hear an old piece of family history reinterpreted so differently after so many years. These stories are how we understand ourselves, after all, she says – the scraps from which we build our ideas of who we are, of family and home. There's something magical to her about discovering this story might be made up, and that by implication every story she has used to work out who she is might also be a form of fiction as well.

We continue talking together on the sofa in the tent on the edge of the lawn for half an hour, till Juliet comes and finds me, clearly alarmed to see me sitting with Amy away from the rest of the guests, the photographer she suspected I was eyeing up a few hours ago. Amy is quick to explain the connection between us before Juliet even has the opportunity to ask; then she stands up, tells us both it was nice to meet us, and slips away.

Juliet watches me. 'You saved her life?'

'Sort of. Not really.'

She looks away. I try to speak as nonchalantly as I can, throw away the significance of that conversation, because as Amy walks back to the party, looking back once to smile at me, I feel suddenly certain it is very significant indeed, and I need to hide that, set that aside, wait till I have time to work out what it means and what might be happening.

'Small world,' Juliet says. The skin around her mouth is tight, and her eyes seem hard and dark as she looks away from me and over at the marquee where the guests are still dancing. And suddenly I wonder whether the reason I've held back from proposing to her these last few years might not really be that I'm saving up money; suddenly I wonder whether that's a lie, and the reason I've held back is something else, some absence I've known was there and never been able to name before tonight. I look at Juliet, and the possibility creeps up on me that I've had it wrong for years.

Strange, how these moments of clarity arrive, how they always comes so suddenly, how it's never when you'd think. Have I been a coward all this time for having known deep down there was something missing between us, perhaps even love, and not raising the issue, not saying anything? Have I spoiled this with my own detachment, which Juliet's had to live with, which she's slowly withdrawn from, until the two of us are walled off from one another now, miles apart with acres of silence between us? I feel almost sure I can hear in the silence between us that Juliet's feeling the same thing too.

How long have we both been feeling this way? How long since she last knew for certain that she loved me, and I knew that I loved her? When was the last time sex between us was a real connection? And how long have we spent pretending? I can't work out why these questions are coming to me now. What's so important about this night? Surely it can't just be one conversation with a stranger, one memory of a childhood holiday long ago? Surely it takes more than that to turn a simple story into a fundamental questioning of the course of one's life? Or does it always seem this quick and easy when it happens, one chapter giving way to another with no more fanfare than the turn of a page?

My relationship with Juliet never recovers after that night. The day after the wedding I put Amy out of my mind, and Juliet and I go home to our flat and on Monday we both go back to work. I don't look Amy up online, don't scroll through her photography website, looking at the photographs she's taken of other people's happiness. I think of her a little, it would be a lie to say I don't. And I mention having met her on the phone to my mum, who remembers the time when I saved the little girl from drowning, and seems curiously relaxed about the fact we've met again, as if this is logical and natural, as if she always expected me to call one day and let her know we'd met. Other than that, Juliet and I get on with our lives, and nothing is outwardly different. There is only the single, crucial change that both of us know, I think we both know, that we no longer want to be with each other. When we're together in the evenings and I ask her how her day has been, she fobs me off with the briefest of answers. I do the same.

A day comes when she gets home from work and tells me she's booked a holiday that summer with her girlfriends, planning a summer without me, and I know we can't go on.

'When are you going away?' I ask her.

'Why? Do you have plans?'

'I'm only interested. I suppose I'm just wondering when we'll go on holiday.'

'Oh.' She shrugs, walking out of the room to go and shower and wash off the day. 'I don't know. I didn't know you wanted to. I suppose we can fit it around things if we want to go away.' She is planning her life after me, I realise.

'You don't want to, then,' I say. It's childish of me to feel hurt by this, because I realise that in a way I must have caused it, but I'm hurt all the same, so I think, fuck it – I'll be childish.

'Why do you say that?'

'I think you've made it very fucking clear you don't want anything to do with me at the moment.'

'I honestly don't know what you're talking about, Ed.'

'Fuck off, Jules.' Listening to myself, I think I must seem pathetic right now, resorting, so early in the argument, to swearing at her. The surest sign of a losing hand. It must be me who's in the wrong here. But it's she who's booking holidays like we'll have broken up by summer, so what have I done wrong?

'You fuck off, I've booked a holiday – why does that mean you're angry at me?'

'We both know.'

'Do we? What do we know?'

'Fuck off, Jules, we both know.'

'I know you've been withdrawn for fucking ages and don't want to touch me any more.' This is true, but seems unfair to me: since we came home from the wedding, she's been turning her back on me the minute she gets into bed.

'Why didn't you get in the boat?' I ask her. The question surprises me as I ask it; I hadn't known that was what I was going to say.

'What?'

'At the wedding. By the lake. Why did you go back? Why didn't you get in the boat with me?'

'That's what you took from that wedding?'

'I just want to know.'

She sighs, exasperated. 'It wasn't ours. It wasn't safe. It was antisocial to be away from everyone like that.'

'We wouldn't have stayed there all night.'

'I didn't want to, Ed. Is that OK? I didn't want to get in the fucking boat.'

And maybe in the end it's as simple as that. We had the chance to be one of three kinds of people. We made different choices. Now a fissure between us is opening up. Probably these choices present themselves to us thousands of times every day, and turn into our lives. I suppose we'd spot them time and again if we looked close enough. But most of the time we're not looking. Most of the time we don't notice the way our roads diverge. It was just something about that night, the lake, the reeds, that made things different, enabling me to see clearly for the first time what was going on, to see we were different people moving down different paths.

'You sure that's all you didn't want?'

She laughs at me, bitterly.

'Trust me, it's you that's leaving, Ed, not the other way round.'

We break up a month or so later, one argument having piled up on another till staying together just doesn't seem possible any more.

She suggests we meet in public for a drink after work, and I guess what's coming. I toy all afternoon with the idea of leaving her before she can leave me, starting the scene myself, or just not turning up, but it seems petty. She's the one who's suggested the drink, she should get to do the talking. We meet in a bar in east London near the office where I'm working, and she looks beautiful, all dressed up, as if she's going out somewhere afterwards. I don't know when we last dressed up for each other – not since the wedding, and even that wasn't really for each other, even that was just what the occasion demanded.

'I wanted to talk to you away from the flat because I think we have problems,' Juliet says. 'I want to ask you a very straight question and I hope you'll be honest with me when you reply. Are you seeing someone else?'

I've never been asked this before, and for a moment it throws me. It feels so like being in a film that responding in the moment is quite difficult. Too many half-remembered lines from the movies come into my head.

'No. Are you?'

'Of course not. I want to ask you as well whether you've been in touch with that girl who took the photos at Leah and Richard's wedding.'

'The girl that I saved from the swimming pool? No. I haven't.'

Juliet nods, taking this in. She's probably disappointed; it would be easier to leave me if I'd actually done something wrong. 'I'm sorry to ask, then,' she says. 'There was something about the way you were talking with her.'

'Nothing happened between us at all, Jules. It was just an extraordinary coincidence; I don't think you can blame me for talking to her about it. We've talked about this already, more than once.'

Juliet picks up her wine glass and half drains it. 'I know,' she says. 'I don't know what happened. I haven't quite come back from that night.'

'I know.'

She looks at me sharply.

'You do?'

'I live with you, remember?'

'It's not anything that happened. I just haven't felt OK ever since.'

I feel as if I would be able to spell it out for her if she really wanted me to. Something about that night at the wedding showed us both that we were treading water, that we'd been treading water for some time, that somehow we'd stopped being happy together, and very soon we weren't going to be living the same lives, our lives were going to travel in completely different directions. I don't know what it was, what forces were pulling at us, but we felt them all the same, and realised they'd been doing that for some time before that evening. It was one of those discoveries that couples sometimes make when they become conscious that things are going to end between them.

'I'm sorry you haven't felt OK,' I say. It crosses my mind that I should reach out and take her hand, but then the thought occurs to me that we might end up staying together if I try too hard, she might lose heart and decide not to leave me. I don't know when that was last what I wanted. 'I don't know why it means you've shut yourself off from me.'

Juliet looks hurt, and my stomach drops a little when I see the cloud pass over her face, because I don't want to hurt her or make her unhappy. But sitting here, drinking with the woman I've shared the last six years with, I know very clearly that I want to end this evening alone.

'Is that what you think I'm doing?' she asks.

'Yeah, pretty much. I feel like we didn't really come home from that wedding. Not as we were. I feel like parts of us must still be there.'

'I feel the same, if I'm honest.'

'I thought you might. I'm glad you've brought it up. I didn't really know how to.'

'So what's happened?'

'I don't know. I think something's gone.'

'Something's gone?'

'Don't you agree?' I can see she's really thinking about this. I watch her working through the implications of the thought. I might still be able to call this back, if I change tack now, if I beg her to love me. A part of me wants to. But it seems that there's a current that's carrying me away, and it keeps me silent when I could speak up; it keeps me from speaking while Juliet realises for the first time that she's not in love with me either.

'I think you might be right.'

'What do you want to do about it?' I ask her. 'Do you think we should have some time apart?' This all feels so civilised, so bloodless, so unreal. I'd almost rather we were screaming at each other.

'Is that what you want?'

'I don't know. You've asked to talk about this; I want to know what you're thinking.'

'I suppose maybe it would be good if we gave each other some time to work out what's happened, and what it is we want.'

I hold out my hands in a kind of shrug, as if I'm pushing all responsibility away on to her.

'If that's what you want,' I say.

She looks at me suspiciously. 'You're taking all this very easily.'

'Am I?'

'Is this what you wanted to happen tonight?'

'Is it what I wanted to happen?'

'I just wondered. You haven't answered, by the way.'

I shake my head at her. 'We don't have to argue, do we? We've both said what we want and we want the same thing.'

Juliet looks away, gets out her phone and checks the time. Perhaps she is going out. Perhaps she'll go on from here for drinks with her girlfriends. Perhaps she's even going to meet another man, someone from work, who knows? I wouldn't blame her. We must both have felt lonely these past few weeks. It occurs to me that I don't feel possessive of her at all tonight. As if that phase of our relationship is already long past. I wonder when it ended. What were we doing the last time I would have bridled at the thought of her with someone else?

'I can move out,' I say.

'That would probably be the best arrangement, seeing as it's my flat,' she replies.

I smile; she meant it as a put-down, but it strikes me as funny all the same. 'Fair point.'

'Where will you go?' she asks.

'I don't know yet. I haven't thought about it.' She doesn't respond. 'I'll be all right,' I tell her.

'Will you go back and live with your parents?'

'At the farm? God, no.'

'She'd want to help you if she knew, you know,' Juliet says.

'Knew what?'

'That you're homeless.'

'I'm not homeless. I'm just moving out.'

She shrugs.

'OK,' she says. 'I just think your mum would want to help if she knew what was happening. And maybe you should let her.' She puts her phone away from where it's been lying on the table, and empties her glass, and puts it down. I think of the Streets, the way this moment has been entirely colonised, at least for my generation, by a song, so that presumably no one lives through a break-up in a bar any more without hearing 'Dry Your Eyes' playing in the back of the brain, no one sees the scene for what it is, they see it through the filter of that music.

'This is all a bit civilised and grown-up, isn't it?' she says.

'I know,' I say. 'But thank you for saying it.'

'Life is too short. This is the only time we'll be alive,' she replies as she stands up from the table. 'I don't mean to hurt your feelings, but I don't think it's worthwhile pretending something's good enough, in the end.'

1911

IN THE BEGINNING there was noise, such noise. Chai sellers in the square and the chatter of hawkers, children laughing, drum of their feet against the stones where they ran and played, the spit and stutter of cooking always at the margins of each scene and the pleasant patina of human life around her house, all drowned, all dwarfed by the coming of the railways, din of their construction through the years of her childhood and the clatter and thrum of the trains passing through and the trains going into their sidings. All those years it was the trains that sang in her ears, changing everything, bringing goods from impossibly far away, carrying the produce of Hyderabad into the unknowable distance, out of the heart of India to who knew where else on earth, far away to the sea and the wide world beyond it, the sea she had never seen and could not even have imagined in those years long lost, so long ago. It always seemed to her like a miracle that the steam and oil and din of the trains brought forth the mangoes and spices and cloth that dazzled her so when her mother brought them into the house after shopping in the bazaar, that the living produce and bright dyes people made with such skill in Hyderabad could be packed away into crates that all looked the same, though they contained whole worlds within them, and loaded on to trains, and turned, as if by magic, into the same steam, oil and din.

Hyderabad was a place in between things, on the banks of the Musi, a city ringed by lakes. It used to smell alive, incredibly alive whatever hour of the day you breathed it in, the richness of its aromas a hymn to the miracle and the dream of civilisation, gathering together all human industry and endeavour into one complex, overwhelming bouquet: garlic and cooking, spices and tobacco, dung in the heat, sandalwood, smoke. All the city's colours were another celebration – the saris and dhotis rippling the surface of each street, flowers in women's hair like stars. The city's wealth rested on its status as a place for diamond trading, and for trading in pearls; though it was far from the sea, it was a great centre for the buying and selling of pearls.

Her father was never involved in those more ancient undertakings, the trading of pearls, the trading of perfumes – he lived among steel and packing crates, he was not a man of the bazaar. He came to the city after the arrival of the railways, when the factories were first being built, to seek his fortune in business while Hyderabad grew around him and new opportunities presented themselves in industry, transportation, infrastructure, telecommunications. He tried his hand at everything, and enough of it proved successful that he came in time to be judged a success. He was a busy man, always chasing opportunities, chasing debts. She never saw very much of him. That was the way it was between fathers and daughters at that time. It never seemed strange to her; besides, her world was built around someone else.

In the beginning was her mother, a woman of extraordinary

beauty. Everyone who knew her said so – a woman people stared at, a woman who was listened to with a different quality of attention from that which was accorded to any of her friends. To Phoebe it had always seemed absurd, really, that the beautiful get more attention. But that was the world she was born into, that had always been the way of things wherever she'd gone in her life. It meant that her mother was used to finishing her sentences in a way few women of her class and background were in Hyderabad at that time, and that she had great influence among her friends. She used to hold parties, welcoming some of the most prominent people of the city into the home she had made with her husband. How she loved those sparkling, champagne evenings. That was how the family came to mingle with the British who lived in the city. Few of them ever came to the parties, but Phoebe's parents were recognised as significant people among the local population because they created that role for themselves, and were invited to the Secunderabad Club and the officers' mess, and in that way they mixed with the white men who ran things in Hyderabad. That was how Phoebe first met Arthur.

She knew from an early age that what her mother wished most of all for her was that she might meet a man from the British army, or failing that a businessman, marry him, and better the lot of the family in that way. As far back as Phoebe could remember, her mother always used to call her beautiful. She believed her own beauty had been reborn in her daughter, just as Shakespeare promised in the sonnets, and she hoped her daughter would secure success for the family by taking advantage of those charms, and meeting and marrying a British officer. She used to talk about that future with

Phoebe, over and over again on the long afternoons of her childhood, until it became Phoebe's own dream, until it became the only future she could imagine. So Phoebe used to go with her mother to the balls and gatherings at the officers' mess and the Railway Institute, which her father had recently been allowed to join, and her mother would teach her about the way to talk to a man so he thought you found him interesting, and by the time Phoebe was thirteen they were searching quite deliberately for a husband for her.

To Phoebe, her mother was the whole world. Of all the people who loved her mother and thought she was beautiful, no one believed it more fiercely than she did. She adored the wisdom her mother had, the elegance and refinement. She wanted to do whatever her mother wanted, to make her proud; she wanted nothing more than to make her happy. So she pursued this dream of her mother's with all her heart, made it her own, never really questioned where it would lead her if she saw it through to the end, because it was what her mother wanted and that was enough. She used to listen to the din of the trains, and watch the thin men in their billowing pantaloons loading all the wonders of Hyderabad into those endless, identical crates and taking them away from the city to distant, other worlds. She watched them and knew one day she would go the same way – packed, or so she imagined, into a crate of her own, her own vanishing act, whisked wherever her husband willed. And that thought used to fill her with happiness, because it was what her mother wanted, and making her mother happy was all she desired.

'Will I still live here with you?' she used to ask her mother when she was very young.

'Of course not. You will go wherever your husband decides.'

'But will I still be able to see you and Father and my brothers and sisters?'

Her mother shrugged. 'It will depend,' she said.

'On what?'

'On many things. On the man you marry, and what he is like, and what he makes of us, and where his work will take him. A family does not have rights over its daughters once it has married them off. I still see my mother, but that is because I am fortunate. I live close to her, and your father understands that it helps me to see my family, and he likes my family well enough. But there is one great difference between you and me.'

'What is that?'

'I married an Indian. You will marry an Englishman. So who knows what will become of you once that is done? No one in this family has done that before; you will be the first, you will be the one to discover it for us, and then we will know what it is like.'

From that single point of difference, their paths diverged so wildly that in the end Phoebe found herself a whole world away from the life her mother knew, and could not imagine the leap it would take for her to recover the young girl she had once been. She supposed that girl was gone.

Once she was thirteen years old she went along with her mother to every party her mother attended, as that was the strategy they had evolved for introducing her to the right English officer.

'You will have to be patient,' her mother would tell her. 'These people have an idea of themselves that is very high and mighty. They do not just go about marrying Indian girls as if it is nothing; most of these men think of going back to England and marrying girls from the villages they once called home. We will have to find a special one for you.'

Phoebe didn't mind that; that sounded much better to her than marrying just anyone. She thought her mother meant that they would need to find a prince.

She met her husband four or five times before it even occurred to her that he might be a man that she might marry. It took her so long to realise because he was so very much older than she was, well into his thirties when he first inclined his head towards her and offered her a smile.

'And what is your name, young lady?' he asked, the first words he spoke to her. At that time he was still a good-looking man, very tall and well built, and his moustaches seemed almost too big for his head, as if the weight of them might cause his neck to ache. Phoebe was most impressed by that moustache, but she could not say she was immediately attracted to him – it was at least another year before the thought occurred to her that it must tickle to kiss him, with so much hair on his lip, which she regarded as the first time she thought about him in any amorous way at all.

'My name is Phoebe, sir.' He did not take her hand and kiss it, or anything like that. He merely inclined his head with a smile, and Phoebe gave the smallest of curtsies, as her mother had taught her, knowing her mother was standing beside her and watching to make sure that Phoebe remembered. He turned from Phoebe to speak to her mother.

'The two of you could be sisters!' he said. Phoebe found this confusing; her mother was much older than her, after all, and they did not look very much like each other, as she had her father's paler skin. Her mother, however, seemed to think he had said something extremely funny.

'Yes, she is very grown up for her age!'

'I rather meant that you are very youthful for yours, madam.' And they both laughed, and Phoebe smiled with them, wondering what they were talking about and wishing that she was at home.

She met Mr French, as she was told to call him, three more times at various functions over the subsequent year before her mother started to talk to her seriously about him. She called Phoebe to her room one afternoon, and Phoebe stood in front of her where she lay on the divan bed, rubbing her feet surreptitiously against the carpet because her mother's room had the best carpet in the house and she liked the way it felt against her skin.

'What do you make of Mr French?' she asked.

'Mr French?'

'The man from the railways that we met last week. We have met him before.'

'Oh, yes. The man with the big moustache.'

'That's right.'

'He seems a nice man. Is he working with Father?'

Her mother thought about this for a moment. 'Not at present, no. He may do in future, though.' Phoebe said nothing to this, not knowing what she was supposed to say, so her mother continued. 'We think he might be interested in you.'

At first, she didn't understand what her mother meant – the thought of his interest being romantic did not occur to her, because there was such a great difference in their ages. 'What do you mean, Mother?'

'We think he might be interested in marrying you. He has said as much to your father. It would be a very advantageous match for all concerned.'

Phoebe, shocked beyond words by this news, began to cry.

'What are you doing?' her mother snapped, apparently irritated by her daughter's display of emotion.

'I'm sorry,' Phoebe said, hiding her face in her hands.

'Really,' her mother said, 'you have no idea how lucky you would be. What a great honour this would be for our whole family, if Mr French were indeed willing to marry you. You should go away and think about being more grateful.'

The next time they attended a social event, her mother let her know that Arthur – or Mr French, as she always called him, even after the wedding was over – would be in attendance also, and that he was hoping to speak to her. Phoebe replied that of course she would talk to him, she would do whatever her mother wanted. So she dressed up in her most beautiful clothes, and went with her father and mother to the British officers' mess, and took a glass from a tray as she walked into the party, feeling sophisticated and hoping she was at least passably beautiful that night, feeling very young and very frail and frightened. Arthur had already arrived, and was standing with a group of other men by an open window. Phoebe looked around for him at first, trying to see where he was, then spotted him at the far end of the room, and took him in, trying to see him differently, trying to look at him as she never had before, and see him as a lover, see him as someone who might become her future. But it was difficult; even as she saw where he was standing, her eyes seemed to slip past him to the evening beyond the window where he stood, the night sky over Hyderabad, the long lawn falling away to the street beyond, India, beautiful home, and the memory of childhood, and the parakeets in the trees, and the stones her brothers and sisters and she used to throw at the monkeys who came and perched on the garden wall, and the feeling that over that wall was a whole world waiting that could quite easily turn into anything. And was it going to turn into this? Was this, and nothing else, nothing more, what was to be given to her – was the rest of life in all its rich possibility about to be closed off? Would she ever see the real wild and teeming world, or was it all to narrow down to this man, those moustaches, the duties of a marriage?

Arthur saw her almost in the same moment as she noticed him, and smiled at her mother, and raised his glass to her father, but did not look directly at Phoebe, and did not come over immediately to speak to her. So she took up a position at the side of the room with her parents, and they all looked around to see who they could talk to. Her father was always keenly sensitive about these social relations, who he might be permitted to speak to of his own volition, who he would have to wait to be introduced to, who he should avoid at all costs. He lived in terror of giving offence, and of losing someone's business because of a misplaced remark, an inappropriate attempt at conversation, a smile or a nod to the wrong person. These kinds of things sometimes go over children's heads, but Phoebe was always acutely aware of the atmosphere of tension around her father whenever they were in company like this. His eyes were always bright with a panic he barely suppressed, and with a kind of desperation, as he tried to work out where he belonged in the pecking order of every room he passed through. It may possibly have marked him out as a small man, this obsession with rank, someone who placed no value in himself except that which was accorded to him by other people. But that never occurred to Phoebe until she came to England. In India, among the castes, rank was everything, as natural as breathing; in business, among the British, how an Indian man conducted himself was always a delicate game.

'Mr French has noticed you,' her mother hissed at her. 'When he has finished his conversation, I am sure he will come over. You remember what we talked about, Phoebe. You will smile and be pleasant to him.'

Arthur spent five more minutes laughing with his British friends by the window, then detached himself from the group he was in and made his way over to greet them.

'Good evening,' he said to Phoebe's father and mother. Phoebe watched him as he extended his right hand to shake her father's, and his eyes flickered for a moment to meet hers, then fixed again on her father's face. Did she feel anything? Any stirring of nervousness or excitement? Not really. Just the same slight sickness and creeping dread she had carried with her into the room. Was that normal in matters of the heart? Who knew? Who knew what love was really like? Not a girl of fourteen trying to negotiate its rocks and shallows for the first time.

'And good evening to you, Miss Phoebe,' Arthur said now, turning to her. She held out her hand and he took it, and kissed it, and a part of her wanted to laugh at them all being so formal together, putting on such a performance, but she kept a straight face and curtseyed to Arthur instead, because she knew it was what her mother wanted.

'How lovely to see you, Mr French,' she said. 'What a lively gathering.'

'Yes, it is, isn't it?' He looked around the room, the people talking, the light on the glasses and the dark falling slowly outside. 'It has been a lovely day, wouldn't you say?'

'Oh, I think they are all lovely days in Hyderabad.'

Arthur laughed at this, as if Phoebe had said something very witty. 'How very true,' he said. 'If you can stand the heat, that is.'

'Well yes, of course; it's no place for someone who doesn't like the sun.'

Her father said something then, and Arthur laughed again, and Phoebe was able to fade back to the edge of the conversation as her parents carried on talking to this strange man who had come looming over to them. She took the opportunity to have a closer look at him. He still looked relatively youthful; there was something quite boyish about him in those days. The trouble had not yet started with his knees, and she had noticed as he crossed the room that he had a strange walk, he seemed almost to bounce as he walked towards them. He seemed at ease with her parents, not too standoffish, and his clothes were nice enough. It was hard to see anything objectionable in him. Of course, he was as old as her father, and that was a little strange maybe, but perhaps that was only a detail. Lots of women married men who were older than they were. And lots of women weren't even that lucky, and never had the chance to marry at all. She watched Arthur as he concluded his conversation with her parents, and tried to persuade herself that the situation she found herself in wasn't really so terrible; there didn't really seem to be anything wrong with him, after all. He was healthy and tall and he had money, and some women never got a chance to marry anyone. Arthur turned back to her once more, smiling, and she made herself smile back at him.

'I wonder whether you would care to dance, Miss Phoebe?' he asked her. She felt suddenly tense and nervous. It was not the done thing for a woman to dance with just any man at a party; to dance with a man was to announce one's intentions. She looked questioningly at her mother, who nodded sternly at her. She realised, with some amazement, that already, almost as soon as she had been acquainted with the idea of Arthur, the moment had come for committing herself to him. It seemed ludicrous; and yet her mother was nodding sternly at her. What else was she to do?

'I would be delighted to, Mr French.'

'Very good. Shall we?' Arthur offered his arm, and they walked together to the middle of the room, where a small group of Europeans had begun dancing to the music of the gramophone in the corner. She felt very afraid. She had not had very much practice at dancing, and she had never danced with a man before, and wondered whether she could do it correctly, or whether she was going to make a fool of herself. Arthur turned to face her, and held her to him, and looked happily at her face, and they began to sway in time to the music. She tried to smile for him. He did not seem to want to try anything more complicated than swaying together, and she was happy enough with that. She became aware, as he pressed himself against her, that he was in a state of some tumescence, which did make her uncomfortable where he stuck into her side, but she did her very best not to notice or draw attention to the situation. She understood that men did sometimes find themselves in this predicament, particularly around young women, and did not want to embarrass her future husband. It was, after all, a compliment of sorts, she supposed. For his part, Arthur did not seem to be embarrassed at all; he smiled heartily, and pressed her close against him, until the song they were dancing to had finished, when they stepped apart, and he led her back to her parents at the edge of the room. Phoebe was surprised to find that she felt quite excited. She knew the whole room had seen them dance, and that was as good as telling them aloud that there was to be an engagement. She realised all of a sudden that she had been announced in public as having been chosen by a European man. It was a conspicuous honour, perhaps a great change in status for her, and, as it seemed to her then, the first thing that had ever really happened in her life. Arthur bowed to her slightly as they reached her parents, and he prepared to take his leave.

'It was very good to speak to you, Miss Phoebe,' he said. 'I hope we will be able to speak again before too long.'

'Thank you, Mr French. I would like that very much.'

He bowed his head to her once more, and then took his leave and went back to the drinks and the men on the far side of the room, who seemed to slap him on the back and whisper to him with bright, snarling grins, and Phoebe and her father and mother blended in with the other Indian guests at the party.

When she retired to her bed that evening, she thought a great deal about the excitement that had rushed through her when she returned to the edge of the room from her dance with Arthur. It had been a strange sensation, one that was not familiar to her. She suspected it had something to do with a change taking place within her from being a girl to becoming a woman; new emotions were revealing themselves as she encountered new experiences, emotions she had never suspected were waiting within her.

Her mother and father broke the news to her the following week that Arthur had proposed marriage, and following a discussion between them, both he and Phoebe's father had found the terms agreeable. Phoebe was told that she should be very proud, that this was a momentous day in the life of her family. The fortunes of everyone in the family would be changed by this match, and it would all be thanks to her, thanks to her beauty and her kindness and refinement, which had so enchanted Mr French. She listened to it all feeling like someone in a dream. They were married three months later.

The ceremony was undoubtedly very beautiful. Her father spared no expense, and for her mother, it really might have been the best day of her life, a day when the dream she had had for her daughter came true. She passed the day in an ecstasy, emotional and smiling, clutching her children to her as Phoebe went to the altar and exchanged the vows that made her and Arthur man and wife. Arthur did look very smart in his suit; really, Phoebe could find no fault with the day, it would be ungracious of her to do so. There was champagne that had actually been ordered from France, foie gras from the Army & Navy stores, and Phoebe's dress came all the way from a tailor in Bombay. It really was marvellous, all she was able to remember of it afterwards; but unfortunately that was not so very much, for she went through it all in a kind of stupor, a daze, and could not come fully to her senses until the end of the evening when Arthur arranged for them to be driven back to his house, and she stepped out of the carriage and into the home that was now to be hers, and found herself all of a sudden alone with a man she did not know, had barely even spoken to, and yet was supposed to stay by the side of for the rest of her life. She experienced, in that moment in the innocent year of 1911, a sense of crippling vertigo that she struggled to believe had ever really left her.

They were supposed to build a life there in Hyderabad, where Phoebe could have lived with her husband but still seen her family and her mother regularly, and still have felt part of the world she came from. However, things didn't turn out that way. Not very long after Phoebe married Arthur, a man named Gavrilo Princip shot and killed the heir to the Austro-Hungarian empire, Archduke Franz Ferdinand, and very soon afterwards the world changed for ever. The changes in Phoebe's life mattered very little, really, in the context of everything else that proceeded from that gunshot, but her life changed unimaginably all the same.

Upon learning that Britain had declared war, Arthur announced his intention to leave India and enlist in the navy in order to serve his country; Phoebe, naturally, had no choice but to follow him. So there was a rushed, traumatic journey out of India, west to Bombay on the trains Arthur had supervised, then by sea past coastlines that thronged with Bible stories.

Phoebe endured the journey in profound shock, hardly able to speak at this wrenching away that was happening to her, hardly able to take in the change that was occurring. She comforted herself as they sailed past the Holy Land with trying to identify places that were mentioned in the Bible, and avoided her husband, because she was speechlessly angry with him, and knew she had no right to be, and perhaps would not even be able to explain herself were he to ask what the matter was.

Her mother had upbraided her the last time they saw each other, and told her it had always been likely that Mr French would want to go home one day, and Phoebe should always have been expecting that. It was almost the last conversation the two women ever had; after that, they never met again, but only exchanged letters till her mother died five years later.

Phoebe recognised with hindsight that she should have realised she would one day go to England. But the suddenness of it, the mindlessness of it, and no one ever asking her what she might want or how she was coping, all of this shook and diminished her in ways from which she never recovered. Years later, she would remember that journey as the breaking of so much that had once been possible for her. Not because she had been taken away from her country, but because of the fractures that change had left in her. After she set foot for the first time on English soil there was less of her, and consequently there was less of life available to her, less to be done. It was not true, she realised bitterly, that experience made you stronger. It seemed to her more like an ebbing away of things, of what might have been possible.

2019

After I've moved all my things out of the flat Juliet's parents bought her, I know what I'm going to do, though I don't feel very proud of it. I wait a fortnight, then call up Leah and Richard and get Amy's number. I call her, and we speak, and we meet, and go for dinner.

I get to the restaurant before she does, crossing Putney Bridge to the far side, wondering why I've suggested we meet somewhere so far from where both of us are living, wondering whether I was seeking neutral territory, somewhere neither of us were likely to have been recently with anyone else, unbroken ground for unbroken feeling. I walk past the church where the Putney Debates took place after the first civil war. 'I think the poorest he that is in England hath a life to live, as the greatest he'. That's all I remember from the Putney Debates. But it's a thing worth remembering all the same. The heart and source of every story, that every life is the centre of the world and weighs the same in the scales of – well, whatever we call God now that we mostly deny him, whatever scales we use instead. All that is etched into history at the Putney Debates.

I get to the restaurant, and give my name, and sit and wait at an outside table, thinking about all the better places I could have picked to meet, and how stupid I'm going to look when she turns up, and how I won't know what to say or what to do because I can never understand or believe this moment, I can never believe someone's interested in me, until Amy walks round the corner of the church and sees me. Then she smiles, and I smile too, and stand up from my seat, then feel ridiculous for having done so, but can't sit down again, so I wait, knowing I'm blushing, knowing I've overthought this terribly. Amy smiles as she approaches me.

'Did they make you stand up at school whenever a teacher walked into the room?' she asks.

'Yeah, I looked weird, didn't I?'

'A bit. Now it's going to be really weird if you don't kiss me, but I'm not going to let you, so we're just going to have to sit with the tension for a bit and see if it dissipates, aren't we?' Her eyes seem to flash with the mischief in her as she sits down at the table while I sit back down opposite her.

'How's it feeling so far?' she asks me, and our eyes meet, and neither of us looks away.

'I'm just sitting with the tension,' I tell her, and we smile, and we're feeling the same thing, and it feels like being alive to be here with her. I can feel my heart beating in my chest: not faster, just harder. The boom of a bass drum I can't always hear. What causes that, I wonder? What chemical is now coursing through me?

'How was your day?' she asks me.

'Fine, I think. It wasn't that exciting. I'm afraid I'm not an exciting person.'

'You should stop talking yourself up so much, I'll think you've got something to hide.'

'How was yours?'

'I stopped a mugging in the street.'

'Really?'

'No, of course not – look at me. But I thought I'd sound more interesting than you. You can tell stories, can't you?' She leans forwards suddenly, looking at me.

'I think so,' I tell her. 'When I've got a story to tell.'

'That ought to be always, if you're any good at it.'

'OK. What do you like to hear stories about?'

She shrugs at this. 'Anything. I'm not picky. People's families, people's lives.'

'Ask me a question, then.'

'No, not like that.' She leans back just as suddenly, as if I'd disappointed her. 'I'm not interviewing you. I just want to know whether you can tell a story.'

I think of the things I might be able to tell her. The family stories I've collected. The little pieces of my own life that might be worth saying out loud. There are fewer of those, it seems to me, though I don't know why. Every day ought to be worth retelling in some form or another, but I can't seem to find the trick of it. So many of my days feel just like time passing by.

'You tell me a story,' I say to her, 'and I'll see if I can pick up the trick.'

She tells me over pasta that she has a tutoring job that's going to take her away to Kuala Lumpur for most of the summer, some rich architect's kids she'll have to spend a couple of months bullying about their grammar and their algebra and the periodic table while they jump off their dad's yacht into the sea. Those endless not-quite-jobs my generation do and call our lives, because the money doesn't add up any more, because the jobs we were taught to dream for don't quite pay and all need to be subsidised by other work. Amy and I have done a lot of stop-gaps: bar work, call-centre work, café work, tearing tickets in theatres, cleaning offices, delivering free papers, clearing houses – all this has come up in the course of our lives. I ask her why her summer isn't filled up with photographing weddings, and she replies that she thought she'd like a change.

'I've done that for the last few years, and the money's great. It's robbery, really, what I get away with charging. But I do these tutoring gigs as well, and every now and then, they're rewarding. You know, if you help some kid understand something they didn't. Or just help some kid feel better about themselves. That feels good sometimes. So I was asked about this job, and I guess I was tired of the weddings on the day the call came in, or maybe I'd had a good session tutoring or something. Or maybe I just wanted to go abroad on someone else's credit card. I half regret it now, I think. But I'm back by the middle of August, and I've booked myself up doing weddings from then.'

What she's saying to me when she tells me about Kuala Lumpur, the story below the surface of her speaking, is helpful to hear. I won't be here every weekend, she's telling me; I'm not going to be free to meet up every time you call – if that's what's going to happen, that won't be what this is. That's all right with me. It seems like it might be what I need. It will be different from the life I've walked away from, and that must be what I'm looking for, isn't it? Otherwise I'd have stayed where I was. Otherwise I would have been happy.

'Do you have any plans for the summer?' she asks me.

'I hadn't made any yet, if I'm honest.'

'Maybe we'll go somewhere,' she says. Her eyes dance, and it seems like the bravest thing anyone's ever said to me.

'That'd be nice. Where do you want to go?'

'Well, I have my summer full of other people's weddings once I'm not in KL, like I said. So maybe we'll end up going to those.'

'Sure.'

'Do you ever want to get married?' she asks me. 'Is marriage something you believe in?'

'I don't think that kind of thing can exist in the abstract. I think it's going to be about a person you meet.'

'A lot of people know what their wedding will be like a long time before they meet anyone worth marrying.'

'No, they don't. Not really.'

She raises her eyebrows at this. 'Why not?'

'A lot of people think they know a lot of things. But it's not them, is it? It's everything around them. People are brought up around so much noise. Shutting it out till you can hear your own self is so fucking difficult. Lots of people never do it. They think they want a white wedding and a beach honeymoon, but it's not them. It's just what the world's told them they should be wanting.'

'The world might be right.'

'The world might well be right. But it's not the person wanting the thing. It's something different. Something else.'

'You talk about it like it's social conditioning. Like it's white noise drowning real things out. You might have it the wrong way round. What you're talking about might really be the evolutionary imperative. A desire to marry that's deeper than conscious thinking. An instinct that precedes our individuality.'

And I don't say anything to this. Because it suddenly strikes me as true, and it makes me wonder what I know about anything.

The evening is a kind of dance I haven't danced in years. I remember what I hated about dating, the uncertainty, the sense of performance all the time. But I remember what I liked about it too. The uncertainty. The unspoken thoughts that bloom between two people while they work each other out. Does that have to disappear once two people get to know each other? Or is it just that things between me and Juliet went wrong? Did we mistake falling into our relationship for the end of the adventure? Did we just sit in front of the TV and lose sight of what we'd thought was about to begin?

After I leave Juliet, I move into the converted garage of a friend. I never bring Amy there; when we meet, we meet in restaurants or bars, and when we go home together we go home to hers. The garage, after all, is never going to turn into my home, and the place is damp, and I've made great piles of everything I own because I'm too cheap to pay for storage. There are always clothes drying on top of boxes of books. I keep this secret, and tell myself I mustn't let this become who I am. When I was a kid I used to get like this about tidying my room. For weeks I'd say to myself that I didn't need to do it, and the mess around me was only superficial, a bit of untidiness, and one quick pass would have things back on their shelves and the room looking how it should. Until the day came when I'd be forced to confront the fact that the mess I lived in was actually several layers deep, that my shelves had been emptied, all my life was on the floor. I want to avoid that in the garage. But I don't do anything about finding a flat just yet.

I don't know whether it's dating Amy or feeling strangely comfortable in the little damp garage, but I don't really want to take another step in any particular direction straight away. I have this feeling that I don't know who I'm going to be in a few months' time, so it would be wrong to commit to anything. When Amy talks about the job in Kuala Lumpur, I wonder whether it will be the end of us, whether we'll drift apart before we've really started. Sometimes when I think of how likely it is that, by the end of summer, I won't know her any more, I wonder whether I've been mad to break up with Juliet for what might turn out to be a two-month fling. Perhaps I've been blinded by the romance of the past that suffused my first encounter with Amy, having suddenly been given access that night at the wedding to the deep dive of time lost and time recalled. When you meet someone who met you or knew you as a child, which to my mind is like them having seen you as you really are, the air between you changes a little. They knew you when you could have been anyone, when your life could have turned into anything, not just this. They remind you of things you've lost, and when you speak to them, the conversation sometimes has a different centre of gravity. Because the kid you used to be is buried under so many years and contradictory feelings. Until the very idea of a coherent identity becomes a bit ludicrous. But there was a time when it wasn't. And it's beautiful to meet someone who gives you access to the memory of that time, so that you almost believe in it again. All of that I feel very deeply, but it doesn't really mean Amy and I are going to be well suited to each other. It doesn't mean that I should have let Juliet go, and retreated from the future I'd been building for myself with her.

That particular door is closed on me before too long, though, and I'm forced to abandon any fantasy about going back. Online, as visibly and joyfully and aggressively as possible, it seems to me, Juliet charts the course of a new relationship that begins almost as quickly as I start seeing Amy. While Amy and I are still on drinks and dinners and theatre one or two nights a week, Juliet moves someone else into the flat we used to share. Her flat, of course, in her name, bought for her by her parents, but I can't help but think of it a little bit as mine, because I lived there; it became my outer layer, it was the shell that sheltered me for a while. I want to feel hurt, but I find that I don't. In fact, I'm glad she has someone with her.

Because what's happening between Amy and me is new, and is moving fast, so that before very long we're spending almost all of our evenings together, sometimes there are bumps in the road. Evenings where one of us is tired or stressed, and the other doesn't know how to navigate around it. If the person I'm with seems to be unhappy, I have a tendency to assume it's because of me. Amy always notices, and calls me out on this, and that tends to turn quite quickly into arguing.

'You're making it about you again, when it's not, when you shouldn't; it's not all about you.'

'Then why aren't you talking to me?'

'I just want to sit on my own for a minute. I just didn't sleep last night, and I was shit all day, and everyone's pissed off at me. I just wanted to sit quietly.'

'But I'm not pissed off at you, so why take it out on me?'

'I'm not, I'm just sitting perfectly still, Ed. Calm down. Can you make us both a cup of tea?'

I meet all of Amy's parents, the people who adopted and raised her, who she calls Mum and Dad, and also, just once, her birth father, the strangest meeting Amy arranges. I never quite work out her intention.

She drives me down there one weekend, tense and quiet in the car, the sound of Sunday morning Radio 2 filling the space between us while she cocoons herself and tries, I suppose, to order her mind, maybe to work out why she is taking her new boyfriend to meet this man, what she's going to say about us both when we arrive. She parks the car on a quiet road in the middle of a nondescript housing estate, and leads me to a low block of flats. Her dad has a place on the ground floor, accessed from a hallway round the back of the building.

She smiles at me nervously. 'I don't know whether I should have brought you now,' she says.

'I know. It's OK.'

'Just don't expect too much.'

'I promise you, it's OK.' I wonder at that phrase, 'don't expect too much'. As if she feels that she's on trial with me somehow. As if she needs to show me this man, this part of her life, before I will really believe in her. What have I done to make her feel that way? What could I do to let her know that's not how I'm feeling?

The council must have been round that morning or the

previous day, because the grass is freshly cut, and I can still catch a trace of its scent in the air. Amy knocks on an anonymous door, and her father shows us in and makes us instant coffee. I look around the room we've been led into. It is a little more lived-in now than the place Amy described that night we met at the wedding: a table, a pile of newspapers, a radio, a TV. But everywhere the air of the charity-shop bargain.

'You're Edward, are you?' he says to me, holding out his hand. I shake it and smile.

'That's right. Everyone just calls me Ed, though. It's Alan, isn't it?'

'That's it. It's good to meet you.' There's a watchfulness about him, as you see in people who've learned the world can fuck you over, who never quite trust that it's not about to do the same again. He lives his life as if he's ashamed of what he's done with it. He reminds me of my own father, who had his own problems in his turn. I'm always interested when I discover I share things like this with girls I'm involved with. Damaged fathers, or summers in haystacks, or whatever it might be. It always feels like an explanation of what we recognised in each other, and makes me wonder how we communicate these secret currents which align our lives.

'Take a seat, all right, and I'll get coffee. Do you take sugar? Do you take milk?'

'Just milk, thanks.'

I feel sorry for him and for Amy as well, because for as long as we visit, the two of them sit in an agony of uncertainty and tension, not knowing what they should be saying to each other, not knowing what they're supposed to do.

'You been all right then, Amy, have you? How was the drive, all right?' All these empty questions. Talk of the football scores, talk of the weather. Anything but the honesty of not saying anything at all, till conversations like this have no meaning, we've had them so many times before. How often do we break through this empty talking into real speech?

'The drive was fine, thanks. Have you been OK?'

It isn't an easy visit, but Alan does the best he can to make us welcome, and when we're leaving he seems to be almost on the verge of tears, grateful we've come. After that first time, whenever Amy visits him, she prefers to go alone. After that day, I avoid bringing Alan up. I get the impression she's said all she wanted to say about that part of her life.

Juliet finds out that Amy and I are seeing each other about a month after we first go for dinner. She doesn't confront Amy, or anything like that; she just calls me. I see her name on the screen of my phone, and it makes me happy at first, because I don't guess why she's calling, which I suppose is naive. So I pick up and say hello, not expecting the coldness I hear in her voice.

'Are you sleeping with her?'

'Sorry? With who?'

'You know who.'

'Oh.'

'I fucking knew it.'

'Jules.'

'I gave you the opportunity to tell me. Why couldn't you be a man and own up to what you were doing?'

'That's not what happened. I didn't lie to you.'

'Of course you fucking lied to me; I gave you a chance to tell me and you didn't.'

'We met up again after you left me.'

'I didn't leave you, Ed – don't change the story.'

'What do you mean? You left me. I remember it very clearly.'

'I just put us down. We did the dying together.'

'Jules, that's a really weird way of putting it.'

'I'm trying to say you made it impossible for us. I just saw it through because you wouldn't. Now I find out you were seeing someone else. You're a fucking snake.'

'I wasn't, though.'

'People who can do that aren't whole people, Ed, you know that? People who can do this to someone else. I'm going to hang up now. You don't deserve any more of my time.'

She hangs up the phone then, and I try to call her back, then text her later a couple of times, but I don't get through and she doesn't reply, and I guess she's probably blocked my number. I try to feel indignant, but realise I can't. The truth is that my conscience isn't clear, not really. This year has caught hold of me and carried me away with it, and I can't say for sure whether I've done the right thing. Perhaps it will be years before I know what happened, whether there are things I should apologise for. All I know is that I can't get back to the place where I started.

Most of the time when Amy and I are together we go to her flat and the area round it, but every week we make sure we do something like a date night – go out and walk after dark by the river, or watch the sun rise over a park, go to dinner or into the city to see a film or a play, go for drinks, just the two of us, and talk to each other.

'Do you want kids eventually?' she asks me one evening.

'Yes,' I say without thinking, and the thought surprises me, and I suppose that surprise must pass over my face.

'What was that look for?' she asks me.

'I just never realised I did till this exact moment,' I say.

'Did you never talk about it with Juliet?'

'No, never. It never came up.' I look at Amy and realise for the first time that one day I want a family. As if I've suppressed this thought for some time, and now it's rushing up in me with great force for having been hidden away. 'I'd like to foster too, wouldn't you?' I ask her.

'What interests you about that?'

'I don't know. A chance to help someone. Like my friend Joe is helping me. He's let me keep my things in the garage. When I move them out again, I'll thank him, and we'll go on with our lives. I'd like to do that for people one day. I'd like someone to know they could always come to me.'

'That's a nice thought.'

'Would you ever foster?'

'I've looked into it actually.'

'Really? How come?'

'I just think it's something you can do that makes a difference.'

'I think it's been on my mind this last year because I haven't had very much for myself. Do you know what I mean? When you're feeling itinerant. You pack up your things and you realise there aren't many of them. You don't have walls around you, you don't have much permanence. And that makes you think about how valuable all that is. And it makes you think it would be a good thing to offer shelter to someone.' It occurs to me as I speak that I'm sounding pathetic, and I start to feel anxious, start to worry that I sound like I'm asking to move in. But Amy smiles, and reaches out, and takes my hand, as if she can see everything I'm thinking.

'I'd say it's strange that we both want to do that,' she says, 'but it probably isn't, really.'

'Why not?'

'Well, I don't believe in soulmates. Soulmates in the abstract. But I do think people are suited to certain other people. And at nineteen or twenty you date whoever you can get your hands on. But as you get older, here we are, we're thirty, basically, we've been in the world a while. Well, it stands to reason that we'd have started to know ourselves a little better. And spend our time in places and around people who are closer to who we'd like to be. So it would make sense if the closest thing we might ever have to a soulmate would be someone who moved in a similar circle. It would make sense if the closest thing we'd ever have to a soulmate were sitting with us, in this room.'

The day I tell Mum that I've started seeing Amy, she hangs up the phone on me. As simple as that. I call one evening to break the news, instinct telling me already that it would go badly.

'Hello?'

'Hi, Mum.'

'Hello, Ed – is that you?'

'Yeah, you OK?'

'We're all right, love. I'm just making dinner. Is there anything you need?'

'Oh. Actually, I just needed to tell you something.'

'Oh right?'

'You know that Juliet and I were on a break.'

She hesitates a moment before speaking again. 'Yes?'

'Well, it's not a break any more.'

'I see. You don't mean you've got back together?'

'No. I'm sorry.'

'I see.'

'And I have some other news that I wanted to tell you.'

'Right?'

'You remember I told you I met that girl, the girl I saved from the pool when we were young?'

'I remember.'

'Well, we've been seeing more of each other. And we've kind of got together, I think.' Mum's silent for a second; then the line goes dead.

I think Mum's first instinct is to reject the idea that Juliet and I might have needed to break up at all. We'd thought we were happy just a few months before; surely we could have gone on being happy together? But life has changed, and she will have to let that go. The life she imagined me having with Juliet was simply one of many alternative futures that are never going to come into being.

For some time afterwards, Mum makes it very clear she's not at peace with what's happened. When I call, it's always Chris who answers, and Mum can never speak, she's always busy. I don't know why she doesn't just want to talk. Perhaps because she knows deep down that she's being unreasonable, and there would be no way to argue out what she's feeling.

This new silence is also complicated because it feels like the continuation and evolution of a different fight we've been having for the last year or so. Although saying we've been fighting for only a year seems disingenuous; it was a year ago I said to her that I wasn't sure I could ever see myself moving home to take over the farm where I grew up and on which she and my stepdad still lived and worked, but that wasn't the beginning of things by any stretch.

I'd felt unsure since I was quite a young child whether I wanted the life I'd been born to, the hardship and money worries and the labour of shepherding. I'd put off thinking about it over the years. Easier to let time drift on without making decisions, knowing there'd be years still before I needed to make my mind up. But a year ago, Mum had tried to talk to me about wills and about inheritance, and that had become a moment of fracture between us.

'I'm just calling because I'm updating my will,' she said when I'd answered the phone and we'd done with the pleasantries. 'And Chris and I have been talking about how to write it.'

'All right.'

'The thing is that it's simpler just to leave the farm to one person, rather than leave it to both of you kids.'

I think in the moment she spoke I was shocked by the assumption that either Rachel or I would want to do what Mum and Chris had done. Phone calls can surprise like that; they come out of nowhere, into ordinary days, changing the weather without warning. I didn't know why Mum talked about us taking on the farm one day as if it was a given. Both Rachel and I lived in the city; we had both drifted away from the world of our childhood, and had never said anything about wanting to drift back.

'I don't know whether either of us is sure about taking it on,' I said. I heard the quality of silence change at the other end of the phone. I could feel Mum's focus intensifying as she sat, presumably at the big window in the cottage, with the wire of the home telephone trailing across the room from where the phone sat on its little table by the door. I imagined her looking out the window at the fields beyond, a cloud passing over her face as she listened to me.

'What do you mean?' Mum asked.

'Mum, we've talked about this before. Rachel and I don't know whether we want to do that.'

'Why not?'

'We're not sure whether that's our life.'

'It's your home, it's the world you come from.'

'No, Mum. You shouldn't think you're there to hand it on. You should be there because it's where you want to be. Don't think about what will happen to it after your lifetime; we'd both rather you thought about what you want to do, about your own lives.'

'But this place is our life.'

'Good. That's good. It's not necessarily going to be ours, though.'

'It's the history of our family.'

'But one day our family won't live there any more.'

The conversation went downhill from there. I suppose Mum had just never listened to me or Rachel when we'd told her before that it wasn't what we wanted. She had shut out a future she didn't want to contemplate, and assumed she might be able to force her wish through if she held to her course, fixed her eyes on what she wanted. But what becomes of your one and only life isn't something you can easily give way on, so I didn't, so Mum was talking about betrayal by the end of the call. Despairing at the thought that she had raised two citizens of nowhere. She then called up Rachel and tried the same trick. Rachel, I think, handled it better than I did, but she stuck to her course as well.

I felt guilty for not particularly wanting the life Mum had laid out for me. I knew it was what she wanted for me, I knew it was something she'd planned all her life. And I knew as well that my reasons for not wanting to go home were not because I had something lined up that was demonstrably better. I hadn't built much of a life at all. But that didn't mean I'd want to move back to Wales and farm sheep for a living. The work had always been hard and draining, the money had never added up; the idea that the land had meant a lot to my family over many years had never counted for ever so much when set against the way I felt about the way it made you live. That lean, hillside farming, losing money on the lambs each year, relying on the single farm payment, out before dawn and back after dark, always lugging dead bodies to fires because so many of the sheep died, and the dogs died, and the farmers died from time to time as well, the dogs in their kennels barking in the night, the cold and the foot rot and the mud caking the whole of you – all of it was a backbreaking life that belonged, it seemed to me, to the past. It wasn't who I wanted to be, it was just the life I had been born into, and I didn't know exactly what I did want to do with my time, but it wasn't that – that hardship, that solitude.

Above all it was the solitude I shied away from. To live around no one but the other old farmers, who all hated each other and all hated you. Nursing ancient hatreds while their lives passed by. In our valley lived a farmer who had run over his neighbour's dog some forty years ago. The neighbour, another sheep farmer, had fired off a shotgun into his chest in revenge. Grapeshot, probably, only meant to wound, but it had happened, and forty years on they still farmed side by side, not speaking to each other, never having gone to the police. There was something extraordinary about living in a place like that. Like living in a myth. But it was essentially mad as well, and I didn't want to go back to it.

Of course, all this wasn't the real fight either. The real fight with Mum was buried so much deeper than that; it was as old as life, fundamental enough that I could probably have sat and thought for a year and never quite got to the heart of it. Something about the scrabble for survival. The way kids end up effacing their parents. The way parents try to ensure their kids will be faithful palimpsests of them, and not rewrite the story too much, not dispel the meaning of the family when it's their turn to decide what that meaning might be. The fight that comes with all our surviving, and the fight of trying to be yourself, not just one bead in the necklace of a family, not just who your mother wants you to be, fulfilling her wishes rather than your own, a thought she had once that lives on after she does rather than a person in your own right. The fight we were really having encompassed everything, and the farm was a face and a name we'd put on it, and now Amy seemed to be about to become a face and a name we'd put on the fight as well.

Just as Amy shared the story of her family with me, I try to tell her the story of mine. Whole evenings pass telling stories to each other; it's something I've never quite done before with any other girlfriend. There's an intimacy to it, a quality of listening that seems to heighten the atmosphere between us. I suppose each person's family and the world they come from is a kind of secret, and the way to let someone into your life is always to share your secrets with them. We lie on the grass in the park near her flat, drinking Rekorderlig and swapping stories, and I try my best to unfold the history of who I am.

'So in the beginning was the farm, kind of thing,' I say to her, lying with my head on her lap while she lies back on the grass as well, both of us staring up at the clouds that are scudding across the light, across our vision. 'That's been ours for a very long time.'

'How long is very long?'

'I don't know completely. Two hundred years? I think the house is about two hundred years old. I don't know whether it was us who built it.'

'How can you not know that?'

'I don't know. Two hundred years is a long time. Not everything survives that long, does it?'

'But knowing whether it was your family who built the place.'

'Maybe my Mum knows. I'll ask her some time. If there's ever a good time.'

'Ask her now.'

I laugh at this. 'Not a good time.'

'Why not?'

'She's decided now that I have no interest in it. If I text her now, I'll just be starting a fight.'

'Or putting a stop to one.'

I think about this. 'Do you reckon?'

'I don't know. Only one way to find out.'

I try to imagine the way it would go. Pulling my phone out, and getting the text right, sending it off to Mum to get the story. I ought to get all the stories from her one day; there'll come a time when I've left it too late. Those sorts of jobs get set aside in families, and they shouldn't. Families really ought to write the stories down. I try to imagine Mum writing this story in a text, and sending it back to me, filling in a gap in the family history. But other scenarios crowd into my mind. The snide response; the questioning as to why I care right now; the silence that gets a bit harder to break every time she stretches it out across new moments. There are too many ways it could go wrong. Better not to write to her, better to say nothing. If you say nothing you can't get hurt.

'Maybe another time.'

Amy doesn't say anything for a moment. 'Fair enough,' she says in the end. 'So tell me what you do know.'

I try to bring my mind back to the story I'd started to tell, having lost the thread for a second. What was I going on about? That was it. In the beginning was the farm.

'So I think my family had already been there for a couple of generations when my great-grandfather, whose name was Arthur, made a break with things and went away to work in India for a while.'

'Why India?'

'I don't know, really. I suppose there was work. This was at the start of the twentieth century. He went over to be involved with building the railways in Hyderabad. It was just that his father hadn't died, I think. And Arthur, my great-grandfather, was quite a bright man, and he didn't fancy just working for his dad till his dad died, so he went and did something else for a bit. And when he was out in India, he met an Indian woman called Phoebe, and married her, and they lived over there for a while.'

'Phoebe isn't an Indian name.'

'I think she was Goan. Christian Indian. She was christened with a Western name. I don't know the whole story, really; I don't know all that much about her family.'

'What was a woman from Goa doing in Hyderabad?'

'Her father moved them there because of the trade. He was some kind of trader. Buying and selling. So she grew up there. She was quite young when she married Arthur. In India then, women married quite young. So she lived with him in India for a few years, and then when the war broke out they came back to England.'

I am watching a cloud cross the face of the sky, a cloud that seems to be taking on the shape of a rhino. I watch its shadow pass over our bodies.

'What does that cloud look like to you?' I ask. Amy is silent for a moment.

'A ship,' she says. I look, but I can't see it. 'They'll have come to England by ship, I suppose; is that why you mentioned the cloud?'

'I didn't see a ship,' I say.

'What do you see?'

'I don't know, really,' I tell her, even though I do. But I don't know why I've changed the subject, and I think perhaps I should go on with the story I'd started to tell. 'They did come back by ship, though.'

'Port out, starboard home.'

'That's it, yes. And then Arthur enlisted in the navy, and left Phoebe living on her own in east London for four years, looking after their son, my grandfather, who was born just after Arthur went away.'

'Really?'

'Mad, isn't it?'

'Can you imagine how alone she must have been? There by the docks in a place she didn't know with a child to look after, and no one to talk to.'

'If I'm completely honest, I can't really. But I agree with you. I know what you mean.'

'And he was at sea for the whole of the war?'

'Yes. Then after the war he came home. And they didn't go back to India again. Arthur took over the farm after his father died, and went there to live with Phoebe and their child, my grandfather.'

'What was your grandfather's name?'

'Leo. Poor man.'

'Why poor man?'

'I don't think he got to have much fun, really. He had a long enough life, but didn't get much out of it.'

As I've been talking, the feeling has been growing that, for some reason I can't quite put my finger on, talking about all the family history is making me unhappy. It's strange, how anxious it's making me feel. I suppose because Mum used to tell me all these stories. But there's also the feeling of time running out on me while I'm talking: all these lives that seemed as long as mine to the people who lived them, which are all gone now, which can all be summarised in half a dozen sentences. I suppose it makes the idea of breaking free of this history seem futile. How could I ever make time to live my own life, and set my own parameters, and choose the person I want to be rather than just inherit where I came from, when lives pass so quickly, when there's so little to them? How can I ever resist subsiding into this long-running story, and being just one more brief anecdote about to be forgotten? Telling my history makes me feel I'm running out of time, and the things I have built up are ending, they are going to go away.

I have found in my relatively short experience that life has a way of giving me springs and autumns, one thing always following another and all seeming to vanish as quickly as they come. Ephemerality is what everything feels like in the end. I think I got the idea from Mum when she told me the stories of our family, the stories that had shaped us and brought us here. What the relatives she spoke about all seemed to share was a life that ebbed and flowed around them, one tide always giving way to another, so they were caught and pulled in different directions, every move they tried to make for themselves beset and foiled by some counter-movement, so no matter what they tried to do to change their worlds, they always seemed to end up back where they started. Back on the farm. What became of their lives seemed to be out of their hands. They were just drawn through time by deep, irresistible currents.

Mum, like Amy, loved to tell stories. In the evenings or on long afternoons when I was very young, she'd sit and yarn with me, remembering, imagining. I'll never quite know how true her stories were; they became the cloak of memories around me as I grew up, so they had that much truth to them, but they might have all been plucked from the clouds. I remember nights when Rachel and I would sit by the fire, while Chris and Mum nursed drinks and Mum imagined the world for us, making it seem so vivid and real, so much more charged than the everyday around us.

'The saddest thing about wanting to find out who you are is that, by the time you start asking questions, it's already getting to be too late,' I remember her saying to me. 'I think the reason any of us get round to asking is a kind of sixth sense that the answers to our questions have begun to disappear. It's when you realise the people who knew them are dying and you've never sat down and asked for their secrets that you wish you'd started sooner in collecting the tale of who you are. Then you set off searching. Or that's how it was for me, anyway. When I was a girl I never thought about who it was that walked round in this body of mine, looking out through these eyes at the world.'

I remember her sitting in front of the fire at home, the old iron stove that heated most of the house through an intricate, arcane system of pipes and pumps, a few drinks deep in her evening, talking poetry the way she sometimes did on winter nights.

'I think the reason my father died the way he did is due to what happened to my grandmother when the first war came. When she was made to move to England from India, and washed up here without her husband, having to live by herself in a place quite unlike anything she'd ever known. That was what drove her mad. I'm sure that's why there weren't more children. After my father, she just couldn't manage it. She didn't have the strength to be a mother any more.'

'Did your dad talk to you about your grandparents?' Chris asked her, careful not to look at her, fixing his gaze on the fire. Thinking back to conversations like these, it seems to me that sometimes eye contact would make Mum think more carefully about what she was saying, and she would discover that it upset her, and then withdraw into herself.

'Not very often. Not ever so much. But I know that when he was a young child it was more or less his grandmother who raised him. Isn't that a strange thing? He must have felt so close to the long ago. His grandmother was born in the 1840s, I think that's right. She'd have brought him up with the values of that time. And he'd have been so out of step with his world, without even knowing it, just because of the start he was given. No wonder it was difficult for him to fit in. The child of an Indian woman, living out here, brought up with the manners of seventy years before. He'd have seemed like an alien to everyone. He didn't say all that much about his parents. I have two photos, though – hang on, let me find them.' She stood up and crossed the room to take a photo album from the shelves. She leafed through it for a moment, then walked back across the room to us. 'Here we go – look at this.'

She put the album down in front of me and Rachel, and I saw two photographs side by side on opposite pages. In the first photograph, two people, a man and a woman, were looking at the camera. He was seated, and she stood beside him: a much younger woman, very beautiful. The man was well dressed, and had a big moustache about the width of his face. In the second photograph, the same man was seated in the middle of a group of about a hundred Indian workmen. He had the same moustache, but seemed much older, his pale suit making him stand out among the thin men sitting round him.

'That's my grandfather with everyone who worked for him,' Mum said. I looked again at the photograph of the couple. The woman standing beside her husband was dark in complexion, but dressed in Western clothes. I had hardly thought of her as Indian when I looked at the picture the first time. More than her race, the photograph expressed the moment it was taken in. She looked more Edwardian than anything else – strapped into the period, bound indelibly to the moment she had lived through. 'They were married just a few years before the war.'

I remember my mum's unease, the tension in her body as she showed us those photos that first time. I try to imagine what she must have been feeling. She was trying to show Rachel and me who we were, of course. And weave that tapestry of inflections and secrets that would shape how the world looked through our eyes, becoming the way we saw, creating the unconscious, instinctive reflexes that underpinned all our actions, that made us who we were. But when I remember how tense Mum seemed as she leaned over us, showing us the photos, I think she must have also been feeling the same way I felt when I told Amy my family's story. A kind of grief would have been roused in her, a panic that soon her time would run out, it would all go, just as it had for the couple in the photo. I think she took the album out in part because she didn't want to die.

'Did your dad never want to go somewhere else?' I remember asking. When I think back to this night, this conversation, I feel sure this was the first time I formed the thought that I didn't want to always live on the farm. So I think it was very important, this question, though I didn't know it at the time.

'He didn't have the chance,' Mum said. 'By the time he was thirteen and leaving school, his grandparents had both died, and his mother was more or less an invalid who never left her room. His father wouldn't look after her. He didn't know how, I don't think. Who can blame him? I think his wife lost her mind. What does a farmer who once worked on the railways know about that? No, my grandfather didn't stand a chance, so my dad looked after her. He stayed at home and kept house, while his father was out on the hills with the sheep, summer and winter, and that was their strange life till my grandfather died.'

'There has to be more to it than that,' I said. 'He can't have just never done anything. Never gone anywhere.'

'The world wasn't like it is now, Ed,' Mum answered. 'He worked keeping the place together till the year his father died. Then he took over the farm, and married my mother, and then his mother died, and then he had me.'

It was strange, how our family spanned the century. My grandfather Leo had been well into his forties by the time Mum was born, so it was only necessary to go back a couple of generations to be speaking of a hundred years ago. He had been introduced to my grandmother by a man he knew at the livestock market in Hereford, so the story went. Grandma was younger than him, a farmer's daughter, without much of a plan in life, and she was happy to move to another farm and continue to live the life she knew. She brought up my mother very well, and in every story Mum ever told about her, the two appeared to be very close, they had shared a lot together. I didn't remember her all that well, because she had died when I was young. A woman who used to give me sweets; a woman with a laugh that shook her whole body, as if it came from deep inside her.

'You try your best to get on with it. But I think life happens too quickly for much recovering; there isn't time. That's what I felt myself when I found out I was having you,' I remember Mum saying as she smiled at me. 'How strange, I thought to myself when I learned I was pregnant. Because I'm still just a girl. And none of the things I wanted to solve have moved on even an inch for any of my thinking about them in the time I've had. But life's going on anyway – now I will be a mother, and I'll just have to go along with it, I suppose. Because it all keeps happening, one day at a time. Sometimes I find myself feeling very small and frightened, and I think of the day my father died, and I don't know how I can ever be all right. But it's happened before. It will happen again. So it stands to reason that there must be a way to keep going on, because others have managed it, billions must be managing it even now.'

Because Amy and I found each other at a wedding, it makes me strangely nervous, just a few months later, to be travelling to another wedding with her, although this time it's different, and Amy's just a guest, and won't be taking photographs of anyone. But this is how it started, I suppose, so it's hard not to wonder whether this could somehow be how it ends. But two of Amy's friends are getting married and she says I should come, so we travel to the coast for a weekend to stay with a group of her school friends in an Airbnb. The place we've rented all together for the weekend is a seventeenth-century farmhouse with a nineteenth-century front built on, surrounded by a couple of acres of grounds and set back from a narrow country road. There's a half moon of lawn at the front, fenced off with elegant ironwork and a scrubby hedge. It was planted as an orchard many years ago but hasn't been maintained. Half the apple trees are no longer producing and the only new tree growing is a young oak. The idea this place exists and yet has been left to fall into neglect is unimaginable to me. When the day comes that I have a home of my own, one of the things I'm most looking forward to is planting apple trees in the back yard. I dream of this moment. I imagine it will feel like coming fully alive.

After breakfast the first day, Amy goes to take a shower before getting ready for the wedding. An hour and a half till the taxi comes. Too soon for the men in the house to start dressing. I take my coffee and a book outside, go into the forgotten orchard, lie down under a russet apple tree.

We arrived the previous day before most of the others, and the couple who had got here before us had gone on already to the wedding rehearsal, so for a few hours we had the place to ourselves. We made dinner, then chose a bedroom, undressed and got into bed together, then dressed again to greet the next couple arriving. For half an hour we all tried to put up the sofa bed one of Amy's friends would be sleeping on that night, then accepted the thing was broken and did the best we could to cover it over with a sheet instead. Half an hour later, two more people arrived on the back of a motor-bike, then the last three returned from the wedding rehearsal. We poured out drinks for each other and sat talking together for a little while, then Amy and I took ourselves off to bed again, this time to sleep. I was tired after four hours travelling up the motorway, weekend traffic, warm Diet Coke from the services. The beginning of summer. In the morning we were woken by the alarm on my phone, and those who had to get to the venue early left us, and the rest of us made breakfast and ate together round the big dining table.

I've been lying on the grass for no more than five minutes when I hear a voice calling my name from the front door, one of the girls asking whether I want a glass of something. The first cork popping will be the sound of the start of the day.

I close my book and start getting up to go inside and help make drinks, then the same girl who called out to me comes back to the door and her voice has changed; there's a sense of real and sudden urgency in the air as she calls out to me. She tells me Amy's hurt herself and I'm needed upstairs right now.

I don't guess at first that it might be serious. I go inside and climb the stairs and walk through to the ancient back of the house where we slept last night, old boards, low doorways, not knowing what I'll find but guessing a stubbed toe, a nail pulled back; I have no intimation of what's waiting for me. Which is strange, because most of the time I tend to assume the worst, but in the summer sunshine where all life feels lazy and welcoming, the idea of real danger seems impossible.

Then I reach the doorway to our room and the day changes. There are four people kneeling round Amy where she is slumped on the floor, holding towels to her head, and all of their voices are panicked and their faces pale, so I walk round to see what's happened and Amy's face is grey, she's shaking and her breath comes in gasps and the towels are soaked in blood and there is blood pooling on the floor and a spatter pattern reaching all the way to the bed across the whitewashed floorboards.

I kneel and ask what's happened and if she can tell me when her birthday is, and she can hardly speak. Someone tells me she hit her head on the doorframe coming back from the shower and there was this crack like a gunshot.

I call an ambulance while her friends start to mop up the blood where it's staining the white-painted boards and the call handler asks to speak to Amy, then tells me to maintain pressure on the wound and that an ambulance will take two hours. I ask where the nearest A&E is and we find it on a map and then we set off, Amy insisting she takes her dress in the back of the car though I can't imagine she'll need it now, driving away from the ceremony we surely won't see, the vows exchanged, the life embarked on, driving through green meadowland past osier-lined brooks and little villages, driving with a police motorbike on our tail for a dozen miles of the journey, following us closely, as if he knows there's something wrong with us, as if he knows I'd be flooring the accelerator if he wasn't there, finally reaching the town with the hospital after forty minutes, funnelled through one roundabout after another on the ring road encircling the town, then parking up at A&E and passing through the sliding doors, and I think of the time I had my skull fractured, a fight I didn't ask for down a backstreet one Saturday night, and the stabbing pains that still come to me sometimes ten years later, like a knife in the skull, and feel a growing panic about Amy, a fear in the pit of my stomach that anything could be happening to her now. We get to the front desk and a doctor takes her away.

The day doesn't feel real. We've all watched too many films; sometimes when things that matter are at stake, we feel as if we've walked into one. Such a sense of detachment is dangerous. It makes people feel they're invincible, when we're not, we're all one crack like a gunshot away from life changing. It is so brief, this thing we're in, so fragile, and only one thing is certain – the end approaching each of us.

The beginning of summer. Perhaps it crosses my mind even now while I wait for news of Amy that something is coming towards us. Like sighting the first slow swell of a wave. And in this moment, I don't know what it's bringing. Because the image of the blood spattered over the floor is still in my eyes, and what if she dies now, what if she's keeled over even now? I press my hands together between my legs, because it feels like they're shaking, and I don't want her to be dead on the other side of those doors, I don't want her to be gone before we've even started, and we had no chance to be happy together; I had no chance to stop her hitting her head on the doorframe, so how could this be taken from us, when we have done nothing?

As I wait, I start to feel desperate, and I want to get up and go to her, walk through the doors, demand I'm allowed to be with her while she's seen, but I do nothing.

I sit and wait. I try to control this urge to make it about me.

She comes back out into the waiting area thirty minutes later, pale and slightly dazed, blood still caked in her hair. I stand up when I see her, walk towards her, and I can feel tears starting in my eyes, because I'd begun to wonder if I'd see her again.

'Are you OK?' I ask her. She looks at me, but not quite at me, as if her vision's blurred.

'Fine.' And her voice is quiet, she seems withdrawn, and I can see she's not fine, she's shaken.

'So what happened?'

'They glued me up. My head, I mean. I can't wash my hair for a week while the glue's in. I can't wash the blood out of my hair.' She raises a hand very gently to her hair, touches the blood that's matted and dried there, then winces, lets her hand fall back down by her side.

'And what are we supposed to do now?'

'We'll go to the wedding.'

This sounds very unlikely to me. Surely she shouldn't be out around people now? Surely they've told her she ought to go home?

'Are you sure?'

Amy looks at me and I can see she's suddenly close to getting angry. 'Do you think we're just going home? I'm not missing my friends' wedding, Ed. They've told me what's safe and it's fine.'

'And it's totally safe? But presumably you can't drink, can you?'

'They've told me what's safe. Come on.'

I suspect her of lying to me, of course. Deciding she's willing to take a risk because she wants to be with her friends. It's her choice, to a point; part of me thinks it's selfish too, but in the end I suppose it's her choice, and I wasn't in the consulting room, so I don't know what they've told her. So we go to the wedding in time for the meal. Amy changes on the driveway of the big house that's been rented for the wedding reception, standing in her underwear on the drive, defiantly alive and determined to be present at the wedding of her friends, the life in her shining, dazzling me, too beautiful to put into language.

In the evening she dances and it makes me smile to see her laugh, makes me feel almost dizzy, because the blood spatter all the way to the bed is still before my eyes while I watch, and suddenly I realise this is happiness, this has been happiness all along. I know this with a clarity I haven't felt in years, and it runs through me like drink, like a chemical high. But I can't join in with the dancing. It feels too ghostlike tonight, this luck we've had, this being here.

When the night ends and we lie down to sleep, I find that I'm holding my breath, as if listening for footsteps, as if something might be coming to claim us. Sleep takes me in the end, but I fight it. Something is waiting at the corner of my vision, and what is it that's coming towards me exactly? What can I almost see? The briefness of this place is suddenly too brittleclear to bear; what seemed this morning like the whole, real world now resembles little more than a dream, ice across a lake that could give way at any moment, plunging us into other worlds, unspoken underneath.

Every minute we live could change our lives. But even though each minute carries the same potential charge, there are nevertheless certain days that seem to shine brighter than others, days when our lives seem to be shaped and decided. Lying in bed next to Amy, looking at the matted blood clotting her hair into ropes on the pillow, I feel like I'm living through one of those days. Right now, right here, my life is changing and I can feel the current that's drawing me inexorably on. I look at Amy as she sleeps and see this is the person I want to be with. Her and no other. Perhaps I hadn't realised that till now. We'd fallen easily into one another's lives, and discovered a rhythm together. But things seem suddenly different tonight. This morning when I saw the blood spattered across this room, for just a moment I imagined she might die. And I discovered as that thought passed over me like cloud shadow that this, the life welling up between us, has come to mean a great deal to me, though it hardly seems we've been together long enough to speak of love, to speak of lasting. It's so new, and it's untested, and if someone had asked me yesterday, I might well have said our relationship was just the two of us going with the flow, but when we were in the car going to the hospital, I felt I simply couldn't lose this woman who was sitting beside me, cradling her head as the blood dried on her hands. We're playing for keeps, I see this now. We have made moorings of each other.

In the morning we wake and eat breakfast with the others, and then I drive us home because Amy is now feeling the effects of the previous night and of the accident before the wedding. The day is a brilliant blazing, bright sun beating down on the apple trees and the house, which makes everyone's hangovers worse. Magpies chatter and flit among the trees. A jay swoops through the shadows, hunting.

'Does your head hurt?'

'Not really.'

'What does that mean? If your head hurts, then we need to see someone.'

'It's a Sunday morning.'

'That doesn't matter.'

'I'm just hungover.'

'Are you sure?'

'No.'

'Then should we go back and ask to be seen again?'

'At the hospital?'

'Yes.'

'It's miles in the wrong direction.'

'That doesn't matter.'

'No, I'm almost certain I'm just hungover.'

'Are you sure that they said you could drink?'

'They told me I wasn't concussed.'

'That's not the same as saying you can drink.'

'They said that too.' I know then that she's lying and I wish I'd gone into the consulting room with her.

Amy stands impatiently, looking at me. 'Can we just go home? I just want to get in my own bed again.'

She sleeps in the passenger seat beside me as we travel back down the M1. At Watford Gap services we stop for coffee. I look up at the bridge over the motorway, and imagine my father standing there. He used to live in a village two miles away, and every evening during his teenage years when he was waiting to escape from this place and make his way into the wide world, Dad told me that he used to walk out to the bridge to smoke his pipe, and look to the north and then to the south, and wonder what was going to become of him, what life was going to offer. He thought by doing this he would avoid his parents, my grandparents, ever finding out that he smoked, but I imagine they knew very well what he was doing, and smelled it on him, and simply let him get on with it. There's no one on the bridge today. This road is so much busier now; I can't imagine anyone ever stops up there any more to look down over it. It's strange to think that if all time was suddenly made visible, and every day in the life of the world was allowed to rub shoulders together for just a moment, I'd be able to see my dad as a young man standing up there, smoking, looking around him, wondering what the future would bring. Like sighting the wave that came before you.

After that weekend it feels like something has to change. I don't quite know what to do about it, but the rhythm I've been in, going round to Amy's and then going back to the converted garage I've been living in, seems suddenly ludicrous to me. Moving into the garage had been natural enough, I suppose; the idea was always to retreat for a time before finding a way to go forwards in life again. But now the adolescence of the present situation feels embarrassing to me, and I'm anxious to do something about it. Amy's due to leave for Kuala Lumpur in a week's time, and I feel like we're running out of something, I suppose we're running out of time, and I don't know how to tell her before she goes that, if she didn't mind, if she didn't object to it, I'd like to still be there for her when she gets back.

How do you say that? Tell someone you love them? Isn't that just banal?

In the end I do the only other thing I can think of, the thing that Amy's already done with me; I take her to meet my parents. Pathetic, really, but it seems like a way of saying, here, look – this is my life. You can share it with me if you like.

Because Mum hasn't really talked to me since I told her Amy and I have got together, I feel more than a little apprehensive when we get in the car to drive to the farm to visit her and Chris. But I know I need to go over there and fix what I've broken, and I can't think of any other way to show Amy that I don't want her to forget me, so I call Chris and invite myself over to Wales for the weekend. I realise after we've finished speaking that it will be the first time I've gone there in almost a year.

Since I left home, I've always gone back in the spring to help with the lambing, but the argument Mum and I had about her will meant that didn't happen this year. It did feel like there was something missing from the year. I stayed in the city and worked instead, and work doesn't feel very much like my real life. All the work I've ever done has only really been a way to pay for living – answering the phone in an agency for a long time, working in the bar at a theatre and, for the last two years, writing advertorial for a website that sells watches and other things people don't need but spend a lot of money on. In the last half a year they've started letting me file my copy for them from home, and I've been able to make some money on the side writing listicles for other websites, but for a long time they made me go into an office every day to make sure I stayed productive. So when I didn't go home for the lambing this year, I sat in a cubicle in east London writing about watches instead.

By coincidence, I hadn't visited at Christmas either; Juliet and I used to have a system of alternating who we visited on the day, and last year it was her family's turn, so I called Mum and Chris and talked on the phone with them, and told myself that was enough, and that they felt it was enough, they wouldn't mind that I hadn't done more to see them. It must be similar with every family, I suppose. Once the children have grown old enough to move away, we all enter the endless dance of how to navigate that week between Christmas and New Year, never in the right place, never all together, all of us wondering how to get that week right. This is where the idea takes hold, I think, that somewhere there's a centre, there's a place called home that's the rootnote of your life. And the search for that starts to consume you, as you try to work out what that strange word means. Home, an idea which is constructed out of place, people, and stories above all. A synonym for love. It's the memory of Christmases when no one had to worry where to spend them, where to go. The memory of a childhood when nothing was complicated. If such a thing ever really existed at all.

Realising I haven't been home to see Mum and Chris for almost a year makes me a little more anxious about visiting, but it doesn't change my decision about travelling out there; in truth, feeling uncomfortable about going back home isn't anything new. Almost every visit I've made out there in the last ten years has been a little awkward, and Mum and I have long ago become used to biting our tongues when we're together. That's partly why Mum liked Juliet, I think; Juliet was nice to her, and wanted to involve her in our lives, so she became a bridge between Mum and me, a way for us to reconnect at a time when we seemed to have lost our connection.

Before it was arguing over wills and inheritance, the face the fight between me and my mother wore was over my father when, in the year after I left university, I let him come and live with me and then looked after him while he died. Dad slept in the spare room for that terrible last six months, and Mum kept her distance, causing a big silence to open up between us.

The way I'd seen it, I didn't have a choice. Dad had already lost his battle with drink by then; his life was already over, and he just needed a place where he could finish the process of dying. He never actually asked me to help him, but we had coffee one day, and I saw the state of him and guessed he'd lost his flat, so I asked if he needed a place to stay, and he moved in with me. I was living at that time in the flat of a friend who'd moved abroad for work and needed a house sitter, so it was easy enough for me to take him in – I had no flatmates to upset.

For the last half a year of his life, Dad sat on my sofa and drank. I'd remove the bottles and take him to the doctor, cook him meals and collect his medication, do whatever I could for him, but I was years too late really. I knew within a month of him arriving that his liver had more or less failed.

After a while he had to go into the hospital, and I would go and sit with him, and then it all came to an end. There was nothing much left for us to talk about by the time he was in hospital, so I read to him instead, a chapter of a book I'd then leave by his bedside with a bookmark in so I could pick up where I'd left off and carry on reading the next time I visited. I suppose I left the book because I hoped someone else might want to go and see him, and find the book there, and be grateful for it because it would mean they could read to him, and wouldn't have to think of anything to say. But no one else ever went, I don't think, and the bookmark was always in the same place when I returned. He liked children's stories. I suppose they took him back to his own childhood, and that comforted him. And I was his child reading to him as well, and I guess he found some kind of happiness in remembering the time when it was the other way round.

When he died, I was reading him *The Magician's Nephew*, about the portals in the attic that led into other worlds. When I got to the hospital that last time, and found that his bed was empty, I took the book home with me. I still have it somewhere on my shelves. He was a bastard, my dad. The things he put himself through traumatised me and Mum and everyone who knew him, and there was a lot we might have wanted from him which he was never able to give. But he was my dad all the same, so I keep the book and I keep the bookmark in the page where I left it. Many years from now, when I die, someone from a house clearance firm will pick up that old second-hand copy of a C. S. Lewis book, and see it was read by someone who never finished it, decide it has no resale value and throw it away. But for now it's a doorway into the memory of my father.

Mum kept her distance all the time he lived with me. I suppose she had to. The fact was that the trigger for Dad's drinking had been their divorce. I suppose it must have been hard for her not to feel some guilt, some responsibility. After the divorce she built a life that made her happy, and looked like permanence, and was filled with children and friendships and the open air, moving back to the farm to live with her mother for her last years, then taking the farm over, and meeting Chris, and marrying him, and moving on. Dad drank, meanwhile, and lost his work because his hands shook, and lived on benefits and odd jobs and moved from flat to dirty flat, and sometimes when I visited him I would take a bottle of gin with me, knowing that he'd kill himself one day, but knowing as well that, until he was two drinks deep, he could barely string a sentence together. I'd sit with him, have a drink myself to normalise the situation. I tried to make it seem like I was keeping him company, like nothing was wrong. After a couple of drinks, his hands would stop shaking and he'd talk in sentences again. It was natural for Mum to keep her distance from all that. But in the last months, that meant she also ended up keeping her distance from me, and after the funeral, which in the end she didn't come to, telling us she didn't think Dad would want her to remember him like that, I found it was difficult to restart things between us.

I don't think we really spoke again till I met Juliet. Then there was someone to introduce Mum to, a new person in the room to listen to the stories, and we were able to build an alternative narrative about our relationship through telling Juliet the story of who we were, rewriting our family history so it wasn't overshadowed by drink, by the marriage that had failed, and other things came into focus instead, parts of our shared history we might otherwise have forgotten. We left out the failures and hidden darknesses, and talked about the farm and childhood and holidays – the stuff of life.

There were things we couldn't get back, of course. There was the problem that even after Dad's funeral I still felt like his representative on earth somehow, responsible for his memory, trapped on his side when the wind had changed. I felt as if I brought him with me whenever I came to stay at the farm. These visits only strengthened the sense I had that one day the farm would stop being part of my life, because it was only half my life, the place where Mum and Chris had lived, not Dad. Knowing that changed the way I saw the place when I went back. It started to seem like a crime scene to me – my childhood was marked out there in chalk outlines, but the body was gone.

My parents had met at college, and got together, and married about a year after they left and started work. Probably too quickly, as it would turn out. After the marriage, they didn't go back to the farm, but tried living away in the south of England. Dad worked in the building restoration trade, and Mum took in people's sewing and worked as a typist for an agency. It isn't so very long ago, but it was a different world; money stretched further, so jobs no one even does any more used to be enough to make ends meet. They made their home in West Sussex in a disused hunting lodge in the middle of a wood, two miles from the next living soul. The lodge belonged to an earl who lived in the big house in the middle of the estate we lived on the edge of, and who had taken a liking to my dad when he did some work on the house, and let him have the lodge for a peppercorn rent because no one was using it, and having someone in it would help to keep it from falling down. It was during this time that I was born and I think both my parents liked the idea of bringing up their child in a wood in the middle of nowhere: the peace, the seclusion, the freedom of no one watching.

For a while it was just the three of us alone there, and I think we were happy. Then Dad started to travel more for work, and then one winter a six-week job turned into the best part of half a year, and the marriage ended, in the way marriages do when a husband and wife are pulled apart like that. Dad moved out, and I stayed in the lodge with Mum for a while, but there was a feeling once Dad had gone that everything was temporary. Mum didn't want to stay any longer than she had to in the ruin of the life she'd tried to build, and money was a problem, and I guess the isolation must have been a lot to cope with once it was just her and me and the ghost of her marriage out there in the woods. So, in the end, she decided to go home.

I remember it seemed to me when we arrived at the farm as if we were walking into a dream my mum had had years earlier. When she was pregnant with me, she had made a blanket that looked just like those hills in Wales. She stitched together squares of wool and felt in different shades of green and russet for the fields, with little border hedges in dark green, and a blue woollen river running through it all, and a road with a bridge in grey-brown, and little sheep sticking up from the blanket made from tufts of white wool that looked a bit like clouds, and this was the blanket I used to lie on in the big room in the hunting lodge before I learned to walk. The farm looked just like the blanket. The same patchwork of fields, the same greens and browns and sheep and hedgerows. I remember taking in the valley we had moved to for the first time, ruined barns that dotted the hillsides and seemed to be caving into the grass like ships going under, like memories sinking back into the long withdrawing furl of time. Of course I didn't take in the meaning of those old ruined buildings at the time, my thoughts were simpler, I doubt I even put them into words, but I do remember knowing those places had sheltered people once, whole families, and now they were nothing. And now we were here, and we'd do the same thing. I remember feeling I could see back in time.

Once we settled there, I learned that time kept different rules in that valley. There were days when changes in the weather seemed to make time move faster; we would watch a weather front scour the valley in the space of an hour, swooping over like a buzzard so that all of a sudden there was snow harrowing the ground. Then it would be gone, and the sun would shine, and the snow would disappear as if it had never happened. The sun burning off the last clouds in the valley would pick out rainbows in the threads of cloud it scattered, so they looked like oil slicks smudging the light. It seemed sometimes as if the sky spent its days in drafting and discarding wild masks of light, riotous and diffuse, the most beautiful show you could ever imagine, searching for a true face, trying to find its real self, never deciding what that might be in time for nightfall, then having to give up for another day when the stars and the moon came out.

It was always the valley more than the cottage that I loved. The cottage itself was nineteenth-century, with an extension built by my great-grandfather, and another lean-to added by my grandfather later on. There were eight rooms, a living space you walked into through the front door where the stove had been joined up to a radiator system through the rest of the house, which was where my grandmother used to sit all day in the short time she was living there as well, before she died and it was just me and Mum again. Either side of that room was a kitchen where the walls were always wet with damp, and the sitting room my great-grandfather had added, which was the biggest room in the house, and heated by a separate stove. At the back, the lean-to served as a utility room, always filled with washing on lines and things that needed to be cleaned, and a small toilet that had been put in and boxed off from the rest of the room. Upstairs were three bedrooms and a bathroom, the older two bedrooms barely larger than the double beds in them, memories of a different time, of the modest spaces claimed by the people who first came here and made this hillside habitable. Stretching up the hill in the field nearest to the house were a few outbuildings for timber and machinery, straggled all the way to the top of the field where the water tank was housed, all of them thrown up over many years as and when they were needed. It was an isolated place, half a mile from the next farm and a mile from the nearest village. In summer it was very beautiful, but in the winter the place became lonely. The cold months always seemed to be trying to drive us out, and something in them spoke to the stone of the farmhouse, enlisted the slate flagstones. Because of this I never quite trusted the farm in the summer. In its heart, I believed that it wanted us gone.

An old school friend introduced Mum to Chris at a dinner party. He was living in the area and had worked on the farm for a time when it was just my grandmother living there, when my grandmother had hired a manager to run the farm, and the manager had occasionally brought in hired labour at lambing time. Mum and Chris liked each other straight away, they've both told me, and Chris says it was the boldest thing he'd ever done when he asked Mum for her number. After they first met, he didn't call for a couple of days, because he said the whole thing just felt too unlikely to him. But an evening arrived when he gave in and called her, and Mum picked up, and everything started.

There followed a strange period in both their lives. The beginning of love, when what you want is in the air but no one's said it. Every evening they'd sit on the phone and talk to each other. Mum said she started to feel as if all day she was waiting for their phone calls, as if that was the real centre of her life. The conversations everyone has when they're trying not to say I love you.

Eventually it happened. It was the phone bills that made them cross the invisible sword that lay between them and find a way to put their dreams into words. Chris said to Mum one night as he stared at the fire in the grate that, seeing as all his money was going on calling her, maybe he'd be better off if they tried living in the same place for a little while. Maybe that would at least help the phone bills, if nothing else.

I was very young when we moved to the farm, but perversely I think of that as the time when childhood ends in my story. I felt like I'd lost some part of me back in the woods after we drove out of them for the last time, the quiet woods that sheltered us for those first few island years, when I have no memory of any other face except my mum's, not even Dad's, as if the world was only two souls wide. The world was never so perfect again, though of course we found happiness out on the hills at the farm; but ever since we left the hunting lodge, I've known there was another life, a ghost life, happening just under the surface of my own – a boy I'd left behind in the wood who never grew up, who no one ever went back to rescue, who couldn't even be reached if someone tried to find him now. Like a record playing in another room. That's what became of my childhood. I've never done anything about it. I've never gone back, or sought out a therapist to talk things through. The only concession I've ever made to the memory of that boy is that every time I move out of a flat or a house and into a new one, I always make sure that I leave a day early. I'll spend the day moving boxes into the new place, and then after dinner on the day I move, I'll go back to the place I've left, and let myself in with the key I've kept, and check the rooms and cupboards one last time. I've rescued some useful things that way. A jacket I left on the back of a bedroom door. A scarf on a coat hanger. A crystal glass that belonged to my grandmother. What I've always hoped I'll find, though, is the real original self I left behind. But that boy is never there waiting for me. I always leave the old places for the last time on my own.

On the day we travel to visit Mum and Chris at the farm, I find myself hoping to put off the moment of our arrival, praying we hit traffic, praying we might get lost down some side road. I think Mum had got the idea fixed in her mind of Juliet as her future daughter-in-law, and I think that particular casting became important to her. Living out in the wilds, the farm being so far from other people, Mum's world can sometimes come to feel quite small, I think, so the people in it take on great significance. I think Mum had imagined the talks she'd have with Juliet in the lead-up to our wedding day, the first visit she'd make to our home when we settled down somewhere, all that. And she thought Juliet brought out the best in me, moderated the behaviour of her son, who she'd been half estranged from, made it easier for us to have a relationship again.

Amy and I both feel the tension on the drive, and snap at each other, but I can't find the words to tell her how I'm feeling. I end up telling her the story of how my grandfather died instead. The story makes me feel ashamed as I tell it to her, and I suppose that's why I tell it. A way of expressing my shame at being irritable towards her as we drive, even if I can't actually explain the emotion.

'Part of why I don't really ever want to live there again is that my grandfather killed himself on the roof,' I tell her.

She turns to look at me. 'Jesus. I'm sorry.'

'It was before I was born. He climbed up there with a shotgun one morning and killed himself. Took half the roof tiles with him when he fell, and he landed in the back yard and my grandmother found him.'

'Why did he do it?'

'Why does anyone do it? He just struggled, I think. He had to look after his mum for a long time. And she wasn't well. She was an invalid, really, her mind had gone. I think that kind of thing builds up in a person.'

'But to kill yourself.'

'It's farming. A lot of farmers kill themselves.'

Amy looked at her hands, and didn't say anything. I could

hear that I was being aggressive, shrugging her off, telling the story so that it would sound shocking. I didn't know how to tell it any differently. 'None of us ever step on the spot where he fell. It just wasn't something you ever did when we were growing up. So the weird thing is that you can see where it happened, because the weeds grow up differently in between the flagstones. You can almost see the outline of the body in the middle of the yard.'

'Jesus. How did your family stay there after that?'

'I never really understood it. I asked Mum about it. She said you can't only see the bad.'

'But that's pretty terrible.'

'She said that leaving would have been like forgetting him.'

'It's pretty terrible all the same.'

'The coroner recorded it as an accident so he could be buried in consecrated ground. And so that Grandma could claim his life insurance. He said my grandfather accidentally climbed on to the roof, took off his shoe, put his shotgun in his mouth and fired it with his big toe. A lot of suicides used to be put down as accidents like that. If the coroner wanted to do the family a favour.'

I immediately regret telling the story, but it's too late to take it back, and I don't know what to say to make us feel better.

We pull into the front yard with sinking feelings, and see Chris open the door to the house and open his arms to welcome us in. Mum follows him outside, smile fixed on her face. Can Amy see the determined look she carries, the watchfulness in her eyes? How well do you have to know her before you can spot that she's acting?

'Ed, hello.' Chris shakes my hand as he always has since I moved away. Mum hugs me, and then turns to Amy and hugs her as well.

'And you must be Amy. I've heard so much about you. It's lovely to meet you. I'm Angela.'

Amy, who has heard too much about Mum, not enough of it complimentary, smiles and hugs her back.

'It's lovely to meet you too, Angela.'

We dump our bags, then all four of us take the dogs out for a walk. We talk about house prices and the weather, public transport and the dogs, then turn for home, and then we're shut in the house for the rest of the night, and just have to hope we can get through it happily. I deal with the tension in the worst way possible, drinking too much, and have to go to bed by ten.

Amy follows me up to bed, but once I'm undressed and horizontal, she says she'll go back downstairs to help wash up the dinner things. I hear her walk back down, the floorboards creaking with each step, and then I hear her in the room below with Mum. Chris has gone outside, I think, or gone to the bathroom, or gone to bed. The two women find themselves alone together, as I suppose both of them knew that at some point they might do, and Amy doesn't yet know how thin the floors are in this house, that I can hear every word they say to each other.

'He'll be asleep in a minute,' Amy says. I can hear the sound of the dishwasher being stacked, and wonder whether Mum has looked up when Amy came down, whether she's smiled at her or turned her back.

'He doesn't normally do that,' Mum says. 'Drink that much.'

'No, he doesn't. But he's home, I suppose.'

'Does that make a difference?'

'Perhaps it means he can relax.'

'I just find it unsettling, really. Because of his father.'

'Oh, yes. Of course. Is he like his father?'

'In some ways. Isn't everyone?'

'Can I do this bit of washing-up?'

'If you don't mind, that would be very kind, thank you.'

I listen as Amy turns the tap on and runs it till it starts to get hot. Then the sound of the water changes when she puts the plug in and the kitchen sink starts filling up.

'I enjoyed dinner.'

'I'm glad.'

'It must have been a strange evening for you.'

I hear Mum stop clattering the cutlery around, a hair's breadth of silence. 'Why strange?'

'Because I'm not her, am I? The person you'd thought he was going to be with.'

'Oh. I see.'

'Ed told me you were very fond of her. Juliet, I mean.'

'I was. She's a lovely girl. We've kept in touch, actually. Just the odd text.'

'I only met her once.'

'At that wedding.'

'Yes. That's right. She was very pretty.'

'I don't know how important that is. She's a very considerate person, that's what I liked about her.'

'Of course. You're right, it's not important. But there's nothing else I can really say about her. We've barely ever exchanged a word.'

'Could I ask you a question? I don't want to seem challenging.'

'Of course.'

'Did you know he was going to leave her for you?'

Amy doesn't answer for a moment. 'That's a difficult question.'

'Is it?'

'In some ways. I didn't know he was going to leave her. I couldn't have really, we only spoke for half an hour and we didn't exchange numbers; I didn't even know if we'd see each other again. But I suppose I did know, as well.'

'It was quite a charged half an hour, then?'

'I suppose so, yeah.'

'I might just dry those so you've got space.'

'Oh, thanks.'

'Thank you for rinsing. Ed never rinses.'

'I know, I criticise him relentlessly for it, but it just makes him more stubborn, I think.'

Mum laughs. 'That's him exactly.'

There's silence below me for a short time.

'I hope we'll be able to be friends,' Amy says, 'even if I'm not her.'

'Of course. Whoever Ed wants to be with is a friend to me, as long as they make him happy.'

'It's so difficult, isn't it? In-laws and girlfriends. I've seen so many people get together with terrible men and women who were awful to them, and all of their family would know and say nothing for fear of causing a rift. It happens all the time, I think. And how do you know the right time to step in and say something? So many relatives must put up with girlfriends and boyfriends they really hate, because they haven't crossed the red line that would allow open warfare.'

Mum laughs again. 'I've seen quite a lot of that, yeah.'

'It's strange to me, really, that people so often seem to get together with people who don't make them happy. It's probably very naive of me, but I'd sort of like to believe that any two people in the world could make each other happy if they tried. I'd like to believe that. Some would be better matched than others, but if everyone was kind, it should be possible for any two people to be happily married. But it isn't, is it?'

'No, it's not.'

'I think I'm sounding very naive.'

'I don't know. Idealistic, maybe. I think you could look at it the other way as well.'

'Yes?'

'I think really, when you think about how difficult people are, and how many fears we all have and insecurities, how much we hate ourselves, how unsure we are, and how jealous we get, and how hard all of us find it to talk or even really to know what we're feeling at any given time, I think really you could argue it's miraculous that any two people do manage to make each other happy. And winkle each other out of their shells.'

It occurs to me then as I listen that Chris still hasn't come back into the kitchen to clear things away. I wonder whether he's stayed away deliberately, to let Mum and Amy have this talk, and whether he's somewhere in the house now, listening like me to what they are saying, and whether Mum knows he's listening, or whether she thinks she and Amy are alone.

Mum's already up by the time I wake the next morning and

head downstairs to make coffee. She's sitting in the kitchen with a cup of tea, watching the steam rise up from the cup.

'Morning,' I say to her, keeping my voice low.

'Morning,' Mum says, and smiles at me.

'Couldn't sleep?'

'No, I never can, I'm not very good at it.'

'I'm sorry.'

She shrugs. 'I'm used to it. Getting up is hard when you're always tired, but once I'm up, I find I can keep going.'

'Mind if I make a pot of coffee?'

'Of course, help yourself.' I put the kettle on and reach into the fridge for the coffee and the milk. 'Amy seems nice,' she says.

'I'm glad you think so.'

'I'm sorry about the way I reacted when I first heard.'

'That's OK. It was a shock.'

'It was. But I understand. Things had reached a point with Juliet, hadn't they?'

'How do you mean?'

'Well, you'd been together for quite some time. So there comes a point where either that's for ever, or it's not, I think.'

'You mean marriage.'

'I suppose so. But more than that, really. You just have to ask yourself at a certain point, is this who I'm going to be? Am I ready to commit to this? And you're a young man. You probably shouldn't have reached that point yet. It's like with this place, with thinking about the farm. You probably shouldn't have reached a point yet where you know what you'll want to do with it when the time comes, because all that's still to come.'

I don't know what to say to this. It seems like a wilful, contorted misunderstanding of who I am and what I think and how I've been living since I left this place, and it feels strange to listen to Mum turn the whole life I shared with Juliet into some subordinate clause of the question of whether I'll ever want to live here again. As if that was the only thing that mattered. But perhaps it is to her. I hold my breath, say nothing. Mum notices that I'm not replying, and glances at me, checking the impact of her words.

'I just mean that I support what you're doing, that's all,' she says.

'So are we OK now?'

'I hope so.'

'I think we are.'

'Well, let's say we are, then.' And she smiles, and I smile back, and the kettle boils, and I make the coffee and take it with me as I go back upstairs, wanting to believe her.

1925

Leo was whisked away from his first world while he was still just discovering it, and though he never did go back, though the call of the past never got so loud he felt the need to act on it, retrace his steps and revisit that lost world by the dockside, a part of him missed it for the rest of his life. Indeed, that might have been exactly why he never returned to Poplar and wandered around. To go back would have been to have seen the place had forgotten him, had changed and moved on, and that it wasn't the place he missed so much as that moment in his life. That state of innocence when the world was just one place wide and he knew all of it. To go back might have taken away the feeling that everything he had left behind was still in the world somewhere, and that he might one day find it again. And he liked his nostalgia, it made things beautiful to him. He didn't want to let it go. Instead he liked to remember the noise of the docks and the faces pressed together, the great shout of the streets of London he had thought of as his birthright. Later in life, when he visited London again, the city came to seem mad to him, too loud to hear itself, and he despaired of the idea of ever trying to live there, but it had been intoxicating to a small child to always be among such energy, such life, as if you were really part of something and not just a person on your own in the world. That lost London, the London of the mind, remained always beautiful to him forever after.

Perhaps that memory of the city was why he felt loneliness so keenly later on; he was introduced to solitude late, so it could never seem natural and fade into the background of his life, as he suspected it did for many others, becoming something they accepted, like the weather. Leo always had a horror of the loneliness that followed him through his years, because he couldn't break out of thinking of it as an affliction.

'We have some news,' his mother said to him one day in 1925, calling him into her room where she sat at her dressing table. Leo stood to attention as best he could in the doorway, hands behind his back, trying to look like the boy she wished him to be. His mother didn't turn to look at him directly as she spoke, but fixed him with a look in the mirror on her dressing table instead. As if she was shy to really turn and face him. Or as if they spoke in some mirror world, not the real world of flesh and blood and bodies. 'I'm afraid to tell you that your grandfather has died. Your father has gone down to Wales to see to his funeral.' Leo felt the rush of shock in his belly, which felt something like embarrassment, and something like being punched quite hard in the stomach. He wondered what it meant for his grandfather to be dead. The thought had never crossed his mind before, but it occurred to him in that moment that he wasn't absolutely convinced that there was such a thing as heaven. Could his grandfather be in some other, better place? Leo couldn't work out why, but instinctively he doubted that somehow. It seemed more likely to him that his grandfather simply no longer existed. He wondered what he was to feel about that. It was difficult, to be sure. He hadn't really known his grandfather, had only met him once. But he supposed it must be important when people related to you disappeared. 'That is going to mean a change in our circumstances,' his mother went on. 'We are to leave London and move to the country.'

'Why are we doing that?' Leo asked, seeing no sense in it. What could the city lack that the country offered? For a small boy in love with the life of the river, it was impossible to comprehend.

'Your father is to inherit your grandfather's farm, and we are going to live there,' Phoebe said, picking up her powder brush to cover up her face, as if the matter was finished.

'Is it very far from here? Will we come back to visit?'

'I don't know why we would ever need to come back here, but it's not too far. It's in Wales, on the other side of England, but it's not so far really.'

'The other side of England sounds like quite a long way.'

Phoebe laughed, but still didn't look at Leo, focusing instead on applying the powder that would make her face seem pale. Leo wished sometimes that she wouldn't do that. There were boys at school who made him feel less than them because his face was darker, as if his skin meant he couldn't fit in. When his mother worked to whiten her face, it made him feel as if the boys were right, and the shame was real, not just his invention. He watched her in the mirror, creating a new self, covering her real self up. Through all the years of his growing up, it would remain his mother's habit to tell him difficult news without looking at him, often while sitting at the dressing-table mirror. He guessed it was simply a way of avoiding him, avoiding the confrontation that is always inherent in admonishing someone, or giving bad news. Years later, Leo would learn that painters sometimes liked to look at their work in the mirror as it developed, in order to see it in a new way, from a new angle, and simulate the moment of its being looked at by others after they had finished their work and gone. When he heard that, he thought of the way his mother and he used to look at each other in the dressing-table mirror, and wondered whether that had been part of what they were doing as well. Rehearsing a time when they wouldn't be together. Imagining the world the other would live in when they themselves had left it. Or if that was at least what his mother had been doing to him.

'Before you were born, your father and I crossed the whole of the world so that he could live in this place. I sat on the deck of the ship each day for weeks, and watched the countries going past. We sailed past all the places in the Bible, and he pointed them out to me one by one. As if we were sailing through the whole of that book and the whole ancient world. Once you've done that, you'll think nothing of moving across England for a better life. And it will be a better life, Leo, I can assure you. Inheriting the farm will make your father a wealthy man, and in time it will make you a wealthy man as well.'

So they moved, and Leo grew up a country boy and not the boy he wanted to be, watched his father struggle and fail to get used to the work he'd grown up around but, through India and the railways, lost all the instincts for. What his father couldn't understand was that, working with sheep, things sometimes just weren't fixable. Sometimes sheep would get maggots breeding in their bellies, and die. And that could not be remedied by an engineer. Failure was simply a part of life, the farming life especially, and it had to be borne and accepted. Leo was young enough to take this on board and see it for a fact, the way that some things just didn't work out. But his father had got too used to being able to find solutions to problems, and he never came to like the work he did, the better life he had supposedly inherited.

Leo hated his school. His face seemed much darker in Wales than it had done in London. He trained for a life on the farm when school was finished. He grew up thinking of life as a series of inheritances that were taken away from you, or otherwise thrust on you when you didn't want them. A place where you had to put up with what happened to you. It was a view he would later discover was shared by many of his generation. Strange, how ideas seemed to move through the air. As if they got into the water supply. On an average day, Leo felt quite independent in his mind, and then from time to time he'd come across something that would make him question whether such independence was even possible.

The little escapes he managed, when he could, were into the pages of books, where no one could get you. There it was possible to hop from world to world at great speed and with great variety – all you had to do was change the book you were reading to go to some new and previously unimagined place. And Leo liked the way that a book, once read, stayed in your head for ever, as if your head became bigger, and gave you more places to hide when you didn't like your life. No one could get to him inside his head. So he could go off into worlds no one knew he contained and kept hidden about his person, like secret stones sewn into his coat lining, and be safe there, and find relief from his loneliness. His favourite worlds, of course, were the island dreams, *Coral Island* and *Treasure Island,* and books like that, where people were given the chance to start their lives over again; he liked that more than anything else, and the heat, and the palm trees, and the light on the water, which were all so many miles away from Welsh rain. But any place could be freedom if no one else knew you were there, so he collected all the secret worlds he could, and went back to London in the pages of Dickens, or back into the past in the pages of Hardy, or over the top with Siegfried Sassoon. He would sit in the garden on dry afternoons, daydreaming his way through these different worlds, and no one ever suspected what he was up to. It was the closest thing in his life to freedom, and it grew all the more necessary as the years went by, because to his surprise the person who did worst out of the move from London into the country turned out not to be him, but his mother. The way she slowly collapsed in on herself as Leo grew up became unbearable to him as the years rolled by. Like a plant that had been pulled out by the roots and left lying on a path somewhere, because someone had forgotten to replant it.

Once they left the city it was like a light went out. Leo had known for as long as he could remember, of course, that England was not his mother's home, that she was having to learn the place just as he was, and finding that harder in many ways because she had to unlearn another country at the same time. When they moved to Wales, it seemed as if some thread connecting her back to the girl she had been was snapped and lost, so she couldn't find her way home, even in memory, even in imagination. Her head no longer seemed to contain any secret rooms that she could escape to, as Leo's did. She hardly ever went out into the local towns once they left London. For a while Leo wondered why she'd wanted to move at all. Only slowly did he realise that she hadn't. Only slowly did he realise that just because someone was a grown-up, that didn't mean they were in control. When it finally dawned on him that his mother was a long way from where she wanted to be, that she hated her life and where she lived and really recognised no part of it as the life she would have chosen, he came to wonder whether anyone was ever in control of anything at all. Who could be powerful, if not your own mother? Life was a series of inheritances taken away from you one by one, or given to you when you least wanted them, and there was no question of controlling any part of it, so it seemed to him.

Discovering how lost and sad his mother was, and watching as she withdrew from the world and spent her time in the house supervising the maid, ensuring that things were kept clean and meals served on time, and not doing much more with her life than that, brought out two strong and strongly opposed attitudes towards his mother that Leo struggled to reconcile. The first was that he came to love her very much. She was so vulnerable, and because she was always forgetting to eat, she turned into this frail and birdlike thing, so easily hurt, always cold, always wrapped in blankets and crying for the memory of her own home, that he wished he could be stronger, with an income of his own, and protect her, and take her back to India, leaving his father behind in this wet place that made his mother unhappy. Then, on the other hand, the more she retreated into herself the more he wondered if really he hated her, and that was the source of all his own unhappiness. Hated her inability to accept the life she had, and get on with it, make something of it somehow. Hated the fact that she needed his strength, when it ought to have been him who needed hers. Hated the weakness as if it might be catching, and pitied his father, who had to put up with her, had to get through all the work of the farm and come home each evening dreading what would have happened, what state he'd find his wife in, and whether she might have broken something in a rage, or whether she would have got out of bed at all that day.

2019

AMY LEAVES FOR Kuala Lumpur a few days later. The period that follows is a strange dreamtime. Waiting for her messages, working out the time difference, staying up late so we can message each other. It gets hard to keep things in perspective when you're worlds apart, and for us, only beginning to know each other, still uncertain, still constantly nervous of saying the wrong thing, the experience is like being caught in a boat in bad weather. I read too much into everything she says; half of our interactions are explanations of what we wish we'd said and what we meant by our last message.

Hey.
Hi, how are you?
OK thanks. Good day?
Only just started.
Course. Sorry. I get mixed up. What day is it there? Thursday?
Tuesday.
Told you I get mixed up! What are you doing today?
Theoretically trigonometry. Actually sunbathing. But I will try!

Try what?
Try to do some tutoring. But they won't listen.
Why not?
Don't worry, it's boring. Tell me a story.
Erm . . .
What did you do today?
Oh, nothing too much. Went for a walk and saw the wild garlic still in blossom.
Did it smell good?
It doesn't really smell that strongly.
Could you do me a favour?
Sure.
Could you drop into my flat and check it's OK? Just been worrying.
Anything specific?
No, just worrying! You can stay there if you like.
Thank you. I don't think I will but you're kind.
Why not?
Just might feel invasive.
Oh.
Sorry, is that the wrong thing to say?
Well, I've said you can stay there if you want, so why would it feel invasive?
Sorry. Didn't mean to say the wrong thing.

I watch day and night for the message that will persuade me she's changed her mind, she's gone away for good, and think I see it all the time, when a message gets left on read, when I send her a joke and she doesn't find it funny.

I feel stupid asking for her permission to be at the airport when she flies back, worried that she will want to see someone else, but she says yes like it's an easy thing.

She comes through the gates half an hour after I get there, and I confess my stomach seems to turn over when I see her, my body betraying the way I feel. I'm nervous as she walks up to me, rolling her eyes at the sign with her name on it that I'm holding as a joke, and kisses me there in the middle of the airport in front of everyone.

The first weekend after Amy gets back to England, she goes and stays with her parents, and picks up her dog, which they've been looking after while she was away. It surprised me the first time I discovered Amy had a dog – I don't know why; I suppose because pets root you in places, and at our age the idea of putting down roots seems hard, anti-instinctive, a luxury most of us can't yet afford. But having a dog seems to work for her, a little Westie called Ivan, and when she comes back to the city after a weekend at home, Ivan's with her again, and he seems to remember me when I see him.

For the next few days, Amy complains of feeling tired all the time, and it's clear the time away has taken it out of her. I get the sense, as well, that she has mixed feelings about coming home. The flat where she lives is in one of the city's more discarded far-flung corners, a place to sleep rather than a home, and she's done well to find somewhere she can afford, but I'm not sure how much she likes it. After a couple of days of watching her stare a little fearfully at the surrounding walls, the idea comes to me of taking her away. A holiday somewhere. A chance for us to reconnect. Perhaps a chance to have the conversation about what might be happening between us, and what we want to be doing together next.

So we trawl through Airbnb till we find somewhere we can afford, then make a few calls to clear the following week, and we leave the city, back in the car and devouring the long tongues of road that disappear endlessly beneath us. How many days of our lives are spent this way, doing nothing at all except watching the road? Are these the stillest hours of our lives now we live the way we do? Sometimes it seems more peaceful than sleep to me, to sit behind the wheel of a car and perform the Rumpelstiltskin trick of turning distance left to travel into time lost, time billowing behind you as it scatters and frays.

These escapes. These brief freedoms that come round like choruses in the song of our long, loving goodbye to the life that has been lent us. I never quite know what they mean. Are we really travelling outwards when we drive into the countryside, or are we trying, somehow, to return home? Is the journey really back and in, a reach for memory? John Berger wrote a trilogy of novels about the drift of the French peasantry from the near-feudal state in which they lived at the start of the last century into the cities, into the dirt jobs and shanty towns that turned into the suburbs as the century ended. If he were still here now, I wonder, would he make his fourth story about Airbnbs? The way those peasants' children pulled themselves up by their bootstraps, and spent their spare money on takeaway coffee, then went out once or twice in a year to look at the places their ancestors worked in, sleep in converted barns where hay was stored once, and marvel at the quality of the ice cream, and feel moving powerfully within them like a current but never quite put into words the hardship and the toil remembered just below the surface of the scene? Is that the fourth act in the unfolding story of the rural working people – to drive out for long weekends, haunt the landscapes they called home?

On the way down to the Airbnb, Amy and I stop at Fleet for coffee. The pines all around us make the place feel unreal, like a film set somehow, like a dream. We are secluded from everything here, and the light strafes through the pine branches palely, as if it were only the memory of light and not the real thing we were seeing. I always feel as if I could spend for ever in this place. I could grow old walking round these shops hidden in the middle of the woods, then return to civilisation after what felt like decades there and find no time had passed at all.

'I feel like these places exist outside of time,' I say to Amy. It's not quite what I meant to say, but I can't find the right words for the feeling I have, so I say what I can instead.

'Like Brigadoon?' Amy asks me. I smile at her. Perhaps I've made myself understood after all. *Brigadoon* is a film I love, a fictional world I would love to walk into or discover in real life. In the story, a man goes away for a very literal-minded stag weekend, shooting deer in the Highlands with his best friend. They walk through the hills all day, and then can't find their way home and walk all night as well, until, at dawn, still lost in the wilds, they stumble on a village hidden deep in the middle of nowhere. What they don't know at first about this village is that, just yesterday, it was cursed by a witch who decreed that, for the rest of time, for every night that passes in the village of Brigadoon, a century will elapse in the world outside. So the man and his friend on the stag weekend walk in to discover a community of people wearing the clothes and living the lives of a hundred years ago, people who are just starting to get to grips with the implications of this new curse. The men spend the day there; the groom, who is on the brink of a high-society New York wedding, accustomed to a life lived in bars atop skyscrapers, falls for the simple, unadorned charms of a local girl, and then night comes, and he has to make a decision. He's been given a glimpse of a different life – a life with a woman he is completely at ease with, and a possible love unlike anything he's experienced before. His own life in New York seems suddenly shallow, hollow, to him – it's that life, not the village, which has come to seem like a dream. So he is faced with a choice. He could stay here with the girl he met just this morning and live in what now feels like the real world, having broken through the surface of his life into a true depth of feeling; but if he did, if he fell asleep just once in this village, a hundred years would pass in the world outside, and everyone he ever knew, everything he ever lived and worked and hoped for, would be gone.

The man makes his decision. He returns to New York. Which of us wouldn't, in the end? He goes for a drink in a bar atop a skyscraper. But the whole place has changed, and he can't believe it's real any more. All of it seems to him like no more than the surface of something, like a dream. So he flies back to Scotland, and walks out into the wilds, even though he knows that because of the witch's curse the village of Brigadoon won't appear again for the rest of his lifetime, and because this is true love we're talking about here, and also a schmaltzy Hollywood musical of a certain era, the mists part for just one last moment, and he sees the woman he met that day welcoming him home. The man – who, incidentally, has been Gene Kelly all along – walks into the mist and vanishes. I hope that once a century has elapsed since the original film was released, someone will make a sequel where not only the Scottish village of the mid-nineteenth century but also Gene Kelly from the mid-twentieth century will emerge into the cold light of the twenty-first century and try to comprehend what we've all done with the place in the time since they left it. The technology will presumably exist to allow Gene Kelly to still play the role by then.

We drive on. Hours pass, and Ivan's sick after a while, so we stop the car to clean the back seat. The roads grow narrower. We know the journey's coming to an end. The sun is ahead of us now, beckoning us into the west. We arrive at the barn we've rented to hide in while Amy recovers her sense of herself, and unpack the car, and let Ivan out into the yard by the farm next to the barn, and he plays with the dog in the farmyard, and we watch them, and we're happy.

On the first day of the holiday, armed with an Ordnance Survey map, we take Ivan to walk on the moor to the south of the place where we're staying. There's a smell of dry earth in the air from the mud we kick up as we walk. Cornwall for me is Radiohead country, I suppose because I know the singer has a house nearby. Something about the emptiness of this coastal landscape seems to leave spaces and silences that long for filling in. What I hear rushing into those vacuums is that spare and spectral music of longing, displacement and desire. Within half an hour of setting off, we take a wrong turn and find ourselves walking through a farmyard. A girl of about six runs out to look at us, as if we might be the circus passing through. A woman who looks like she might be the little girl's grandmother comes out of the farmhouse.

'You two all right?' she asks. She seems friendly but her voice is raised almost to a shout, as if she's mainly used to talking to people who are half a mile away.

'We were following the bridlepath, but I think we've gone the wrong way,' I say.

'People do that. You wanna go back along the path and turn left down the lane you passed.'

We thank the woman and turn to leave. The girl watches us go. I wave goodbye to her. I know what it's like to start your life so remote, what this solitude and silence does to a mind, to an imagination. She is like a glimpse of someone I used to be. I want to take a moment to tell the girl: all your life there's going to be a secret room in your head no one else will ever know exists or know how to get into, a room filled with the silence and freedom of your childhood. Sometimes it will seem like a miracle to you, and sometimes it will seem like the purest loneliness. There's nothing you can do about it; the secret room will always be part of you, it will always be there, and sometimes you'll need to go into it and sit quietly for a little while. It will be the only way you ever find to feel like you've come home. The rest of the wide world with its sound and fury is never quite going to feel like home, it will always resemble a dream, and you'll never truly convince yourself that all of that noise could be real.

We turn away from her and retrace our steps, then open the gate for the left turn, and the lane beyond is shadowed by trees overhanging us. We walk on for half a mile until we come to a tree that's fallen and been left across the path, blocking the route. I try for a moment to find a way through, but the branches are thick and we can't fit under. So we clamber out of the lane into the field on our left, walking round the tree. In the field a few dozen young bullocks are grazing. They watch Ivan, uneasy. Amy slips back into the lane, and I follow her out of the bright light of the field back into the shadow of the trees. The bullocks come right up to the hedge as we walk away from them, but they don't come through.

We come to a fork in the path. There are no signs, so I look at the map, and we take the right branch that should lead us up on to the moor. We walk into dense deciduous woodland, the light on our faces dappled by oak leaves, the ground soft and loamy under our feet, and the path begins to peter out as bracken and moss encroach and claim the space, until all we can see are a few scuff marks from other feet that walked here before us. The ground grows steeper, and after a while we find we have to start climbing, grabbing on to branches and roots growing out of the hillside and making our way ever more slowly towards the light we hope will mark the edge of the moor, which ought to lie just past this wood's liminal margin. We stop for breath, and I get out the map, because it seems clear now that we've taken the wrong path; I've misread our location. I look at the map, and don't understand why the ground here is so steep; the lines on the page give no indication of this climb. It seems as if we must have been on the wrong path all this time, and travelling in a different direction; but I can't see where we've gone wrong. I realise the map's no use to us any more, until we get out of the wood and see where we are. Drowned in this woodland, there are no landmarks to orient us. So we keep on climbing. After another ten minutes we pass out of the wood into a clearing of long grass, parched by the summer heat, and fall down on our backs, and stare at the way the grass falls away from us till it reaches the next hedgerow, where trees rise up again beyond it. I look at the map once more, and now I can see where we must be: another path, almost parallel to the one we should have taken, has brought us out half a mile to the west of where we thought we were walking, to the same stretch of Radiohead country, the same place that's been awaiting our arrival all this time.

'Isn't it strange?' I look at Amy, and follow her gaze to see what she's staring at. She only seems to be looking at the space ahead of us, the grass and the trees and the sky. 'All this was water once. All of this was underwater. Not even that, it didn't exist. There was water here instead where this view would appear one day.'

'And one day this won't exist again, and this will turn back into water.'

'Will there be anyone here, d'you think?' she asks, turning now to look at me. 'To see it when it goes?'

Neither of us speak for a little while. Neither of us need to say anything, as we lie back on the grass together with Ivan lying behind us, as walkers have rested on their way for thousands of years, and imagine the end of the world.

After a while, when we've got our breath back, we stand up again, heave our packs back on to our shoulders, and go on.

I try and imagine a future with Amy, and it plays out compulsively in my imagination, like a movie rising up unbidden. The film of our life would be made up entirely of these holidays, these adventures, our lungfuls of freedom away from the rest of the world. That's how they'd tell it in the movies, the romantics' version, and up to a point they'd be right – that's how we try to live. Always the next adventure to be planned and looked forward to, always the memory of the last one just gone for us both to retreat into when work gets hard, more secret worlds that are ours alone, where no one else can reach us, just like the pool where our lives first collided. In the film of our lives, we'd take that idea even further. You'd never even see our home, our families, the offices we worked in. We'd be played by two very beautiful actors who would walk together through one European city after another, through forests of vast redwood in backwater Maine, talking all the time about how hard it is to feel you belong anywhere on this earth, talking about the way we met, and the sacrifices we made in getting together. It would be pure Richard Linklater. Beers and weed on Prinsengracht in Amsterdam, rye bread and tomatoes from the little supermarkets, padlocks on the bridges, Amy wanting to linger in the red light district and take it all in, me wanting to get away from the women in the windows and the tired, lonely figures queueing to go in and see them. Dinners on Kollwitzplatz in Berlin, days lost in the English-language bookshops and among the tattooists who ravelled their stories in blue ink over our skin. Then a train to Leipzig, the wide-open square in front of the beautiful station, and going from church to church to visit the graves and trace the lives of great composers round that city. And on again, further east to Prague and soup served in bread bowls and walking up steep hills to look down on the city, then to Dubrovnik, baking in the sun, diving off concrete platforms busy with Croatians selling beer to each other from cool boxes, diving and losing ourselves in the sea, the sea. Then back west to Ireland, walking out from Knocknarea to Sligo. Stopping the car to watch the Glencar waterfall fly into the air. Sitting in the bar of the Grand Hotel while the Irish dancers come in and out with their parents, young girls dressed like nothing you've ever seen, their hair done up like wedding cakes. Orkney in the pouring rain. Then south again and the view from the slopes of the Atlas Mountains, lasting for ever, lasting till the end of space and time. One image of freedom after another, and the two beautiful actors walking through all of it like Adam and Eve, sharing all this life, talking beautifully and filling the screen with ideas, but none of them really mattering, because the real narrative would be the move from one location to another, the passing of time, the change from scene to scene. Perhaps when we're old that will be how we'll remember our lives. All of the dailiness melting away, only the red-letter days still shining.

When we've finished exploring the fields around the village where we're staying, we get back into the car to travel further afield, and make our way, inevitably, to the waiting sea.

English summer weather rifles through its moods and many faces over this stretch of coast like a spell. Over these rocks the weather of childhood still dances changeably and seems to be always drawing you back into memory, like a radio left playing in another room, music reminding you of something you'd forgotten when you hear it through the walls, down a hallway, through an open window as you walk in the garden.

Change down into third gear for the hill, foot always poised over the brake in anticipation of the vehicle coming in the other direction that will mean you have to stop and back up to the last passing place. These old lanes are maps of the history of a place as much as they're a way of getting anywhere. The route from one village to another the cowherds once took, or farmers with their carts, or trudging labourers. Now they are made to take the mad, impossible strain of this century, too narrow for our needs and not getting anywhere quickly enough. Emerge from the tree cover and see, ahead, the ocean, the idea that can never be caged within words, the largest thought that's ever put to us until the day of our deaths. Amy spots the car park to the right while I'm still distracted by the sat nav, and we slow down too quickly, turn off the road. There's no signal on our phones, as if the paraphernalia of our world were losing its grip out here. I feel as if I'm in the middle of some enchantment. We scrape together enough cash between us to pay for parking, get Ivan out of the car, and head down the hill towards the old fishing village.

'Do you know which way?' Amy asks.

'I think just follow the steepest road down and we'll get there.'

'Everyone's going the same way, aren't they?'

'Yes. We'll follow them.'

'Is it how you remember it?'

'I don't remember this car park at all.'

I have been here before. A friend's birthday in a field by a house overlooking the sea that his parents had bought when they retired down here six or seven years ago. I thought of looking the family up while we are here, but in the end it seems too complicated, and I worry they won't remember who I am. While we've been in this part of the country, we've been revisiting places. Twice we've gone to a place whose name Amy remembered from a childhood holiday, and found she didn't recognise it, then driven on to the next town to find it was in fact the place she had in mind. These are memories dating from when she was eleven or twelve years old, and the mind doesn't keep complete tapes from those years, or any years, I suppose – it compresses and cuts out and sticks things together, so our memories are montages of things that have no more to do with each other than the fact that they happened about the same time. What we find Amy has remembered each time is the name of the town where she stayed; but her richer memories, the places she recognises and in which she feels she has been happy, seem to have been day trips she went on with her family on that holiday. They were the exciting days, the prettier places, out of the ordinary, vivid and new. Each time, in the memory, for some reason she's given them a different name. There is a pleasure for both of us to hunting the real site of what she remembers, seeking out the places that feel alive to her, trying to second guess where she might have been happy, in what feels to her like a different life.

On my previous visit to this town I never made it down into the harbour. Amy has seen this place in a film, though, so she knows what to expect: the shelter of the harbour cleft deep into the coast, streets of old cottages rising like wings on either side up the cliff-like flanks that shape the village like a potter's hands. Every second person walking down the hill has a dog on a lead, and ours is still practically a puppy, and desperate to play. He yips and strains at his harness, skittering his claws on the pavement. The road grows steeper and turns to the left, and then we see the harbour lying below us, the gift shops, ice-cream parlours, local crafts and pottery, tourists making their way up and down the narrow streets as if on pilgrimage. And this to me is everything beautiful I love in people, this little postcard spread out beneath us: all of us dutiful and patient, making our way through one place or another on our holidays, soaking up what's been laid on for us and finding in it the peace and freedom we need to go back to our real lives and face them next week or the week after that. An ice cream, a mug with the name of the village on the side, a walk on the beach; we take these small offerings and somehow find in them the restoration and the courage and grace we need to face the world's indifference. Here, in a place like this one, you can see the agreement we've all made with each other playing out: that we'll observe some kind of system to keep things moving; we'll be civilised, and lay these small rituals over the untamed surface of the world, and lend some pattern to our time here. Holiday towns always fill me with love. We all appear to have made a pact with each other: I won't stove your head in, and you won't stove in mine; instead we'll agree to set boundaries, say that this is a place where we come to get away from things, and that is a place for farmers, and that is a place for office work, and we'll accept these limits on our lives because they will make our lives possible.

The shops here sell the merchandise of three different franchises which have been filmed around this harbour, an electric shock provided to the local economy by storytelling. As we walk round the horseshoe of narrow streets, we hear people talking about each of the shows in question, pointing out one house or another to indicate that this is where a particular scene was filmed on one of those shows. People chasing the ghosts of stories over cobbles, in and out of the light and shade of the cottages. Halfway up the hill on the other side of the harbour from where we came in, the home of a doctor in one TV drama stands right beside the B&B where a record producer stayed while visiting the town in a different film. People gather to stare at both, as though celluloid characters might become flesh and walk out into the street to be among them. What are we hoping to see when we go on pilgrimage to former film sets? We all do it, when visiting those places that have been turned into stories and sold to us elsewhere. We stare at the spot where a shot we know was captured. Is it that we want to see some ghost of the magic? Do we want to be able to see as if through the eyes of the director, somehow acquire her fierce clarity by looking at the same things she did? Or do people just like collecting things, and collecting places is as good a hobby as any other?

We take Ivan down the harbour slipway and on to the sand while the tide's out, because he's burning to be let off the lead and allowed to run round. There are boats lying beached on the sand as if dropped there by children; by the water, a jellyfish is in the same state. Ivan takes no interest in the jellyfish; it's dead and can't be played with. Instead he hares over the warm rock pools and ridges of barnacled stone and the soft sand to be among the terriers already playing there, so there are three dogs suddenly together in the belly of the harbour, suddenly running, springing into action like a flock of pigeons leaving a square, breathless mad energy bursting around us. We stand and watch them, laughing, with no intimation that the day holds anything for us but happiness like this. Amy's eyes drift past the dogs, and now focus on the sea.

'There must be a moment somewhere out there in the water where the tide turns and an ebb becomes a flood again,' she says to me. 'When the tide meets itself coming back the other way, you know what I mean? How does that happen? What does it look like, do you think? I think it must look like the centre of the world, the place where the tides change.'

I stare out across the water with her. 'They're always both out there, aren't they? Just pulling in different directions all the time.'

She turns to me. 'How do you mean?'

'It's always high tide somewhere. And low tide somewhere else. Everything just gets pulled from one to the other.'

'But the water we can see must get turned around somewhere.'

Ten minutes pass with the dogs dancing in and out of the water, attracted by the water, yet also afraid of it, shaking themselves when they get wet, then one of the owners has to leave, so we catch hold of Ivan and put him back on the lead, and it's while I'm doing that, ruffling his head and giving him a treat, that my phone rings.

I take it out and see that it's Chris calling. I answer the phone, already uneasy, because he never calls me; whenever I speak to him it's because I've called the phone at the farm.

'Hello, Chris.'

'Hi, Ed. Sorry, I know you're on holiday.' I can tell from the sound of the call that he's out and about, not at home. He sounds as if he's walking.

'Is everything all right?'

'I think so. I just wanted to let you know that your mum's gone into hospital.'

'What's happened?'

'She was having breathing difficulties over the last few days. And she assumed she just had a cold – well, we both did – and she hoped it would pass. But she hasn't been able to sleep, because when she lies down it feels worse, so she went in to see the doctor about that, and they've said she's got pneumonia.'

'Right.' The call feels suddenly unreal to me. Dad got pneumonia too, before the end.

'She's in Abergavenny hospital, and she's totally fine, she's on oxygen and they're putting her on antibiotics.'

'Are you with her?'

'I'm in the hospital but I've just stepped out to get a cup of tea and make some calls.'

'Are you OK?'

'I'm fine. Bit scared, if I'm honest.' It occurs to me that this might in fact be something serious; I don't know whether I've ever heard Chris describe himself as scared before.

'What are the doctors saying?'

'Not much, really. I mean, it's too soon for them to say much, that's what they say. They've put her on antibiotics, but it'll take a couple of days before they know they're working. In the meantime, they've said that she could be in hospital for a few weeks.' I think of the work that Chris is going to have to do while Mum is in the hospital: the endless, backbreaking work of the hill farm where they live, and the visits to Abergavenny, forty minutes in the car each way. My sister and I both miles away in the city. Should we be dropping everything, I wonder? Should we be going back home?

'We'll come and see her.'

'She doesn't want you to cut short your holiday.'

'It's all right. We're due to travel back. We'll come to you instead.'

'I know she'd love that.'

'Of course.'

'I'd better go, I think, better call Rachel.'

'Do you want me to call her?'

'No, it's best I do it.'

'OK. Will you give Mum our love? And we'll get to her as soon as we can.'

'Absolutely. All right.'

'Love to you both.'

'All right.' He rings off then, and I look at Amy, who has guessed what's happened from hearing my side of the call.

We walk up off the beach. The day has turned against us now, the rain is lashing in from the sea as we drive back along the coast towards the place where we've been staying. The trees bowing low over the road loom larger in this weather, darker against the shifting sky, the progress of the afternoon bringing different things into focus. The day we knew two hours ago has vanished, scattered and drowned in wind and rain. The hedgerows seem closer on each side, windows of the car steaming up, all colour drained from the face of the sky.

'Do you want to go tonight?'

'No, there's no point. We won't get there till after visiting hours.'

'You're sure we shouldn't go anyway?' I know what she means. Am I sure we don't need to get to the bedside? Am I sure visiting hours still apply? In truth, I don't know. But if I pretend this isn't an emergency, then perhaps it won't become one.

'He hasn't said that. He just said it was too soon for them to know what's going to happen.'

'And you don't think we need to be with him?'

'He doesn't want us to be with him tonight. Turning up in the middle of the night.'

'If you're sure.'

I'm not. But I don't want to go, and I don't know what to say to explain that irrational feeling, so I say nothing, and the silences stretches out between us.

Along the cliff road with the sea roaring to the left of us, incoming waves volley and thunder, Atlantic breakers tearing at the strand below, a few lonely cars huddling down in a car park by the side of the road on a gorse-littered hilltop, people eating their sandwiches in front of the sea, or having sex, or making calls, or waiting for their shifts to start. Whatever people do in parked cars. All these lives like islands we'll never set foot upon. As we drive home, we see an arrow of Canada geese heading north-west, out over the sea and carving fearlessly into the weather. In the car park we left behind, there were seagulls stalking up and down as if they were guarding the bins. Is that what it will be like when all the humans are gone? On these islands, the bigger predators wiped out long ago, will it be only the birds still stalking the deserted landscape, pecking at the rubbish till even that has been consumed? Perhaps the birds as they eat the last remnants of who we were will become a kind of forgetting, a benediction. And will the ghosts still be there for the birds to see, the ghosts of our lives that seem to be always trailing after us – are they part of us or do they stay behind here, trapped and lonely, when we leave?

A ghost can appear to you anywhere. I am certain that ghosts are walking with us everywhere. But there are also places where ghosts are more easily seen. At the edges of things. The coast, the first fingertips of a forest closing round you, dawn and dusk, and time away from the familiar. In liminal places and times like these, where we are shaken out of the stupor of the everyday by the prospect of things changing, a great deal can appear to us more clearly, as we are forced to look more closely at what is around us and take life in.

We get back to where we're staying and I sit in the main room of the barn in silence, thinking of the gulls in the car park and the geese in the air, like lost souls crossing the earth, and the day wanes and disappears, and I know I won't sleep, so I tell Amy I'm going for a walk and head outside.

I pull on my jacket and set out into the dark with my head down, listening to the crunch of gravel beneath my feet. The absolute dark of a moonless night in the middle of nowhere. I leave Ivan inside to keep Amy company; even though it's stopped raining, he won't want to be out in the dark, and I don't want to have to entertain him, reassure him, rein him in. At first I can't see my hand in front of my face. But there's always a light source somewhere, even on the blackest night, so as I stagger forward my eyes adjust and my pace gradually increases as I start to make out the shifting gradients of the ground underfoot. I am listening to the different qualities of silence: the sudden rushes of sound like the sea that come from the hazels and oaks surrounding me when the wind picks up, the rustle of mice among the ground ivy audible in the lulls. Out the gate and left up the hill, and I suppose I might as well visit the church as it's only a short walk and unlocked all night, and that will allow me to sit somewhere silently. Above my head the clouds are moving quickly, and now they are starting to fray, and here and there I catch a glimpse of stars. Should I feel afraid of this dark I'm in now? Is there something in it that's waiting to meet me?

I come to the church and open the gate and walk into the graveyard. I listen to the wind in the trees sounding like the sea, and watch the skies clear till the stars are spangled all above, layer upon layer of faint yet brilliant ancient light lapping like waves across the darkness. When does it start? A day comes when you lie on your back in the grass and wonder whether this is the closest you'll ever come to happiness, whether the long slide away from this moment begins now. The rest of your life a falling away from this point. When do we first know that might be what's happening? Is that what's happening to me now?

It gets colder the longer I'm out here, but I don't want to go back to the barn just yet. I open the door to the porch of the church, and step inside, looking for shelter. The view of the sky through the open door is shadowed by holly trees blocking the night. The leaves of the holly trees' higher branches are smooth-sided, with none of the spikes on the lower leaves. As I watch the silhouettes of the trees moving gently against the night, a different movement catches my eye: a spider is moving over the porch doorway, trying to spin a web across it. The frail bright threads are visible and sharp against the darkness. I watch, still and silent in the church porch, for what feels like an hour but might only be ten minutes, as the web spools out and shuts me in, like a blanket, like a concealment. I am alone in here. No one can reach me. No one else has ever stood like this before and watched a spider stitch them into this place.

1933

Arthur never did quite work out what he had done wrong. Except that he disgusted her, except that he wasn't what she wanted, except that it turned out long after it was too late that he had taken her away from her life. And that was his fault. Somehow, though he hadn't known he was doing it, that would always be his fault; there was nothing to be done that could change that simple, sad fact. Eight years after he moved the family back to Wales, a day came when he accepted she would never get better. She would live upstairs in the cottage, and continue retreating into herself, until finally there was nothing left.

He remembered the way they met in Hyderabad. Of course, she had been much younger than him, of course he could see that was so, but no younger than the women many of his friends had been marrying at the time. And she had seemed to like him, she had seemed to want to marry him back then; she was kind to him and seemed to think he was an interesting man. It was only later he discovered that, in her eyes, he very much wasn't. In her eyes he was just a conqueror who stole her and took her away, like a looter, like a common thief. That hadn't been the way her mother and her father talked about it when the marriage was negotiated. They talked about her kind nature, the way she would grow to care for him as they shared their lives, just as she had always cared for every person she was close to, just as she was always kind to animals or the poor. And she would bear him children, which was the reason Arthur could not have married a woman of his own age; the women of his own age were past childbearing by that time, and it was his responsibility to his family to try and carry on the line. He remembered the way Phoebe's mother and father talked about the opportunity he was giving to her. And if he had made a mistake, if he could put his finger on one moment when it all went wrong, perhaps it was then, when he assumed their feelings would be hers as well.

Of course it had started slowly. The idea of intimacy between them had been as embarrassing to him, he guessed, as it had been to her; at least she was beautiful, after all. At least she had no reason to feel any shame. Whereas Arthur, trapped in the prison of his middle age, had a very great deal to be ashamed of. He knew going to bed with him couldn't possibly please her; he tried to ask as little of her as he could, and respect her instead, let her have her own bed and her own room, let her spend her days as she wished, and go back to visit her family, where happiness seemed to lie. He had believed in time that kind of respect, that kind of understanding, would lead to a deeper connection between them. But perhaps he had done all that wrong as well? Many years later, she would tell him he had never shown her love, and he would think back to those days, the way he tried to give her space. And he wondered whether he should have done it all differently, whether things might have ended up better for her in the end.

The trouble was that he did come to love her. He really did. His beautiful wife. Her life, her fragile life, that he had been tasked to watch over. It might have been easier if he had never fallen in love.

Had it been wrong to heed the call of the war, and come back to England? He supposed that it had. He supposed he should have stayed out in India and supervised the railways, and then Phoebe could have stayed in the place where she was happy, and even if he never became someone she loved, at least there would be love around her that kept her safe. But he had never intended to stay in India for ever. And he had said that to her parents, back when they were negotiating, and they had raised no objections to the idea of her going to England with him. They had said it would be a great opportunity, he seemed to recall. And yet, even as they got to Bombay, even as she took in the men working naked on the docks and the way the dogs scavenged round them for scraps, and were chased away, the savage starving animals, he saw a light start to go out in her. Some kind of connection to the soil of home. Some faith that the world was a good and decent place. Such faith struggled to remain strong in the face of the evidence of Bombay, and the subsequent stink and sickness on the ship, and the docks of Poplar where they made their home.

That, he admitted, had lacked imagination. They had rented a house more or less where they first alighted in England, and he accepted it must not have been the best place to have a child and start to raise him. He rented that house at the time because he was in a hurry, he was going to the navy and didn't have time, and a friend of his father's owned the house, and let him have it with a maid for a good rate. He thought Phoebe would be safe there, and to an extent he closed his heart at that time to the thought of her unhappiness. There was a war on, after all. Many people were unhappy at that time. It was a mistake to think of life as all spices and roses. But then when he came back, once the war was over, perhaps they shouldn't have stayed so long. She withdrew a lot from him then, and seemed to give up on the youth he'd always loved in her. Though she was a young woman, she acquired more than a touch of Miss Havisham in that time, always alone and flitting round the rooms, always staring like a ghost through the windows. He used to watch her reading and rereading *Wuthering Heights*. Is that what she saw reflected in the glass when she looked out over Poplar, he wondered? Did she imagine the glass shattering, rude hands reaching in and snatching her away from the silent world of their home?

By the time his father died, and he decided to move back to Wales and take up the birthright he had expected for so long, it was already too late, he came to realise. Her mind was going, her happiness was already gone; nothing he could have done would have helped her. It was those years in London when things went wrong, and the poison of that time simply seeped out once they had got away to the hills and the farming. He was too old for it by then, of course, and his father had half bankrupted the place without telling him, mortgaging and remortgaging it to get through the post-war depression, so Arthur couldn't afford the help he would have wanted to make a success of the place. He knew very early on that it would be the work of the farm that drove him before too long into the grave. But he didn't regret that. It became very hard to do so. At least he wouldn't be here to hurt her, was all that he thought. At least he wouldn't torture her any more if he was under the grass. It was enough to make a man think of taking his own life, but Arthur had no more interest in suicide than he did in divorce. A life was a series of responsibilities. You took them on and then you saw them through. These things were not to be backed away from. That was not how to be a man.

And anyway, he couldn't have left; Phoebe wouldn't have managed. This, always, hung heavy over his head, as she withdrew to the upstairs rooms, as she walked round the house at night and he was left with nothing but the memory of her brown eyes when she was young, and her hair, and the way she first looked at him those evenings in the club when they danced together, and the air was thick, and the scents of India came in through the windows. He couldn't give up on her now all that was gone. The light had gone out, and his leaving would not have reignited it. His leaving would have just left her alone. She was his responsibility, and he had to make sure she ate and washed and stayed alive. Who else was going to, after all? There was only Leo, and one thing he could still do was save his son from having to do this for as long as he could. He had nightmares about predeceasing Phoebe. He knew it was likely, but feared it all the same. It would pass all the weight of this care on to Leo. It would pass all this lovelessness down the generations. He dreamed of lasting long enough to get his beautiful wife to the end of her life, though she didn't love him, though she would never thank him for being here, just staying in her haunted attic, day after day. That was the only way he could see of making sure this sorrow lasted only one generation. And preventing a longer cycle setting in. And after all, why should he let her go? He loved her; he couldn't help that. He wanted her near him. So he stayed, and he worked, and felt it wear him thin, and said nothing of their poverty, and nothing of his misery. If he could take it all upon himself, then perhaps he could take it with him when he came to the end. That would be right, he liked to think. After all, it must have been something he'd done.

2019

In the early morning, a light rain falls till it has exhausted itself in patterning the gravel, till the sky is drained and quietened, then clouds are scudding over the lonely farms. We pack without saying much to each other, and walk through the rooms doing idiot checks. The morning is gorgeous and pristine; we imprint nothing of our own on to it, no thought, no inanity, no disagreement. I start to imagine the air I'm moving through as something perfectly white, tablecloth white, wedding-dress white, which my thoughts spoken out loud could only muddy. Like dirty fingerprints on the sleeves of a shirt. How could any thought of mine add anything to this place, this quiet? My head's full of things that could never matter like the morning seems to matter as I live it and watch it vanish and prepare for the car and leaving this moment behind me, the sound of the birds outside, the heat rising up as the day develops its themes. I hope Amy is feeling the same things too: the preciousness of this hour spent packing, the day like pure clear water we are holding cupped in our hands for as long as this silent moment lasts, before saying goodbye to it. I hope she is alive to the magic of this farewell to our holiday, and loving the feeling, loving the intuitive choreography of our shared packing, our quiet dance through the rooms as we check them one last time. The peace of the morning is broken only when the farm dogs bark to each other across the fields, and Ivan joins in. At the end of the lane where we've been staying, two Basset Hounds make sounds like Judgement Day.

We walk Ivan one last time round the woods, under the apples ripening early in this strangely balmy climate, and pass the church on the way home, and I say nothing to Amy of having sat there in the porch last night, and a small scar of silence forms between us, a part of my life I'll never tell her. But love is not the act of consuming the whole of a person. These scars and silences are also part of love. Amy had wanted us to get straight in the car and leave, but I insisted we should walk the dog first, or he'd grizzle in the back seat. The reality is that I think I'm trying to put off leaving. Trying to persuade myself this isn't the emergency. People will do anything to locate the emergency later than it is.

Cutting through the woods is the filled-in ghost of an old railway line, closed off and shut up before we were born. On our first day here we followed it through the fields until it broke away from the slope of the ground it had been passing through, a bridge to nowhere, a raised escarpment built long ago by men who will all have vanished now, who broke their backs to throw this bridge up into the sky, and whose work came to nothing when the railway line closed. It must have taken months, chucking up enough earth from the surrounding fields to keep the train travelling level through this shallow valley. Now the overgrown spit they made jut into the air seems to grieve their memory, the time they lost and wasted, the time they could have been doing something else. Still, at least they were paid for it. And the work would have been hard, but they would have gone home at the end of the day knowing the bills were paid, and there are worse ways to make a living.

Strange, how the labour of a handful of men who were simply doing a job of work for the wage it earned them can become the landscape you walk through, shaping the hills and valleys. Every place we pass through is so much more than the scene as it appears to us. Every place is held up, patterned and formed by a latticework of choices, decisions, memories. Everywhere is made out of ghosts.

I think of the road running past the school that I went to. To walk down it today would offer the casual observer one or two points of interest – the restaurants, the B&Bs. But the life under the surface of that street is infinitely richer. I can pass its houses knowing a marriage ended in this room; a drunk threw a spice rack at a group of boys from that window; a boy was killed crossing the road just there; a priest was arrested in that house, for the reason priests are always arrested. All this only a heartbeat, a fraction of the life of that place. All these chance happenings become our history, more or less random, more or less unplanned, but growing all the same into the reason a place is like it is, and the world is like it is.

How far does that history reach into us, control us? Which of us ever really knows whether we're making our decisions for ourselves, or whether our days are finally shaped by these ghosts? If we knew the whole stories of every family in the world, I think we would discover the secret sources of everyone's actions. If most of the history of the world wasn't lost, allowed to vanish because no one wrote it down, we might be able to understand how it came to be what it is now. But the world is too big to ever catch all these stories. We can only observe the way these memories work like pain bodies for ourselves, the way we retreat back into the pain body of family memory whenever we confront something important, and act out of fear of what's hurt us before, and guess at the way that affects everyone else around us, all the time.

Life like a coastal shelf, built up, layer upon layer, like minute upon hour upon day, till it looms over you, till you come to fear its falling, because when the end comes and it finally falls, it will cut you back into the ribbons of minutes and hours and days that made you, and you will be dissipated, and ebb back into glimpses, fractured and diffuse, and you will be nothing at all, scattered memory, a ghost.

Days that feel like going home pattern the years like clouds, like occasional rain. The visits to parents, the visits to graves, the occasional return to childhood places, like finding tucked away at the back of a drawer something you thought you'd lost. Or simply coming together with the people you feel closest to in life – that becomes a kind of homecoming after a while as well. As I get older, I feel more and more as if these moments of togetherness, of happiness, provide the real and secret rhythm of each year. They take me under the surface of my days into the real story. In the company of friends who really know you, who know where you came from, what you used to dream of when you were young and how it measures up to this life you're living now, your world can take shape as you see it through their eyes, and you can make out more clearly where it is you might be heading.

Amy drives today, which is always the best option really, because she's a better driver than me, and a worse passenger – she becomes angry and irritable sitting shotgun when I'm driving. I sit holding on my lap the new teapot we bought in one of the ceramic shops clustered round this county, and the plates and bowls we bought a day earlier in between my feet, and we listen to the radio, and I try and chart the way my legs seize up, the stages of stillness, stiffness, discomfort. When we stop to refuel at a service station after about an hour and a half on the road, I limp like a pensioner.

There's a closed-down, slowly collapsing old diner by the petrol station, windows with signs still hanging in them that haven't been lit for what looks like a year or more. When I see the old adverts for chips and beans, I feel a rush of nostalgia for that disappearing old culture, the world of bad fry-ups, fat swilling on the plate, cheap bacon and the ketchup in the Heinz bottles replaced with own-brand stuff that tastes like vinegar but costs less money. One by one those roadside places will all shut down, replaced by franchised Jamie Oliver sausage rolls, and Costa Coffee machines. And people will forget the terrible filter coffee you used to pay a quid for in the Happy Eater, and the kids' slides shaped like an elephant that I used to play on in the deafening fenced-off spaces people called gardens that sprang up outside diners on the side of motorways. Shit Britain, old Britain, where the commercial travellers and football supporters would nod to each other, and hold the bathroom door while avoiding eye contact, because they knew what they'd just done. I miss that world. Even as it's disappearing, I already miss it. Not because there was anything good or wholesome or life-improving about it.

It just reminds me of when I was young, and nothing had gone wrong yet, and things were easy. It reminds me of my grandfather taking me out for the day and letting me get a buzzcut at the barber's, then buying me a milkshake in a roadside café and taking me home to Mum, who almost cried when she saw my hair.

And I think, as well as the memory of youth, there's a kind of innocence to all these shut-down cafés that we'll never have again. This is where we gulped down bacon rind, and never thought about calories, never thought about sustainable, ethical meat or where our eggs came from, or the ecological holocaust we were creating. We were idiots. But it was a very simple time, and I know that we'll never live it again. When chocolate bars were massive, and a two-thousand-calorie breakfast seemed OK. And then we'd get back in our cars and motor on down to the seaside, to leave litter on the beach. Imagine being so thoughtless, so carefree. Of course, we can't now. I can only see the damage it's all done. But it must have been wonderful while it lasted. Once, people used to worry about E numbers. That was the problem that needed solving. I'd give a lot to have a conversation about E numbers over a Big Mac in McDonald's again. In the windows of those old, shut-down diners, I see the equation between ignorance and bliss. There'll always be traces of it, of course. The cafés on industrial estates, the little roadside vans, and the places outside football grounds. There'll always be people who need real fuel for a day putting up scaffolding, or just don't care about the modern world's discoveries, the modern world's attempt to take back some of the things that were said and done in the wild, American moment of the eighties and nineties. But for most of us, for those of us who separate our rubbish for recycling and only get takeaway once a week or so as a treat we regret later, those days and that innocence are gone.

We look for something to eat in the petrol station, but none of it seems edible, so we head into one of the towns the road takes us close to and where we guess there'll be better cafés, and while Amy shops I walk Ivan round the multi-storey car park, trying to find a way out and into the town centre that doesn't take me through the shopping centre, where dogs are banned. It's difficult, and I have to turn back twice before I find a back staircase that gets me down to a service road, and follow that round till I get in among people again. Clearly, no one who planned the car park or the shopping centre gave much thought to what people would do if they were travelling with dogs. I have half a mind to stop searching for a way out and just let Ivan shit on the car park floor. Once we're out in the streets, I distract myself with being attentive to Ivan, and wait to catch Amy on her way back into the shopping centre. This is when dogs do the greatest good for their owners. It helps at times like this to lose yourself in another life, to be kind, and not need to speak, not have to put what you're feeling into language. It's immediate and present to be kind to Ivan, anchors you in the here and now, and keeps you away from the twin, grim precipices of the future and the past that are lurking always at the edge of your vision.

Another dog approaches, young like Ivan, straining on the leash to say hello. The woman holding the lead is missing some teeth.

'Don't mind him, he's friendly,' she tells me. 'He's only nine months. Ten. Sorry, I'm not sure. He was my partner's dog, but my partner died last week, so I'm taking him on. Keep him in the family.'

'I'm so sorry your partner died.'

'Thank you.' She watches our dogs as they playfight. 'Yeah, I took him to the morgue to say goodbye.' I don't know what to say to her. She doesn't seem to want me to say anything; she says it like it's merely a statement of fact. 'I better go now. Have a nice day, yeah?' She walks away then without looking back at me.

Amy finds us as she walks back to the car park from the shops and we get back in the car, and the rest of the journey passes in podcasts and toilet breaks, stopping to take out Ivan and walk him, the traffic disappearing once we cross the Severn Bridge into Wales, the empty bridge, no toll booths, no money changing hands, just the long grey tongue of the road leading us on into a new emptiness. Up through the country on the winding roads past ancient slate-grey pubs. Every town disfigured by the bad architecture of the late twentieth century. Every 'For Sale' sign has been up for months.

We clean our hands at the door to the ward and walk inside, and I see Chris sitting in a blue plastic chair before I see Mum lying in the bed beside him. Chris stands up when he spots us. Mum can't. She has a mask clamped over her face, plugged into the wall, getting her oxygen through a tube. As we approach I can see that her face is red and there's sweat running off her. Her breathing is quick and shallow, like a fish on the bank. She looks emotional when she sees we've arrived, and reaches out an arm towards me. Her hospital gown is hanging off her shoulder. She turns her head to look at us but doesn't raise it up off the pillow. I sit down with her, take the hand she's holding out towards me. Amy stands behind me and the thought crosses my mind for just a moment that this must be so strange for her, very new to this family, pitched into this bedside *pietà* in reverse.

'Hi.' She doesn't speak, but smiles instead, and I realise that perhaps with the mask and shortness of breath, speech is difficult. I turn to Chris while Amy leans in to smile at Mum and say hello.

'I'm sorry we didn't get here sooner,' I say to him.

'Don't worry. It's wonderful that you've come.'

'How are things?'

He searches for the right words for a moment. 'Pretty scary right now, actually. They've pumped the oxygen up as far as they can go without putting her in intensive care. She's running a temperature and she feels very hot. We don't really know what's going to happen.'

'What's she on? What are they giving her for it?'

'They've put her on antibiotics, but apparently it takes two or three days before they know if it's working. So for now we just have to wait.'

'But once the antibiotics kick in, she'll start to recover?'

'That's the hope. As long as they're the right antibiotics. Different forms of pneumonia need different treatment. They won't know whether they've got it right for another day or so.'

'So they might have to try her on something else?'

'That's possible, yes. We just have to wait and see.'

It's hard to know exactly what it is I'm feeling as I listen to him. So many of the most dramatic moments in our lives can feel very ordinary, because they happen too quickly for us to take in. And we've seen them all so many times in films that sometimes we can't help feeling like we're in a dream, watching ourselves from above as we act out our lines as best we can. I feel numb, almost calm, as if none of this is real. I turn back to look at Mum in the bed.

'Are you in pain?' I ask her. She shakes her head.

'Just my breathing.' Her voice, when I hear it, is shocking to me – all the strength stripped out of it, all the life. She is speaking with the voice of an elderly woman. Now I've heard her speak, she seems suddenly much more unwell than I thought she was a moment ago. As if I've just discovered that a part of her has vanished.

'They're looking after you, though. They're making sure you can breathe OK.' She nods. There's fear in her eyes. Her gaze wanders. It occurs to me that she might be a little delirious. 'Are you able to sleep?' I ask her.

She shakes her head, listless, exhausted, terrified. 'I can't. Not for days now. I'm so frazzled, I feel like I can't see straight. When you came in just now, I thought it was a dream.'

A nurse comes and talks to us, checks Mum's oxygen levels and her blood pressure and asks if she's feeling all right. Mum does what everyone always does, and says she's fine, though it's clear to all of us that she isn't. A porter brings a plate of food and I chop it up so it's easier for Mum to eat. Watching her try to eat is agony. She has to take the mask off her face to get the forkfuls of food to her mouth, but without the mask she struggles to breathe, so she can only take a couple of mouthfuls at a time before she has to pull the mask back down and get her breath back and recover. So the food cools as she eats it slowly, slowly. I remember the way she used to tell me off at mealtimes when I wouldn't eat what was in front of me. 'Don't you know there are children starving in Africa?' 'Well, why don't you send it to them, then?' The hospital food disgusts her. Before long she gives up, pushes the plate away. She still feels hot, so we hold a cup of water to her lips, and she sips at it. Chris finds an electric fan, and turns it to face her, and turns it on, and that seems to help a little. The water makes her calmer. She stares into space and shakes her head, and the look in her eyes is desolation. We are sitting around her in postures of supplication, leaning forward, hands resting on the bed. We turn our faces to her like moths to the light.

'I don't know what's going to happen,' she says to no one. 'I don't know what's happened.'

I find it hard to stay in this moment, not to think ahead, my mind is racing forwards now to the troubles I feel sure this illness is going to cause both Mum and Chris. Pneumonia is one of those illnesses that takes a long time to get over. When she gets through this, I wonder whether it will be possible for her to recover on the farm, or whether she'll need to stay somewhere else. Surely there'll be too much work waiting for her if she goes home, too much struggle? And surely it must have been the farm that made her ill in the first place? I think of the black mould on the kitchen wall, damp and cloying from lack of ventilation. Just stepping through the door of the place made Amy start coughing when we visited. Rachel's the same these days, though she grew up in that environment; years in the city have made her sensitive to it, and she coughs whenever she goes home. Surely that will be why Mum picked this illness up as well?

I know part of my reason for asking myself these questions is selfish. I've always feared the farm would one day become too difficult for them. For a moment I entertain the possibility that there won't be years between now and having to set about selling the farm, and the picture seems different, and I feel panic gathering in me. Things that are going to end some indefinite time in the future look very different from things that could end any day. I know as I sit by the bed how much of a betrayal it really is for me to be resolved against ever coming back here, against ever taking it on.

We spend perhaps an hour and a half together, trying to reassure Mum that she's going to be all right, trying to talk about ordinary things so she doesn't feel like the whole world's ended, telling each other stories about what we'll do when everything's all right, the family gatherings, the reunions. Amy disappears a couple of times to let Ivan out of the car and make sure he's all right. Then when the plate's been taken away again, Mum starts talking about going to the toilet, and Chris suggests that perhaps we should leave her now to rest. She's having to use a bedpan as she's too weak to move or stand at the moment, and doesn't want us around to watch.

I don't really want to leave. It feels like I've only just walked in, and I know once we get home there'll be five hours of driving between me and her, and getting to her bedside will become more difficult. I don't know how to say goodbye to her. What I want to do is open up, say how I'm feeling, talk about love and things that matter. But I hold back. I don't want to make a big deal of this leave-taking. If I say too much,

I worry it will seem as if I think she's going to die. So I kiss her on the forehead, as she must have kissed me on the forehead when she used to tuck me into bed as a child, and tell her I'll visit again as soon as I can, and we leave with Chris, and say goodbye to him in the car park of the hospital, and tell him we'll call him that evening once we're home, again not saying enough because I don't want to say the wrong thing.

Then we let the dog out for a minute, and get into the car, and turn for home. Neither of us speaks for the first mile of road. Neither of us knows what we ought to say.

'Look,' Amy says to me, eyes on the road. 'Don't go home to your place tonight. Actually, don't go back there again. You don't want to be on your own right now. Come and be with me. If you want, I mean. Why don't you come and be with me?'

The offer strikes me as almost impossibly romantic. I realise that she had hoped we'd have this conversation out on our holiday, too; she had also been wondering when we'd get round to mentioning that.

'I really want that,' I say. 'But I don't want you to feel you have to because my mum's not well. We should only do that if we would have done it anyway.'

'Would you have done it anyway?' Amy asks.

'Yeah,' I say. 'I would. I don't know when I'd have asked, but I wanted to ask you.'

'All right, then,' she says, 'let's do it. Because that's what I wanted as well.'

'It changed while you were away, didn't it?'

'Yeah. It was always going to, though. It was always going to end or get more serious. Being apart does that.'

'You're sure you're up for it?'

'If it's where you want to be too.'

I want to say to her: I would go anywhere you wanted. I would follow you anywhere, because you want me with you. And to know someone cares whether or not you're around is the heart of all meaning, the heart of belonging; that's what people search for all their lives. I would go anywhere if you wanted me to go with you. But I don't know how to say it without sounding like a greetings card.

'I'm up for it,' I say to her instead. And we drive on together. And just like that, the world is different. I glance at her. Something happens that's never happened before.

'I love you,' I tell her.

She smiles. 'Yeah, I think I might love you too actually, but right now I'm going to concentrate on driving.'

1952

YEARS BEFORE HER husband killed himself, Mary was just a young woman from Llandrindod Wells who wanted to be happy, who met a man at a dance in Builth Wells who said he was going to take over a farm near Erwood, and fell in love with him, and fought with him sometimes because he had black moods but always loved the making up together. Who looked after her parents-in-law until they died. Mary was a young woman who had a daughter with her husband, and she loved the raising of that girl, her angel, her Angie. She was a young woman who kept the house while Leo kept the farm. As the years coursed through her, she gathered in the store of her memory a trove of things which seemed to her to have the gleam of love, and life became more and more about the act of remembering for her with the passing of each year, as she went on collecting up these things that gleamed like prayers, one beautiful image after another that made her grateful to have been alive. The day she found a shrew with all its babies in the pantry of the house, and lifted one of the baby shrews up on the palm of her hand and watched it groom itself; the day she travelled with her parents to St David's, and for the first time saw the sea; the first time she helped birth a lamb;

the feeling of biting into good beef bought from Builth market and carted the miles home for the family after Lent; the feeling of sitting at Evensong in church, looking up at the stained glass in the windows while the organ music seemed to speak to her, catching chords in her heart she'd never previously heard, lifting her up out of herself. Like the feeling she got when she climbed up mountains.

Her life on the farm was one of unremitting labour, but each of the thousands of tasks she carried out were essentially straightforward in what had to be done, the number and constancy of them being what really wore her down. If people ever asked her, she'd say she had a simple life, though each morning she woke before first light to put fires in the grates and open the shutters, let the chickens out and feed them grain, take the bread dough from where it had been proving under its cloth overnight and get water from the well and heat a kettle and make breakfast for her family, clean the house and keep the fires stoked and get her child out to school at the top of the hill in time, clean clothes in the big tub with the washboard in front of the fire, and wash herself, and change the sheets, and make her husband's lunch, and make bread and churn butter, and maybe go down into Erwood for provisions, and mend things, always patching or darning, and help Angie with her reading, and make the dinner, and get her child to bed and then help her husband clean up from the day, and a thousand other tasks besides this. Leo always knew this and was always appreciative, always grateful for the work she did keeping the house together while he was out on the hills with the lambs or mending fences or feeding the sheep, all the daily work of a farm. It was barbarism really, she thought sometimes, but that was life in that part of the world in that moment in time, and she accepted it. It wasn't as if there was anything else. Or rather, there might have been once, when she was young, and could have gone anywhere or fallen in love with anyone, but that never happened, and now was long gone. She was in her life and she decided she would love it. Years later, when Angie's marriage ended and she came home to the farm, Mary would sit with her grandchild Edward while Angie and the man she'd hired to run the farm were out doing Leo's old job on the backbreaking land, and tell stories about the lives she hadn't lived, the things that might once have been different.

'It's the pattern with the women in this family,' she'd tell Edward. 'They follow the men and that becomes their lives, for better or worse – that's been the pattern. I followed your grandfather back here and now I will die here, I suppose, and your grandfather's mother followed her husband the whole way across the world when he wanted to come home, from the place where she was born in India. And the cost it took on her, you wouldn't believe it, she was a very ill woman, but that's what happens in this family; we all come to the farm, the women following the men.' She shouldn't have, really. Probably sowing trouble like dragon's teeth. But that was the story as she understood it, and she liked to tell her stories to them; she thought love was storytelling, the sharing of a life the meaning of love.

All the time she told this story of herself, there was another life happening within her that she never knew how to share with people. These feelings, these vast feelings that she could not fit into language, would assail her every day as she reeled, dizzy sometimes, with how much she loved being alive for this span of time. The sunsets at the end of the valley, and the way the hawthorn foamed with flowers upon coming into bloom. The trees seeming to speak to her in the wind, the shelter of tall oaks, the shelter of beeches. It was all breathtaking to her, and she wished she could have found more ways to say it. Instead she satisfied herself with telling her family that she loved them, trusted that they saw the world the way she did, trusted that they would know what she meant when she spoke of love.

Leo took a lot of looking after. Sometimes he would sit and cry in the mornings before he went out for the day, and for many years she kept her distance from him, afraid he would become violent and strike out, but that never happened and as time passed she realised what he wanted was to be comforted, because there were things terribly wrong with him. It was the legacy of his mother, she supposed, the years when she had been mad but nothing had been done about it, when she used to sob and scream and try to throw herself from windows, the cost of that on this poor boy who should have been looked after by her, not the other way round. He had to do it all, right till her dying day, because his father didn't know what to do, and there was no one in the area who could have helped her. Really she should have been sent away, but asylums in those days were not places for anyone you loved, perhaps they still weren't, perhaps they never would be, so she stayed upstairs in her own private kingdom in the attic and looked out at the alien hills and the abandoned farmhouses falling down, and Leo would cook for her, wash her, keep her living, although Mary doubted that was what Phoebe herself really wanted. She would have rather been dead or gone home, but no one can ever go home, not really. That was what she thought Leo might have been doing the day he died, those many years later, when he fell from the roof. She remembered Phoebe's funeral in 1952, the two of them standing side by side in the churchyard in the village, holding her husband's hand. She was looking down into the grave as the coffin was being prepared to be lowered down into it, as the young men who had dug the grave started to take the weight of the straps wrapped round the box, and she glanced at Leo, worried he would be appalled by this, traumatised by the physicality of it, the huffing and heaving, and saw to her surprise that he wasn't looking at the coffin at all. He was looking at the tower of the church and the sky beyond.

'Are you all right?' she asked him, knowing she had asked a stupid question, because of course he wasn't, his mother had died, and just as difficult as the sorrow of this was the sheer relief, the knowing she wasn't in pain any more, and that all the work of keeping her alive had finally ended; the guilt of that relief would be as difficult as the sorrow.

'She used to love to look at the tower from her bedroom window,' Leo said to her.

'It's very beautiful.'

'It wasn't so much the tower itself. She liked to be up high. When she was high up, she could see further. I think she dreamed of one day getting so high she could see all the way home. Of course, she got it all wrong. She could see further from the farm, she could see for miles from the top field over the valley, and if she'd climbed the tower, she'd only have seen the valley from the bottom. But she loved to be up high, my mother, she loved a tower, loved a spire.'

Mary looked up at the little church tower, which seemed so pathetic when you thought of ever getting high enough off the ground to see all the way to India, but of course she knew home wasn't a place, it wasn't somewhere physical in the world you could return to. What Phoebe must have liked, she suspected, was the look of distance, the blue of distance falling over hills, which must seem beautiful from the top of the church tower in the estranging wind. A chance to see out to the edge of the vision, not to spy any particular place, but just to know the distance and take it in. She watched Leo watching the tower. She knew as the years rolled on, he might fall more and more in love with the look of distance too, a way to take in what had become of him, to remember his mother. And she was right. And then he fell. And then he was buried in the same graveyard where they had stood together in 1952, newly married, not yet parents, barely begun on the journey they'd share until he took it away from them, because the black moods became the whole of him, because no matter how hard he tried he couldn't outswim the current any more, which had been pulling at him ever since his mother left India, before he was even born. She had the strangest feeling later, after he had gone, that she had seen it all coming, as early as that day in that churchyard. It had all been contained in that moment when she watched him staring fixedly at the church tower while his mother was lowered into the ground. She remembered how she used to wait to meet him from the bus into Llandrindod when they were courting, standing on tiptoes to see in the windows of the bus as it arrived, to spot him looking out at her. She remembered the crackle of the air when he got off the bus, the joy in both of them, their faces lighting up with smiles and him shyly leaning down to kiss her on the cheek, and him taking her hand, and her heart in her chest as they walked into Llandrindod together, or out the other way into the fields to be alone together. The glory of taking a man's hand, and loving him, and knowing as you did that he loved you, that you wanted the same things, that one day you were going to be together. Couldn't life have been that? Might there not have been something she could have done to make things different?

2019

We travel home. In English we don't have enough words for 'home', the precise nuances of what we mean are never spelled out clearly enough. The same word has to stand for this place I'm from that I'm leaving behind, and this place where I lie down to sleep each night. The traffic of London slows us down for the last hour. The city we live in rises to meet us, funnels us along its faceless roads flanked with dirt-caked houses and the walled-in soundproofed lives lived inside them, the people hiding. I feel the city climbing into my head, making room for itself, overturning one thing after another, setting everything spinning. The ceaseless noise, the light, the fear, the anger. In this place we cling to each other and try the best we can to survive the huge indifference of the metropolis all around us.

All cities are built like maps of a mind, and when you spend time in them they come to map your own, you can't help but fall into the rhythms offered up to you. As we return, I feel all my thoughts start to press together. This jealous city where no one looks anyone in the eye. We crawl through the leafy outskirts, then on to the concrete and empty shops that make up the place where we live, the part of the city where things are sent that people want to forget or ignore or cover over. This is us for now. We find what life and dignity we can in this place where voices are not heard, where memories are being obliterated.

We reach Amy's flat and I get Ivan out of the car while Amy brings the first of the bags inside. I look around the place with new eyes now, imagining moving the things I own into this space, becoming part of it, for however long we stay here. I try to imagine my books on the shelves.

It's growing dark and for the first time in a week I find I can't feel the weather. Behind this double glazing under the low growls of the road, under the flight path and disoriented as the orange lights turn on outside with the nightfall, I can't feel what's happening in the air in the evening. This is living in the city, desensitized and numb. I hadn't noticed how numb it made me feel.

So this will be us for a little while, then. Four rooms to go round, the big living room at the front, the bedroom, the kitchen and the bathroom. The flat was once the first floor of a house on the end of a terrace built at the end of the nineteenth century; all those houses were cut up into flats many years ago. Amy lives above a Spanish family with a three-year-old child, who I have learned loves nothing more than to run up and down the length of the house, screaming at the top of his voice. It seems to me sometimes when I stay here and listen to him as if there must be something emotionally wrong with him: the child seems to cry at the slightest provocation, and his parents, who are kind people, and can't be blamed for the noise their son makes, don't know how to calm him down. If we pass in the front hallway, we greet each other like friends, but in the back gardens, our garden being the one nearest the house and theirs being the scrap of lawn beyond it, we pretend not to see each other, and get on with our reading or sunbathing in silence. This is how I've come to characterise life in this city – impossibly close together, yet somehow miles apart.

Before Amy lived in this flat it was, I believe, a cannabis farm. Both the downstairs and upstairs flats had stood empty for some time, as this part of the city, though still undesirable now, was practically dangerous five or ten years ago, and flats could often be hard to rent out. At some point, someone must have noticed the flats were abandoned and found a way to break in. I've only been able to piece the story together by reading around online, but the pieces seem to fit. Our building, being on the end of the terrace, borders the playground of the neighbouring primary school, and I came across an article one day describing a police raid on a property next to the school that discovered a farm with a hundred plants growing in it. As all the refurbishment work done on this flat to make it habitable dates from about five months after that raid, and the only other property next to the school has been a family home for many years, it seems likely to me that the owners of this place, having been informed by the police of what had been going on, had decided to give the flats a lick of paint and persuade some more legitimate tenants to live in them. Very little sign of this chapter in the life of the flats remains to be seen today; only the front doors seem to give a hint of it. The outer door, which contains several glass panels, has two very different kinds of glass in it, the panels nearest the door handle being much newer and more recently installed. The inner door, meanwhile, is a cheap fire door installed very recently. These, I think, are the traces of the police raid that ended with Amy's flat being reclaimed for human habitation. The outer door was opened by breaking a couple of glass panes; the inner door had to be kicked in completely.

We eat a light supper, take Ivan for a last walk round the woods up the road, phone Chris and tell him we hope he's able to sleep tonight, and promise we'll call the ward for an update in the morning. Then we watch an hour of TV sitting side by side, take our books to bed together, and make love, then sleep.

For a little while after Amy has fallen asleep, I lie awake and watch her. I used to laugh at people who talked about watching someone sleeping. I didn't understand how it could be a tender moment. It was a moment, after all, when the person you were watching wasn't really there. It was just that I hadn't loved anyone back then. In these quiet moments of looking unselfconsciously at someone else, taking time to take them in, the mind unspools the life you have together, the things you've shared in the last hours and days, and you find out what they mean to you as the feeling creeps up and makes itself known in all its depth and complexity, the feeling swells because it's given its acre of silence to stretch out, like light falling lazily through the window of a kitchen, taking a whole day to roll across a table, loving slowly, tracing every knothole and lineament. I watch Amy while she sleeps and the feeling is almost like grief, that once I didn't know this woman, I missed so much of her life in the years before I knew her, and one day not so far from now our togetherness will end again, it is all of it ending every minute we live.

When I call the ward the next morning and ask to speak to the nurse in charge, then apologise for taking up his time and ask how Mum is feeling, I don't get the reassurance I hoped to hear. Strange, how in these times we always seem to expect the best. I had called up thinking whoever I spoke to would tell me that things had improved with the passage of time. People, given any reasonable inducement, will look away. The rubbernecking traffic that builds up on motorways is misleading, it's not really a marker of human behaviour at all; when the accident happens in their own lives, most people don't slow down to look at it if they don't have to. Most people will deny it's even happening.

'Your mother's been moved to intensive care; she's no longer here on this ward, I'm afraid. You'll need to redial and speak to them.'

'What's happened to her? Why was she moved?'

'In the night she needed a boost in oxygen, and she's continued to need that today. She can get that more easily on intensive care, so the decision was taken to move her.'

'But she's not getting worse?'

'She wasn't getting worse, no. It's just that she wasn't managing to get any better, so it was decided a stronger intervention would help her turn the corner.'

'All right. Thank you. I'll call intensive care now and see how she is.'

But I don't. I ring off, then decide to call up Chris instead, guessing he'll know all this already and just hasn't got round to calling me yet, guessing I'll learn as much from him as I could from the overworked nurses. It makes me uncomfortable calling the hospital; I feel like I'm taking people away from their work. I call him straight away without going to find Amy, because I'm looking for quick reassurance. The memory comes to me of the last days of my grandma's life, my father's mother, when the hospital kept sending her back to the nursing home and the nursing home would simply send her back to the hospital, because within an hour of getting there she'd need oxygen again, and they didn't have a ventilator. Three times it happened; there was nothing technically wrong with my grandma when she kept getting sent in, so the hospital would send her home, then six hours later she'd be back again. I was there for two of them, and watched her being wheeled along on her trolley bed, tiny and birdlike, looking suddenly fifty years younger without her glasses on, her face stripped of old age, perhaps because she had lost a lot of weight, and she looked so like my dad that it was frightening. In a corridor waiting to be given a ventilator room, she shifted and moaned, and I asked her where it hurt, and she roared out to me with all the strength left in her body in a voice that seemed to come from some supernatural depth the one word 'everywhere'. There was nothing I could say. I held her hand. I told her we were all so proud she was our grandmother, that she'd set us all a wonderful example. She looked very deeply into my eyes and nodded, and the pain seemed to clear while she thought of that. Then the pain came back again, and she lay on her back, and all life had shrunk down to focusing on her breathing, the whole world, which had once been hers to travel round and explore and visit on cruises, reduced down to breathing in and out. She died later that same day. I'd left the hospital, and wasn't with her when it happened, and I wish I had been, I wish I hadn't gone home that afternoon.

And remembering her always leads me back further to the death of my grandad, her husband. One memory always spurring the next. His death was even more horrifying to me, in part because it was the first; he died before Dad died and I had never gone through it before, I had never seen how hard it was to die till then and the knowledge shocked me, the knowledge made me far less certain than I had been that it was a fortunate thing to be born into the world, when there was so much pain waiting for us all in the leaving of it. And there was the fact that there was nothing really terminally wrong with him either; he seemed to just decide he couldn't go through with it all any more, so he stopped eating and drinking, and starved himself to death, and was overcome by waves of fear and panic in the last days when we sat with him and asked him to drink a little water, and begged the nurses to help him with the pain.

I think of them both, my beautiful grandparents, the kindest people in the world to me, who never deserved the way their stories ended, and I can't believe Mum could be next along the line to face all that. It's ludicrous to me, at her age, in her robust health, it's unimaginable. Although I realise, having seen her lying in the hospital bed, that it will happen one day; and I realise that now she's one of the people in my life who might be next, impossible as it is to really take that disturbing thought in. So I call Chris's number and he picks up, sounding a little out of breath. I can hear that he's outside, and I guess he's in the hospital car park again.

'I'm sorry I haven't called yet,' he says, once he's heard that I know she's been moved to the ICU. 'When they told me, I just got in the car and drove. I've just parked up.'

'Of course, don't worry. I'm guessing you don't know any more yet than I do?'

'Not really, no. I don't think your sister knows yet.'

'I can call her, don't worry.'

'Are you sure?'

'Of course. You just want to be with Mum, you don't want to do all that.'

'Thank you.' He's silent for a moment. 'I thought I'd be stronger, you know.'

I don't know what to say to that. I still don't know what conversation Chris wants to have, how much further he's thought than this moment, whether thinking past this crisis and getting Mum back home would just be an irrelevance to him. I want to ask him how long she's been ill, and whether he's cleaning the house for when she gets home, where she'll sleep while she recuperates, how his work's been affected, whether he's getting help in. All of this might just be chaff to him, could even make him angry while his wife's there in the hospital and that's all he wants to be thinking about.

'Why don't you go in and see her, see what's going on?'

'All right. Thank you. I'll call you in a while, then.'

He rings off, and I look out the window and don't know what to do. I can see the back of the allotment site beyond the gardens, a line of trees dividing the allotments from the gardens of the houses. I can see the light falling on the trees, and catching the high fences of the gardens, picking out the slats of the fences in stark dark and light. Amy is in the next room. I go through to her.

'I'm guessing you heard all that?' I say.

She nods.

'Do you want to go back?'

'I don't know what to do yet. It might just be she needed the extra support, and that will mean she turns the corner. I don't think we should do anything till he calls back.'

'All right.' She stands up and crosses the room to me, and we kiss. 'Are you all right?'

'Kind of.'

'Can I do anything?'

We smile at each other, because of course we both know she can't. Absurd as it is, there's nothing to be done. Even travelling to see her might be more for us than her, really. But what else are we supposed to say at times like these? What else can we offer? Is it better to stay silent and say nothing at all? The words are really just a form of kindness, just a way of telling someone you love them.

Ten anxious minutes pass, time I spend in the kitchen putting the washing-up away, then Chris calls again, and I answer. I'm slightly surprised he's called so quickly. When the phone rings my stomach drops, as if I already know it's going to be bad news.

He tells me he didn't stay long, because she's not conscious any more. He came back outside to tell me so I could call my sister and get in the car and start driving. She has sepsis, and for some reason he can't explain she's not conscious now. I hear the news through a dim, deep roaring, as if there's a waterfall crashing down to drown the air between Chris and me. It's the blood in my ears, I think, the panic, the urgent heartbeats. He hangs up. Amy has come to the kitchen doorway. I turn and we look at each other.

'I thought she was recovering,' I say.

'She might still be recovering. She might just need more help than she was getting.'

'But why is she unconscious? What does that mean?' I try, but I can't get my head round it. I didn't ask what he meant, whether she'd passed out or whether her unconsciousness had been somehow induced. Did he mean sleeping? Did he mean a coma? She's still a young woman, my mother, she's just turned sixty; it's going to be a long time before her health fails. There's going to be a long time yet for us to plan what to do when this kind of thing happens. We don't have to be thinking about days like these, not for a decade yet, not till she's older. What on earth is happening? How could this moment be real? I call my sister and she answers on the third ring.

'You OK?' she asks.

'I'm OK. But I think we need to head home.'

'What's happened?'

'I'm not completely sure, but Mum needed more oxygen so they moved her to intensive care. Your dad's there with her but I think we should go.' I finish the call, and ring off, and again I don't know what to do, I feel frozen by the significance of what might be happening even now, right now, even though the day outside the window looks unremarkable to me.

'Shall we go?' Amy asks.

'Is that OK?'

She smiles as if in exasperation. What passes unspoken between us is my apology for still behaving as if this might not be an emergency, still pretending we might have some say in what we do with the next few hours, when in fact we've fallen somehow into a crisis, and none of the normal rules are going to apply for a while. I'm still pretending a drive back to Wales might be putting her out, because if that were true, if there were still any say in the matter, maybe the situation wouldn't be as frightening as it suddenly seems.

We get the dog back in the car and drive, only stopping at a service station once the fuel light's come on. There's a text from Chris to tell us he's still with Mum. No more than that.

Rachel is my half-sister, though I've never used that term about her. She went through a phase of calling me her half-brother. I didn't understand why at the time. It was a long time before I realised she must have been upset when I left home, and relegating me to the status of half-sibling must have felt a bit like what I'd done to her when I went away. Because she was born after Mum and I came to the farm, the place is closer to being the whole of her life. I always find that strange to imagine, because in many ways we're extremely alike, and it's easy to imagine we think all the same thoughts, share our memories. But there's an essential difference between us. Her image of the world was never broken. She never lost the geography of her childhood, never experienced being uprooted and having to accept a new place as her own. Her first memories belong to the farm, so for her there's still one place she can call home, one centre. She's never even had to work out what it means to have divorced parents. I can't imagine what it would feel like to live her life. I suppose there are things I distrust that she can never have doubted. Because she doesn't have the same grounds I have for believing the world could suddenly end at a moment's notice. It occurs to me, thinking of this, that she might respond more calmly to this current situation than I have. It may be that I'm catastrophising, expecting the worst because I always look out for it.

Amy drives, worried I won't be able to concentrate on the road, and I sit in the passenger seat beside her and think of the past. I remember the first time I ever needed stitches, falling from a tree and impaling myself on the stump of a low branch Dad had sawn off at the base of the tree I was climbing. Mum and Dad rushed me in the car to the doctor's surgery, my lower half covered with only a towel because the cut above my coccyx was open and bleeding. While we waited, I sat on Dad's lap and Mum crouched down and put her face in front of mine so that I could see her smile, I could see she was calm and listen to the soothing words she was trying to say to me, persuading both of us at once that I was all right. They took me into the doctor's room and I lay on my front on a bed, and the doctor sewed up the cut. I screamed as the needle went in, but it was mostly for show because Mum was holding my hand and I knew that I was safe and that I'd be all right, and the local anaesthetic the doctor had applied, a cold gel I remember him rubbing on, meant that I couldn't really feel any pain. I remember falling on a walk, and my front tooth cutting right through my upper lip, and the screaming, the blood and the pain, my mashed lip, and Mum kneeling down to pick me up and carrying me away again, back to the doctor's. This was the rhythm once, falling and being picked up. I watched her do it with Rachel, when Rachel broke her arm so clean at the elbow that when she held it out to show us all, it swung the wrong way. We would fall and she'd pick us up. And then, ever so slowly, everything changes, and it's her turn to be falling, and all of us feel like the same person we used to be, we hardly realised any time had passed at all. But everything is different and we can't go back.

When we get to the hospital Mum's awake again, and I can't get a straight story from Chris about what he meant when he said she was unconscious, whether she was sleeping or delirious or something else. The tension he feels is written on his face now, the colour all fled from it, the lines gouged deeper than I've ever seen them. He looks decades older than he did the day before. Rachel is there with him, holding Mum's hand. Mum tries to smile, but seems afraid, and I worry the fear on all our faces must be making it worse for her. So I try and see the positives. The new breathing machine Mum's been hooked up to makes it easier for her to speak and drink and eat; because the tubes go into her nose now, there isn't a mask to cover her mouth, and this makes talking easier.

'It must be such a relief to be able to drink without having to take a mask off,' I say.

'What?' She speaks like someone who's been up for a week – which she has, more or less, the shortness of breath and the other patients previously lying alongside her in the hospital ward making sleep impossible.

'The tubes. These must be so much better.'

'Oh,' she says. 'Yes. That's right.'

'And it's calmer in here, isn't it?'

She has her own room now in the ICU, a window that looks out, comically, on to a brick wall about three feet beyond the glass, like something from a movie, a cliché of a hospital view. The walls of the room are painted in that blue that people call either duck egg or eggshell, I can never quite remember, and the nurses are in earshot beyond the swing doors, which are pinned open. Through the doors we hear the nurses speaking and the beeping of machines, but there's quiet around Mum, where before there were five other people in beds on the shared ward, visitors, the scraping of chairs, nurses fending off questions. Mum growls in the back of her throat at the memory of it.

'Fucking place.'

We laugh.

'Yeah. Was it really awful?' I ask her.

'This woman opposite. I don't know. Theresa. Seems to have had a difficult life, and fair enough. But my God. All night, she wouldn't stop.'

'Stop what?'

'There was this programme she was listening to. About jazz music in England. About jazz music after the Second World War. And it was all about the kinds of jazz and where people heard it, and the kind of venues there were and the record shops, that kind of thing. And Theresa listened to this whole programme, and the thing is that after the war there was a lot of motorbike manufacturing. People made a lot of motor-bikes because they were cheap to produce and cheap to run and because they were popular as well. And Theresa thought there wasn't enough in the documentary about motorbike manufacturing. And she was calling up the station for hours and hours to complain.'

Rachel and Chris laugh uneasily. I lean towards her, try to catch her eye.

'So this was a programme on the radio, was it?'

'Yes, but she kept calling in.'

'She was trying to complain about a programme on the radio.'

'Yes, again and again and again.'

I try to look her in the eye, make out whether this really happened or if she had been delirious. She seems to doubt what she's saying herself, already what had seemed so clear a moment earlier becoming dim and cloudlike.

Chris leaves the room to go to the toilet, and Mum beckons to me and Rachel, drawing us closer, so we both lean in around her.

'You have to look after him,' she says.

'We are, Mum, don't worry,' Rachel tells her, taking her hand.

'But you have to make sure he's all right.' This time neither of us speaks, because it's clear she doesn't mean just for now; she doesn't mean till she gets better. It's shocking, to see her planning for life after she's left it. And neither of us knows enough, neither of us knows whether she's truly in danger or whether she's just frightened. 'He won't be able to look after himself on his own.'

'He won't need to, Mum, you'll be home with him,' I say.

'But if he couldn't look after the farm,' she carries on, determined, a little out of breath now from this speaking.

'We don't need to think about this.'

'If he couldn't look after the farm, would you help him?'

Rachel and I share a wild glance, and don't know what to say.

'Of course we would,' I say.

'He can't just leave it. It's his home. You'd have to help him keep it going.'

'We'd do whatever we could, Mum.'

'No, but I mean it. You can't let him leave. Couldn't you take it on? For me, couldn't you do that? He can't do all his cooking himself, you know.'

I lift up my head again and this time share a look with Amy, trapped at the edge of the room, not knowing how to help me. 'We'd do what was best for Chris, Mum, don't worry.'

'You'd live there with him?'

'We'd work out what was best. Sometimes when people get older it's better for them to move somewhere easier to manage, it's not just a case of saying we'd help him stay. But all this is years away anyway, Mum, we can talk about all this another time.'

'You don't want it,' she says with sudden force.

'What do you mean, Mum?' Rachel says.

'We built it. We all built that life.' Her face seems to fall in on itself, with the sad sullen rage of a child. She has seen it for the first time. She's taken it in. And we should be changing our minds to reassure her. If I was a better man, I'd say what was needed. But I say nothing. None of us says anything for a moment, because I can see Rachel feels the same way I do; Rachel doesn't feel like the farm is her life, and neither of us wants to lie to Mum just to make her feel better. Perhaps we ought to, but we don't, and then Chris comes back into the room, and the moment passes.

After a while, the nurses tell us we have to leave. It's different here to the rules on the ward, where we were allowed to stay late and no one noticed. The ICU is full of people fighting for life. So we say goodbye to Mum, trying to keep it light, trying not to say too much and frighten her, and I leave with Amy and Rachel while Chris stays behind for one more minute. Mum seems frightened, under the surface of her saying goodbye, but she tries to be brave, she tries to hide it. We tell her we love her and she says the same. We kiss her on the forehead and then we leave. We go outside and see to Ivan while Rachel uses the loo.

'She's pretty scary,' Amy says.

'I know. The machine she's on seems better, though.'

There is a fear that's taking me over, and I don't know how it got so strong, or whether it's rational, and whether I should mention it. The feeling of having no more control over what's going to happen, the knowledge that even Mum can't make it on her own now, and needs the machines to help with her breathing, makes me feel suddenly very weak. I wonder how many times in my life I'll have to feel this. I wonder how often I'm going to have to cope with this feeling of weakness. I can't quite dismiss the thought that this, now, is the beginning of a long and drawn-out ending that will slowly build up till it encompasses everything, drowns out everything. In and out of hospital for one person or another, turning the years into a long goodbye. I could see it stretching ahead of us. The world going round in ever-decreasing circles for my parents as they grew older. One thing after another becoming impossible, the walks they used to take getting shorter, the back aching worse first thing in the morning. Before they knew it, they'd have bought their last overcoats.

'Do you want to stay?' Amy asks. I guess we've both assumed since the moment we left home that that was what we were going to do, for a while at least, though neither of us has mentioned it, though neither of us actually packed a bag.

'What do you think?'

'I think while things are scary, it would be the supportive thing to do, don't you?'

'Would you mind?'

'Of course not.'

'If we're welcome, of course.'

'Of course. But I think we will be.'

Rachel comes back out of the hospital. 'What are you two going to do, then?' she asks.

'We thought we'd see if we could stay for a few days. If we wouldn't be getting in the way.'

'I think that'll be good for Dad, yeah. He's not dealing with this very well, is he?'

'Understandably.'

'Told me he spent all of last evening online looking at houses in town.'

'Did he?'

'He said it was a useful distraction.'

'Really?'

'He's worried the farm will be too hard for Mum.'

'Jesus.' I don't know what to say to this – I ought to feel glad we're thinking along the same lines, but in fact a kind of panic sets in.

'We'd been talking about that,' Amy says. 'You can't know with these things, can you, but we wondered whether the lifestyle could have been what made her ill.'

'It's so fucking hard there, in the winters,' I add. 'I don't know whether now's the time, because there might be too much else to deal with, but it's interesting that that's what Chris's doing.'

Then Chris comes along the hall from the ICU and joins us by the front door. We smile at him, tentative, and he smiles in return.

'Shall we have a cup of coffee?' he asks. So we go to the hospital café and I order drinks, and we sit down.

'We were actually wondering whether we might stay with you for a night or two?' I ask once we're all seated. 'If you didn't mind.'

'No, of course. I'd be really grateful,' he says. 'I know your mum would be too. That's really kind, thank you.'

'All right. That's great. Thank you.'

We finish our coffees.

'Did she seem OK when you left her just now?' Rachel asks.

Chris shrugs. 'I think so. I hope so. I think maybe she had a wobble this morning, but things are levelling out. This is going to be a long road,' he says.

'Yeah.'

'The doctor tells me maybe six months, before she's properly well again. And while she's recovering, there won't be that much she can do.'

'We could make up a bed for her downstairs, so she doesn't have to go up and down too much.'

'That could be good.'

None of us speaks for a second then. I have a feeling that all of us are holding back. All of us scared, and imagining different futures. But none of us wants to be the first to say these terrifying things out loud. Eventually my stepdad looks up and smiles.

'I spent the whole of last evening on Zoopla, you know. Looking at cottages in town. Silly, I know, wrong time to think about it, but it was where my mind went. Seeing if there were easier places for us to live while your mum recovers. God knows how we'd ever sell the farm, though, selling it would take years. I was only distracting myself.'

We walk to the cars, putting Ivan back into the back seat, and Amy and I are alone together once the doors close and the silence closes round us. While we travel, a buzzard flies low over the road, and seems to stare in through the windscreen at us both. The sun catches its wings as it passes, so it looks like it's burning, and I feel as if the world's trying to speak to me. Perhaps that's just the ghost of religious faith making me read significance into a bird in the air, and light on its wings. Sometimes I can almost hear God singing through these landscapes, though I don't believe in that story any more. But it's hard to start life in a place like this and not believe the world has secret currents, because of the cold, heart-stopping sunlight on the grass. After forty minutes we come to the road that leads to the farm, and drive through the village, slow and easy, then on up the lane till we come to the left turn, and bump over the last few yards of unmade track till we come to the gate.

I half expect the house to be a mess when we walk in, but Chris has been cleaning up to keep himself busy, and the house actually looks better than I can remember it in a long time. Mum and Chris's dogs are overjoyed to see Ivan, and they race out into the garden together, chasing each other, inscribing circles in the grass and the quiet air and the afternoon. I make tea, and we take it out to the garden and sit by the vegetable beds, the three of us together.

When we first came back here, I think Mum saw the farm's history as a challenge, a story she could try to rewrite. For a long time she managed to pull off that trick – we all did it together, made the place where we lived fill up with noise and life and the clatter of living. That had lasted a long time. I don't think I'd ever noticed till now how long we'd held all that life in the air. A quarter of a century is a long time to make anything work. Was it going to end now, I wondered? Was this what it felt like to enter a new phase of the life of your family, for everything to change? People don't seem to age at all till they get ill one day, and suddenly they realise they're getting old, and then they can never get back to before. Would the farm reassert its true self now, its real face, and cast a shadow across us again?

'We could go back later today, I think, but I'm not sure that we ought to,' Chris says. 'Not unless they tell us we need to. I worry that what your mum needs most is rest rather than visitors.'

'We can leave it for today and go tomorrow. What can we be doing for you for the rest of today?' I ask.

He smiles weakly. 'You don't have to do anything. It's just great having you here.' He drinks his tea, and no one speaks for a minute. I watch a red admiral fluttering past us to settle on the flowers of the pea plants in the bed beyond. There are other butterflies feeding there already, blues and coppers and a swallowtail. 'The thing I need to start thinking about is what your mum will need when she gets home,' Chris says.

'Shall we set up a bed downstairs?' Rachel suggests.

'That would be good.'

'And if you wanted us to really go over the house and hoover all of it, I don't know whether that might help her breathing.'

'It's made me wonder whether we're getting old.'

Amy glances quickly at me, then looks away again. 'I don't think you're getting old,' she says to Chris. 'But it must make you realise how hard the life is.'

'That's it,' he says. 'Even a couple of days, when it's just me on my own, it's too much really. All the time you're out in the fields there's nothing happening at home. There's no way of keeping up. It makes you think.'

'We could come and help a bit more,' I say.

'You're kind. But it's not a solution, is it? You can't be always making that drive.'

The swallowtail catches my eye as it leaves the pea shoots and takes flight.

'It makes me wonder whether perhaps we might be coming to the end of this story.' He throws his arms wide then, and looks around him, to indicate that it's the place he means, the farm he's spent his life on. 'We've talked about it before, the two of us.'

'In a few months she might well be fine.'

He shrugs. 'Maybe.'

We finish our tea then, and talk of other things, work and our plans for our house move, unimportant stories, ways to distract us from talking about the thing that makes us all afraid. Even the talk of selling the farm is no more than that really, no more than a way of steering clear of the thought of Mum in the hospital, fighting the infection that wants to kill her. We all feel useless, because in the end we all are. We have all realised there isn't really anything we can do, and that shames us.

As the day passes and the shadows lengthen, we convert the sitting room into a bedroom in the hope that before too long Mum will be able to come home. Chris hopes it won't be too long, and talks about hospitals being dangerous places, where one infection might follow another. Then we spend a couple of hours in the garden, fixing the wooden frames on some of the raised beds and trimming a hedge, and mending a fallen section of dry-stone wall. It's good to find work to do with our hands, and in a small way all of it feels useful. Everything that makes Mum's home an easier place to live might help with her recovery. Chris calls the hospital to check what's happening, and the news is neither positive nor negative, in that it seems nothing has changed. He asks if we ought to be going back in, and the nurse in charge tells him Mum's stable, she's OK. We start preparing dinner when the evening comes, and don't need to light a fire because it's been a hot day and stayed dry, for the first day in weeks, Chris says, so we all work together on a chestnut casserole. When it's cooked, Chris starts serving the casserole on to plates while we lay the table, and that's when the call comes.

He goes to the phone with the ladle still in one hand, and answers, and asks who was speaking. These are the last moments. I try to remember what they looked like, the end of that world. Dust in the air and the cobwebs shadowing the roofbeams, logs piled up in the baskets by the hearth. The lights bouncing off the wood of the dining table, the wicker chair catching at Amy's top as she leans forward to fill a glass with water, a single candle flame on the table the centre of the scene. The phone is just round the corner from the kitchen, just out of sight, and none of us stop talking to listen in, none of us suspect. Then Chris comes back into the room, and we see his face, and stop talking, because we all know suddenly that Mum has died.

1964

ANGELA WALKED OUT into the wood beyond the home fields on her birthday, dreaming of knights in armour, dreaming of learning to fly. She threaded her way through the trees past the camp where the old soldier had slept last summer, past the old stones where the barn once stood, and watched the leaves weaving over her head in all their autumn glory. She saw how, when the clouds passed over, the colours of the wood hid themselves all away, and the place became damp leaf mould, deep shadow, shivers up her arms, so she hugged her cardigan tightly round herself and wondered, irrationally, if someone was watching. And then she saw how, when the clouds cleared once again, the colours of the wood flamed out once more, as if there was some wild light hidden in the trees, and the sun brought it out of them.

A thought struck her for the first time in her life that day that would haunt her for all the years that came after. A thought that would always remind her of this birthday, this moment in the wood when the clouds cleared, just before she heard her mother's voice calling her home for cake and presents. It occurred to her, watching the trees wake into beauty once again, that perhaps the same wild light might be hidden in everything, only waiting for the sun to bring it out. Years later, she would think that must be what people talked about when they talked about God, and why people went to church and bowed their heads, to feel close to moments in their own lives just like the moment Angela experienced in the wood. Years later, she would take comfort in the memory of that day when hard things happened to her or the ones she loved, and remember that sometimes in the world you did glimpse divinity, you did glimpse peace, and perhaps the passage of time was all a falling away from those moments, but that didn't mean such moments never happened.

She stood in the wood and drank in the reds and yellows of the autumn, watched the leaves twist and twirl in the air. A year later, at school, she wrote her very first poem about that moment, and felt a rhyme happen in her head for the first time, the way the words seemed to dovetail like a knitted stitch. 'Autumn leaves are falling down, whirling whirling to the ground.' Nothing so special about that, really. But the words seemed to go together because they echoed each other, and Angela felt very deeply, years before she had the learning to understand it, that words, when you strung them together, were like a map of the world, and the rhyme, the act of rhyming two sounds, was just what it had felt like to stand in that wood. As if the world wasn't just one thing after another. As if there was a shape to her different days when you looked at them together.

'Angie!' She heard her mother's voice filtering distantly through the trees, and turned to look for her, through the shade of the autumn wood to the light beyond and the home fields and the cottage. She saw her mother waving from the other side of the fence, leaning on the fence in a blue dress like a smock, as if she was living in a painting. And she thought nothing of it. She was just a little girl, five years old today, and wandering through this world that had been given to her to make the most of. Her mother was there, and she loved her. Inside the house her father might be washing his face, or perhaps he was still working and would get home soon. It didn't matter. They were together. And their lives were a dance like the leaves that fell through the endless blue air all around her. Back at the cottage there was poppyseed cake, and five candles for her to blow out when her father was with her. She started to walk back through the woods towards home. Years later, she would remember that walk towards the light, towards her mother, and wonder if that was the journey that she had been making ever since.

2019

Hard to remember the following few hours. The moment we knew Mum had died was filled with agony the first time I lived it, but I've lived it so many times since then that I seem to have drained all the blood from the memory, so it hardly feels like my life at all, more like a story I've told too many times. What happened to me next seems to exist now on the other side of a glass separating my past from my present self, and I can't get back to it. It was a moment when my life changed, I suppose, when I became a different person; so perhaps it's natural I can't think my way back into the body of the man I was when that happened. This must be why people who've been through pain will sometimes talk about it so much they seem proud it happened to them; they've relived it so many times the shock of the story has died. And they go back into the story just to check there's no way of crossing back into the past and recovering the person they were before.

Rachel lets out a cry that seems to last a long time as she crosses the room to Chris, and they hold each other, tears in their eyes. I look at Amy, and then we seem to get up as one and go to Chris and Rachel, who part as we approach them and hold out their hands, so I take my stepdad's hand in one of mine and Amy's in the other and for a moment, almost absurdly, we all stand holding hands in a kind of ring, and everyone is talking; perhaps I might have spoken too, but I don't know what I said, and no one else's words go in. Again, the rush of blood is roaring in my ears, and I hear nothing of the outside world. I stand in the dark stone room instead with my left hand in Amy's hand and my right hand holding Chris's left, and feel very close in that moment to all of the darkest days of my life. They all come rushing in, because they all felt like this, it always felt like this; when trouble came, it always hurt me in the same way, so that new tragedy always had the strangest way of feeling simultaneously like a retreat into old pain.

I remember the blood spattered over the floor in the rented farmhouse where Amy hit her head, the blood on the floor and the shock in her eyes and her fast, shallow breathing, and listen to her breathing now and hear the same sound, all of us drawn back into the same pain body by this grief, it seems, and then absurdly I find myself thinking of Tolstoy, who said all happy families were alike and all unhappy ones were different, and how wrong he was, because happiness had always seemed so infinite and various to me, whereas pain always seems to gather life back into the same narrow darkness. Each of us knows exactly what the others are going through, right down to our secret fear that it won't affect us as much as we think it properly should, each of us caught in the tide of sudden mourning that sweeps over everything and then retreats, emptying us all and leaving only a hollowness, leaving only a silence behind. Radiohead country. It was the same when Dad died. I'd worried for so long that, when it happened, I'd feel only relief. Then the day came, and I walked home in shock from the hospital along narrow pavements by myself, down quiet shabby backstreets linking the hospital to the estate where I lived, and went through the house and found the bottles he'd hidden, and emptied them into the toilet, then sat alone in the dark on the sofa where he'd slept till he went into hospital, and wished I could have my dad back again, and felt like a child, felt so small in the world, and wished I was young, wished that none of this had ever happened, because in that moment all life felt like an unravelling, a long litany of things gone wrong.

'We just saw her, though,' Rachel says. 'We only just saw her.'

'Oh my God.'

'She was fine, she was talking to me.'

'My God.'

'Jesus fucking Christ.'

'I don't understand.'

'What are we going to do, Dad? What are we going to do?'

'Should we go? Are we meant to go there?'

'They said that we shouldn't.'

'Jesus Christ.'

'They said that it's late; we should go in the morning.'

'This isn't possible.'

'What did they say happened?'

'I don't know, I don't know.'

'Fuck.'

'Oh fuck.'

'Oh Jesus Christ.'

I sink back into my chair and stare at my hands, and think of the time when Mum and I weren't speaking, while Dad was dying, the things we didn't say and the things we hadn't mended, and I feel my lips peel back in a rictus snarl as something takes me over and pulls back the muscles of my face till I bare my pain and show it glinting in the bright, broken snarl of my mouth. I feel welling up inside me a need to do violence, some desperate violence, to kick out and reject what I've just heard.

And there are no words for it. Language stops short here.

The nurses hadn't seen it coming, we learned; if they had, they would have told us to stay, or called us and asked us to make our way back. It was her heart that failed, they said. That was why they didn't see she was going to go downhill; if her breathing had deteriorated, they would have had more warning. Her heart had been under strain for several days, and all of a sudden it gave out and stopped. They attempted to revive her but didn't succeed. It seems almost impossible, in this day and age, that a whole hospital can muster its resources to try and jumpstart someone whose heart has stopped working, and somehow not manage it. But that's how it goes, I suppose, every time someone loses a loved one. It seems impossible that it could have ever happened. I was angry when we first knew what had happened. It seemed outrageous to me that, all the time they were trying to save her life, no one called us and urged us to get back there. They waited till the death had been pronounced before they called. But of course, there was no one free to make the phone call. And we'd never have got there in time. And perhaps we'd have died trying, killed by some blind bend, killed trying to overtake and running into another vehicle while driving on the wrong side of the road. Heart trouble ran in her side of the family, they'd seen on her notes. A couple of relatives who'd gone that way. As if that made it normal. They told us that because she had turned sixty, she didn't even count as having died young. Just a fatal heart attack in someone with a family history of cardiovascular weakness whose age made them vulnerable to the same fate befalling them. They made it sound so normal, when it wasn't, when it felt like whole continents had been hacked away from us, as if all of our memories had been torn out.

I had learned already what it felt like to lose a parent. The loss of a father had left me thinking of the future, the world I would have to live in without him in it, the man I might become as a result, the way his story ended and the way I wanted my story to be different. The loss of a mother was something else. Somehow it drew me in the other direction, back into the past, into memory. She was the shell I had sheltered in whenever things went wrong. She had always been the place of safety. Now there was no safe harbour to turn to, only the life I would have to make for myself, and I thought with sudden grief of all the ordinary afternoons we'd spent with one another, all the small acts of connection that would never come again. The loss of a mother was like all the lights going out on the shore, and I was left alone on the waves, turning back in the hope of receiving some encouragement, seeing only the dark instead.

We stay at the farm for the next seven days. A neighbour agrees to keep an eye on Amy's flat, and Amy and I stay with Chris. There are a lot of phone calls and paperwork that need to be done and that we'll try and help with. Chris goes to the hospital and sees Mum the next morning. The doctor warns him he might not want to, but he goes all the same. We don't travel with him; he comes home, and says nothing, and needs to be alone for the rest of that day. I try not to think of what he must have seen, but of course I think of her, and the way bodies look in the movies, and the room he must have seen her in, and the corridor he must have walked down to reach her, and then had to walk back the length of it to get back out into the light. I can't stop seeing it the rest of that week, and I almost wish I'd gone with him. Perhaps that would have broken the spell, I don't know. Numbness. Like paralysis creeping through me, turning me into a statue, killing me cell by cell. Shock, someone tells me. It's OK not to be able to cry. I try to tell them I have been crying, I've done nothing but crying, but then I realise I don't know what I've been doing, because of the shock, because I'm living in a kind of fog. Rachel stays for a few days, then says she has to travel back to the city. I think of asking her why she isn't taking the week off work, but she seems determined to leave, so we say no more about it.

The injustice of it all makes me speechlessly angry. That she just got ill, and was taken in, and never got the chance to go back home. Never got to climb the hill above the farm for one last time, and see the view, and fix the place where she had lived her life in the mind's eye for a last time, for ever. Never got to sleep out in the cold beneath the stars one final night, or go to the bluebell woods in May and lie down among them, the river of their scent and colour, dousing her senses in the world she had loved before she left it. She would have deserved that. Anyone would. A deliberate goodbye to what they were leaving, all they had loved and lived among, everything that had shaped them.

It feels like we spend a week on the phone, then just as the first wave of work is almost finished, the funeral date is set and we have to do it all over again, sending out cards to people to let them know, preparing an order of service for the funeral directors. It's relentless, remorseless. It's shocking to me, the way that time goes on, and the world seems to be speeding away from what's happened without our having had time to stop and examine and understand it, so that already, before I've even taken this moment in, it seems to be turning into part of the past. I can't believe how quickly the moment is moving away from me. Chris spends most of his time in the garden, staring at nothing, trying to write a speech. He was determined from the moment we started planning that he wanted to deliver one. Rachel and I will stay silent, letting him speak for all of us, that's the plan; and a colleague of Mum's will say something, and a childhood friend. I don't envy any of them. When I go to funeral services, the speeches people make just sound like rain. I wish the whole thing could happen in silence, because all anyone wants to do is sit with the feeling of being there, surely?

'You don't mind if I say something, do you?' Chris had asked me, and we had looked at each other, and the moment had seemed absurd.

'Of course not. What do you mean? If you say something at the funeral?'

'I just mean you kids won't mind if I speak.'

'Of course not.'

Every second has become an unravelling, a shredding of the narrative order of our lives, the sense that we knew who we were to each other, the sense that we knew what to do. But now none of us knows, it seems, who's supposed to be in charge here. Rachel and Amy and I had assumed it was Chris, but something had been holding him back too, preventing him from feeling that he could take whatever decision he liked.

'I don't want to say a lot.'

'You don't have to. You should just do whatever you need.'

'Whatever your mum would want.'

'Yes. Of course.'

Day by day we navigate around each other, leaving space for one another's silences. Then after a week, Chris suggests Amy and I should go back to the city till we have to come together again to face the funeral. Again, I feel the world beneath my feet spinning madly, barrelling on.

'You've done so much,' he says, 'and I'm so grateful. But you shouldn't have to stay here with me for ever. I'll be all right for a week. I'll be all right.'

'We don't want to leave you on your own if there are things you still need help with.'

He looks into his tea and I realise he might have reached a point where he doesn't want people round him; he might want to spend the next week alone with the ghost of his wife before he has to say goodbye to her for the last time. The strange, in-between weeks after a death and before the funeral, when nothing seems final, nothing seems certain, everything seems to need to be done. Life at its most provisional, life as survival.

'I know. And you're kind. But I'll have to be on my own at some point, won't I? So will you both.'

I worry, once we've agreed we'll leave the next morning,

that we've somehow ended up outstaying our welcome; that Chris has grown tired of our voices and wants above all to be on his own. When we heard the news, it seemed the only thing we could possibly have done was to stay and do whatever we could, and I didn't want to leave and head home. Perhaps we should have left when Rachel did; perhaps Chris has been wishing we'd leave ever since. Amy does her best to reassure me.

'He's trying to do something to help us,' she says. 'He can see as well as I can that you're not processing this, you're not taking this in, and you need to get home and try to work out what's happened. And maybe he does want to be on his own as well, but why does that matter? We were always going to have to go at some point.'

'What do you mean I'm not processing it?'

'I just mean you're in shock. You know you are.'

'Do I?'

'OK, maybe I'm wrong. I just mean what's happened is a lot to take in.'

'Do you think I'm not doing that?'

'I think it will take you a long time to do that.'

So we leave, promising to come back for the last few days before the funeral. Chris hugs me when we go. I hug him back. We get in the car and I feel as if it's gone so fast, that week, it can't really have happened. Perhaps I won't believe in it till the day of the funeral comes; perhaps I should have gone to see the body after all, because the time since Mum died has all seemed like a dream, and I don't know what's going to shock me out of it. It is so brief, this thing we're in, so fragile, and its disappearance is so sudden, so impossible to bear. We drive away from the farm and I look back once, see Chris still waving at us from the gate. Next to him stand the dogs, who have no idea yet about what's happened, who will take a long time to accept they won't see Mum again, who will be months still rushing to the gate when they hear a car passing, always hoping it might be her. The lane leading down from the house is rutted and uneven. I look at the farm standing behind Chris, and it seems to me that it's become like all the other empty barns around it; one more vanished life disappearing back into the waters, as time closes over, as time moves on.

A week passes. Another week in the city, feeling like life lost, life half lived. The heat of the city in these days of apocalypse, the shirt clinging to your back, the news screaming murder, and no bugs to clean from the windscreen, no water running in the brooks that ran year-round through my childhood. In this heat it's difficult to think. My skin is tight over my face from being out in the burning sun. Mosquitoes rule the park and the wood at the end of the road where we walk Ivan morning and evening, and bats raid the air when night comes. In the dark of the trees, chicken of the woods stands out, luminous among the fallen tree trunks, the wild garlic has died and disappeared in the heat, and the other dog walkers loom up out of shadows, slapping at their legs where the mosquitoes bite. I work as best I can and stay out of the centre of London, walking Ivan and catching up with emails, plugged in, trackable. I feel the weight of this working life like an anchor.

Chris says there's no more to do for the funeral, so I move

all my things into Amy's flat instead. Anything to distract me, any way of turning my mind elsewhere, because I find I can't talk, I can't let out what I'm feeling. I lose hours rereading Marcel Pagnol. I make a pile of all my old CDs. I haven't listened to any of them for years now; no point keeping what we don't use any more. Moving house a lot in my early twenties taught me only to keep what I couldn't bear to lose. In the end it turns out that's not ever so much.

Moving house will reveal things you'd lost and hadn't noticed. As I move my things from the converted garage into Amy's flat, I go over what I'm going to keep and what I'll give to charity. The grandfather clock my grandfather made in 1976, the hottest summer. The bookshelves he made for my dad. The coffee table he made in 1988, the year after I was born. His harmonium, which I can never play now I'm at Amy's because the first time I try I find Ivan barks at it, thinking it's another animal. The guitar he made, which never comes out of its case because I can't play it. The carpet I stole from the theatre I worked in, a beautiful old rug they were keeping in a store room no one ever looked in and which I claimed for my own when I left. The armchair my father gave me because I never got out of it and he said it didn't suit him, which I think he only really gave me because he knew I was in love with it. All these were days once, now they're the memory of those days. I lug the things across London, sweat in my eyes, and hope they won't overcrowd the flat, hope that they'll go with everything else Amy has gathered around her already.

When thoughts of what's happened begin to overwhelm me, I go out into Amy's little scrap of garden, and sit there quietly, and stare at the sky. This is the one small space I've found in my day-to-day where something like peace is sometimes possible. In the garden I can still hear the planes overhead, the ice-cream van at weekends, boy racers, the football ground nearby on match days, drills and electric saws from the home improvers, the traffic noise underlying everything. But all I see is stillness around me, and that's something, that's precious. Sun on the back of my neck, the fence shifting in the winds, oak leaves whispering, blackbirds and wagtails calling to each other, crickets in the grass, the bees coming and going from an apiary somewhere nearby. There are hedgehogs living along this row of back gardens that crawl under the fences at night, there are admirals and whites, jays and green woodpeckers coming and going. There is life going on here under the radar of the big world and it comforts me.

Rachel texts me and asks if I want to go for a drink. I read her message, and think for a while. The truth is I'm not sure I do. Since we've got back from the farm, the best way I've found of coping is not to talk any more than I have to. Going to see Rachel will just mean having to talk about it all over again. And there's a part of me that resents Rachel for having left so quickly, when I know she could have got the time off work and stayed at the farm a little longer if she'd decided that it was the right thing to do. I resent her because we stayed, and she didn't, and I resent her because we were wrong to stay as long as we did, I feel sure of it now; we ended up being a burden on Chris when he needed to be on his own, saying nothing, seeing no one for a few days, and Rachel saw that coming and left when we should have done too. I resent her because when Dad was dying he came to me and I had to help him, and Rachel never had to deal with all that, because he was nothing to do with her, he wasn't her father; it was me who had to watch my dad die, I faced that alone. Rachel kept a distance then as well, knowing when not to be around, because really Dad's death was nothing to do with her, but it felt like she was taking sides, avoiding the flat I lived in for as long as my dad was in it out of some kind of loyalty to Mum. I didn't mind at the time: I would have liked to have nothing to do with all that vomit and shaking, either; I would have enjoyed the privilege of being able to remember Dad as he had been when I had lived with him originally, when I was very young, and not how he was in the end. But he came to me and I took him in, and I did that on my own, and Rachel was no part of it, because, really, it was nothing to do with her. But now Mum had died, I found I resented her for that. It seemed to me now that, during that year, she had become closer to Mum than I was, because I was living with Mum's ex-husband while he died. So Rachel ended up in league with Mum, while I looked after Dad. They had shared things that I hadn't. Now Mum was gone, and I'd never catch up with Rachel on that missed time. That was that. I had thought there would be longer, and there wasn't, and that wasn't Rachel's fault, but I felt angry nonetheless, and in the moment of getting her text, I focused that anger on her.

'Rachel's asking if I want to go for a drink,' I say.

'You should,' says Amy.

'I'm not sure.'

'Why not?'

'I don't know whether I want to go through it all. Talk about it all right now.'

'It'll be easier to talk now than it will be when you get to the funeral. There'll be too much happening then to think. And you should be there for her if she needs it. If she's asking to see you, it's because she needs it. You're her big brother. You should help.'

'I think it's easy to say that if you don't have siblings,' I say, and instantly regret it. Amy gives me a look. A lot of the time this last week, she's found herself needing to be patient with me while I say the wrong thing.

'How do you mean?' she asks.

'Well, I can see that you're right,' I say. 'In black and white, that's what I should do. But it's not black and white with your sister. Because there's so much between a brother and sister. We're still furious at each other over things that happened fifteen years ago, or hurt by something the other one said that no one else ever heard, that no one else would ever think was important. That's how it works between siblings, isn't it? All these things that seem so small, except to the people involved. Things we couldn't even remember any more if someone asked us, which make everything political.'

'But not so political you'd refuse to have a drink with her when your mum's died and she needs someone to talk to?'

I shrug. I know I'm wrong. Whenever I start to feel angry I know that I'm wrong, and I know that the person I'm feeling anger towards is actually myself. So I swallow my unhappiness, and text Rachel back, and we agree to meet in a pub halfway between our flats the next evening before dinner. I don't want to see her, because I know things will be different now. The world has given way to something new, and I can't take it in, I don't want to. Not least because I worry that, spoken out loud, it would all seem small, it would prove inexpressible. A break-up for me; the loss of a parent for both of us. These are things that everyone goes through. But they seem like the whole world for now. It's the same stake as Lear's, except for the scale of it, except that we have to fit the worlds inside us into these stories, these lives.

Rachel is the eternal student, working on her doctorate, still living on beans. She tops up the funding she got to finish her studies with teaching work at the university, and lives in one room in a shared flat in the far-flung south of the city, on the fifth floor of an old block of flats overlooking the train station that connects her to the centre of the capital. One day the work will have been worthwhile, but it takes a long time to make your way in academia, and I can't really say I envy her the years spent waiting. Too much of your life is spent waiting to start. I get to the pub first and sit outside in the afternoon sun, and see her approaching, the bob of her walk.

'How are you?' Rachel asks, as we embrace.

'You know. Want a pint?'

'Thanks.'

I go inside and get the first round, then bring it back out, and we sit down together at a pub bench in the sun.

'How long did you stay for in the end?' she asks.

'Till the end of the week.'

'Was that OK?'

'You know. I think we stayed too long.'

'I just felt like I couldn't be there any more.'

'You didn't feel like you were closer to her there?'

'I can't be closer to her anywhere. That's the point.'

'What have you been doing since?'

'Nothing, really. I try and work. I've been teaching. Then when I get home I stare at the wall. You sleeping?'

'No.'

'I've been angry with myself,' she says. 'That's part of why I wanted to see you, really. I can't talk about it with Dad, but I can say it to you.'

'Go on.'

'I've been thinking that I should be doing more.'

'I don't know about that.'

'No, but I should. I should be doing more. But I've found there's a limit I can't get past. There's a point where I have to stop. Because I can't support you or Dad or anyone. Because I have to look after myself.'

'I know. It's the same for everyone. It's all right.'

'It doesn't feel all right.'

'No. But it's the same for everyone, all over the world.'

She tilts her head back and drains her glass. 'There should be a way for us all to be together now, though, don't you think? A thing like this should mean that just for a little while, for as long as it takes to come to terms with this, we become one unit, like we've never been before, or not since we were young. And I don't know why that isn't possible, why it feels like we're just as far apart as we were. I want it to have changed more than it has. Because otherwise it's just loss.'

'But that's what it is, Rach. There might be no positives to it. It might just be loss.'

'Yeah. But I hate that. Another?'

'I don't want to get drunk.'

'No, but you'll have another.'

'All right.'

She stands up.

'Want me to get it?' I ask.

'Fuck off,' she says, and disappears inside. When she comes back out with the drinks she's silent for a moment, looking at her pint. 'Is it true that in Japan they pull down a house when someone's died in it?'

'I don't know. I think they pull down houses because it's humid and they rot.'

'I think we should do more of that. I'd like it if everything was got rid of, and nothing left behind after you'd gone. Every time I go back home, I feel this guilt that I wasn't a better kid to Mum and Dad, and I wasn't kinder, and I didn't say thank you more often, and I wasn't nicer to them. I feel this shame that I didn't get it right, that's what the place reminds me of. And I feel this sadness because when I go home, it's not like it was. It just never can be. Even when Mum was still there, it never could be. The times I've spent there since I moved away always remind me of those shadows of people that get left on walls after nuclear bombs, you know what I mean? Those ghost people. I'd never feel all that if the place wasn't there any more.'

'Is that really what you want?'

'Maybe. I don't know. Did you like going back there? Before Mum, I mean, when they were both there and you went home. To the land of lost content.'

'It's too complicated to say yes or no.'

We finish our drinks, and in the end we agree not to have a third, and we say goodbye to each other, and go our separate ways. I walk away thinking how cruel I was being, to think I shouldn't see my sister. How cruel of me to think we should keep apart at this moment. Why could I not see straight away that that was just what I should have been doing? Why could I not have known instinctively that the best way for each of us to break our own silence would be to start sharing one another's? The selfishness of grief, maybe. Or maybe more evidence I'm sleepwalking through life.

2000

ED HAD MADE the treehouse with Chris's help the previous summer. That meant it wasn't particularly well made, because Ed had only been twelve back then, but he'd hammered nails in as best he could, Chris finishing off the job after he'd done his bit, and tied string round things, and got a platform together. It had stubbornly refused to cohere into a whole, remaining instead like several planks of old wood that were up in the tree, and that he could sit on, not a coherent house at all, but Ed was still proud of it because it was his. There were many sheds and outhouses in the farmhouse garden that he played in and out of. They included Chris's workshop where all the tools were kept, which Chris had started talking about padlocking this year, because he was worried the tools might be stolen, and because Ian from down in the village had taken to sleeping there on nights home from the pub if he couldn't face the whole walk back to his farm. Mum had first mentioned it six months earlier, her suspicion that someone was sleeping in the workshop some Saturday nights. She'd find things disturbed, and the dogs would bark. Eventually Chris woke early enough to see Ian slipping back out of it to finish his long walk home, and then they knew what had been happening. Ian was a drinker, especially on nights off, so in order that he could have his preferred skinful he'd walk from his farm to the nearest pub on Saturday, a walk of about three miles down to the river at the bottom of the valley. This meant that at the end of the night he had to walk three miles all the way back up, usually with a dozen pints in him. Ed's home was just off the road he walked back up, on a little lane that split off invitingly just before the steep hill up to the school and the Buddhist retreat centre and Ian's farm. Clearly, on some nights, Ian gave in to temptation and found temporary shelter among the tools. Chris and Mum didn't mind this at all, it seemed, and would have been happy to let Ian sleep on the sofa, as long as he wasn't sick, they said; but it had got Chris thinking about security, about whether tools were even insured if you left them in an unlocked building, because maybe there needed to be a padlock for the insurance to kick in. It was one of those jobs he said he always meant to get around to doing, which never quite got to the top of his list.

Next to the workshop there was the shed inside the chicken wire, which contained nothing but grain for the chickens and a huge old chest freezer Chris had run a cable up to under the ground, where the family kept bags and bags of frozen lamb they'd set aside for themselves to eat. This wasn't a shed Ed particularly liked to go into – rats got in to eat the grain, and had to be dealt with by the farm cat because you couldn't leave rat poison in with the chicken feed. The shed was damp and starting to rot away, and he thought it was spooky, though he didn't know why any ghost would go in there.

Above the workshop, further up the hill, there was another shed, very like the grain shed in the chicken wire, where Chris kept the lawnmower and tubs of varnish and paint and twine and manure and bamboo poles and forks and things for the garden, except this one wasn't rotting away because he'd put a cement floor in, and then at the bottom of the hillside, right by the house, was the woodstore, which was open on one side, covered only with a tarpaulin. Here, the family stored everything they could burn, because fire was life and they needed a lot of wood. This varied in character, from old junk, old furniture, to trees they'd chopped down on the farm and some firewood they ordered in to make sure they had enough in the winters. Chris didn't like ordering firewood in, but the fact was that theirs was a sheep farm, and all their land was grass, so they just couldn't get by on the trees they could grow. And the man who brought the firewood was the doctor's nephew anyway, and Mum liked to say it was a good thing to send some business the way of the doctor's family, because then they'd look after you when it was needed. Ed didn't know why the doctor wouldn't look after you anyway.

All of these could be the sites of various games that Ed would play, whether that be simple hide and seek or gangsters or World War Two, they all had their uses, and were tolerably full of interesting things, but Ed was also aware that none of them were his. He could be turfed out of each of them at any minute, and wasn't really allowed to change anything, and he wanted a place of his own, high up above everything, where he could look down on the farm and feel as if he was sailing away into the distance far from this place, someone on a spaceship, someone on a plane. He'd been on a plane once, flying to Guernsey, a little yellow plane called Joey that Mum had bought him a book about at the Guernsey airport, and it had been the most thrilling experience. Far better to be up in the air and strapped into one of the rattling seats looking down at the miracle world below than enduring the drive to Cornwall, the catamaran to France. Guernsey itself had been so-so – the most memorable event of the holiday had been Ed cycling downhill into a wall and sending himself flying over his handlebars, barking both his knees and his chin and his elbows as he fell – but he had been very in love with the plane, and that was in his mind when he asked for his treehouse. A way to be up high above everything. He asked if he could build one, and Chris picked out the sturdiest tree, and they worked together to get a platform up there. Ed had initially imagined walls and a roof, a little window to look out of, but Chris was always busy with the farm and could only help in little bursts in the evenings, and in the end Ed decided just sitting up there on dry days was enough for him. He could tell he hadn't made the platform very well, and had plans to ask Chris to make him a better one the next summer, when Rachel would be old enough to play up there as well, and the treehouse would have to carry more weight.

Rachel had been furious to be banned from the treehouse in its first year, of course, but Mum was determined that it was too dangerous and she couldn't go up there in case she fell. But this year, Rachel had been given permission, news that she had initially met with joy. Once she was up on the platform, though, she found the whole thing less impressive.

'There's nothing to do here,' she said. 'There's no walls on.'

Chris said that perhaps one weekend later this summer, they could all work together to improve the treehouse, which Ed and Rachel agreed to readily. So Chris said they'd spend a day on it next weekend, and make a really good one with walls and a roof and a door and a ladder. It would be easy for him to do, Ed knew; he'd held back the year before because Ed had been in charge, and Chris hadn't wanted to take the job off him. He felt a little embarrassed now he was older that his efforts had come up so short, but it was understandable; he'd only been twelve at the time, and would be better placed to help Chris make a really good treehouse now he was a year older.

In the meantime, he tried to encourage Rachel to enjoy the one they had. It was difficult; she had noticed straight away that Ed felt responsible for the treehouse's shortcomings, so poking fun at them was a way of poking fun at him, and she pursued this mercilessly. But he showed her there were games that could be played. You could, of course, be a pirate in the lookout post on a pirate ship; or you could be a fighter pilot in a plane; or you could be a panther, stalking puny humans, looking down from the trees to jump on them. Rachel attempted all these games, but enjoyed making fun of Ed much more, so their attempts to play up in the treehouse didn't get far. The third day Ed tried to play pilots in the treehouse with Rachel, and she refused to be a rear gunner and protect their tail, preferring instead to pick bits of splinter off one of the platform planks, he lost his temper and climbed back down to the ground.

'You're stupid,' he shouted up at her, not really knowing what stupid thing she'd done.

'You're the one who's stupid; you can't build a treehouse – how am I meant to play up here?' Rachel shouted after him as he stormed inside. Ed didn't look back, but went into the kitchen instead and poured himself a glass of milk. He took the biscuit tin down from the high shelf he could reach now, and got himself a biscuit, and took that and the milk through to the sitting room where his Mum was typing at the work table on her old typewriter with the radio on. Ed sat by the bookcase and thought about taking down something to read, but he was too angry to concentrate, so he just ate his biscuit instead. A bite of biscuit, then a sip of milk, then mixing them together was his favourite thing, the best meal in the world, the meal he'd ask for if he was on death row. He'd tried McDonald's at a birthday party in Hereford, and it wasn't anywhere near as good. Biscuits and milk was the best meal imaginable.

'Everything all right, darling?'

Ed looked up at his mum. 'Fine.'

'Where's Rachel?'

'In the treehouse.'

'You're not fighting, are you?'

'She says it's no good.'

'But next weekend you'll make a better one.'

'I suppose so.'

'Why only "suppose so"?'

'I don't want to play in it if she's up there.'

It was at this point that Rachel came into the room, and it was immediately clear that something was very wrong. She was deathly pale and her breathing was fast and shallow, as if she was trying not to cry. Ed watched, stomach lurching, as his mum stopped what she was doing and turned round and then stood up.

'Are you all right, darling? What's happened?'

'Mum,' Rachel said, and then couldn't say more. She held out her arm instead, and Ed recoiled as her arm from the elbow down fell back the wrong way, as if it wanted to stay by her side, snapped at the elbow and hanging loose from the rest of her. Rachel saw what had happened and screamed, and then Mum became a sudden whirlwind of action, bundling Rachel out of the room, grabbing her car keys, thinking of the hospital. She turned once to Ed before she left.

'Will you go and tell your stepdad what's happened? And he can take you with him to the hospital.'

'Where is he?' asked Ed.

'He's out in the fields.'

Then Mum and Rachel were gone. Ed drained his milk as he stood up from the chair by the bookcase. He looked around, shocked by the sudden quiet, queasy because of what he'd just seen. He shouldn't have drunk the rest of the milk really, but it was automatic, he hadn't been thinking. He put the glass down on the table by the typewriter and went outside to the garden. He wondered whether he should lock the front door, but he had no key, so he didn't know how to. He could get the spare one from under the flowerpot, but maybe Chris would want to get things before they left.

Halfway up the garden, he could see the treehouse. He stopped and looked at it for a moment. He knew already what must have happened. Rachel, on her own up there, had decided she was bored, and started to climb down, or otherwise she'd tried to test her bravery by leaning over the edge.

Either way, she'd overbalanced somehow, fallen to the ground, and landed on her arm and snapped it badly. He looked at the treehouse, tried to spot some malevolence in it. He was very afraid this was all his fault; that he had wished this on her somehow, when he left her alone. Had the tree-house hurt her because he was angry? Or was she just too young to be up there? Either way, he shouldn't have left her alone. He realised he should have looked out for his sister, and his heart sank at the thought of the telling-off he'd probably get later. He decided then and there that he wouldn't go up in the treehouse again, and he wouldn't say any more about Chris building a new one. He turned his back on the abandoned island he had hoped to make his own, and went to look for his stepdad.

2019

A DAY COMES WHEN I'm supposed to go into the office for work, the first time they've asked me to go in for a few weeks. I walk the mile to the nearest train station, and find it's closed, the area cordoned off for half a mile around. On the roof of the flats looming ten floors over the station a woman is standing on the concrete edge, her back to the police negotiator trying to talk her down, doing little practice jumps, visible to all the crowded street below, her eyes fixed straight ahead of her. People throng the streets to watch. I turn around and go back home. She wears a blue cardigan over a T-shirt, and looks cold up there in the wind keening over the city, which must blow stronger and more frightening up there above the buildings. I can't watch the fragility of the woman, desperate to be noticed, desperate not to be invisible any more, but powerless to end her silence any way other than threatening to throw herself down that endless drop. Why do people watch these atrocities? Does it make us feel better that we're not her? Or is she really a part of all of us, acting out something we've all thought of doing?

I get back home and call the office and tell them I can't make it because there's a jumper above my train station so all the lines are closed. They commiserate with me, and I say I'll go in tomorrow, and then I put down the phone. A whole conversation come and gone as if what I had seen was something normal, as if it happened all the time and it was just one of the many reasons meetings are rescheduled every day. Because where we live, it is. I remember a woman who had stood next a jumper saying to me once on a station platform, 'They always put their bags down on the platform before they get on the track. What I don't understand is why they bring their bags at all if that's what they're going to be doing. She wasn't even dead after it hit her. She was screaming and the bottom half of her was gone. She wouldn't have made it. Poor woman. I wish she hadn't done it, though.' In a place like this, sometimes the only way people can think of breaking out of their silence is to do something so terrible no one can look away. Among these atrocities we make our lives.

I pick up the car keys and leave the flat again.

As I try to go forwards through the story of my life, the feeling takes hold that somehow I am going in the wrong direction, that really what I want to be doing is going back, not flicking through the picture book towards its ending. I can't find it, the secret of myself, the person I'm supposed to be; the key is lost, and I feel it must lie deeper, I must have lost it earlier, it must be buried longer ago. What I am trying to fight against is a sense that I regret having lived my life, that I would almost rather my life had never happened than for so much of it to be lost and unrecoverable. I don't want to feel like that. I want to feel like I'm glad about where I'm going.

The drive south feels like travelling back in time. Money has preserved these places more or less as they must have looked in the nineteenth century. The green south of this island, repository of the most extraordinary wealth ever collected by people almost anywhere. The vast estates sprawl out, the beautiful cottages, tree-lined roads. I listen to Bill Evans as I drive, thinking he'll keep me calm, but it's been a long time since I heard *Undercurrent* and the rhythms surprise and mislead; I find myself listening uneasily, not knowing what's coming next. The music is a journey back into memory as well, songs I listened to as a student, songs Dad introduced me to as a child. An hour's drive and I pass the village where I first went to school. It is still the place I knew, and yet entirely different. New buildings have sprung up around the old schoolhouse. Past the school is the village green where we used to go in November to see the Guy burned, the bonfire stacked up on the grass and the mannequin sitting at the top. He tried to burn us down once, so now each year we burn the memory of him. I've seen his signature on display in the Tower of London, the shaking, ruined hand of a man stretched and broken on the rack. I used to stand hand in hand with my parents, watching the flames lick their way to the sky till he was consumed once more. How many years till he's burned for the last time, I wonder? Or will people still burn his image after no one remembers who he was? I drive on through villages I called home a life ago, but there's no sense of belonging to any of these places, no point of connection between them and myself. It unnerves me to see the buildings that have changed. For decades I left this place behind, and never revisited, and the buildings seemed only to live inside me. Their independence from the way I imagined them is a reminder of the smallness and hubris of my life. I come to a wood and leave the road, changing down into first to bump along a rutted dirt track through shadows that darken the middle of the day and beckon me back into childhood. An avenue, dark, nameless, without end. I turn off the music, watch the silent woods on either side of the track till the sky opens up again ahead of me and I see the lodges waiting.

We were here for a few years, living in one of the two hunting lodges at the edge of this wood. There are photographs and home videos of my family together in this place, the only place we were together, on a bright day in summer. Is that why I've thought of this place today, and felt compelled to return for the first time, because this seems like the closest we ever came, where the idea of family and the idea of home once almost cohered into some clear meaning? I drive up to the gate between the two lodges and turn the engine off, and there is the view I remember from childhood, the silence of the birchwood, empty fields stretching away, grass in the sun and the hum of crickets. I walk through the gate and there is the house where we once tried to be a family. Empty now, panes missing from two upstairs windows. I walk around the building, looking in through the windows and the glass in the doors to the bare living room with its red-tiled floor, the bedroom where I used to sleep just visible to me on the first floor through its quarter-moon window that we curtained off with spaceman curtains, and the stairway curling round three sides of the hall as it descends, the cupboard under the stairs where Mum hid Christmas presents, and the little porch over the front door and the white Formica kitchen. I stare through the kitchen window for a long time, because the fittings haven't been replaced since we left, and I am transfixed by their dim familiarity. I turn away and stare into the garden. At the end of the lawn I'm standing on, two apple trees, a russet and a James Grieve, with fruit already ripening. I walk towards them, take them in. I take a russet from the tree and bite down, the dryness of the skin and the acidity of the flesh sharpening the day as if it's being etched into me.

I turn back to the house, walk towards it again. A pane of glass in the kitchen window catches the light when it shouldn't, and I realise the window is slightly ajar. I walk back to it, open the window all the way, stick my head through. There is a sound sensor plugged into one of the power sockets on the kitchen wall. I reach across and turn it off, then clamber up on to the window ledge and into the kitchen, my feet in the sink, before lowering myself down to the linoleum floor. I walk out of the kitchen and into the hall, take in the living-room fireplace of rough brick, turn to the staircase and begin to climb. At the top of the stairs I walk through the first doorway on the landing and stand in the room that used to be mine. Let the stillness settle for a moment. No one speaks, nothing happens. No one is waiting for me. I bend down to look through the quarter-moon window. I look at the empty field falling away towards the blue of distance. The colour we can never know or ever put our hand on, the light that never reaches us, which spends itself on what is far away instead.

I am cast down in the flood of remembrance.

I could have been telling her all this time that I was grateful, and that I loved her, and that I was glad I'd come into this world, and been her child, and lived this life and no other. I could have been telling her that all along, and driving to see her, it wasn't so far really; a hundred years ago the distance would have been insurmountable but I have a car, it wasn't all that far to travel. I could have stayed closer to her, or at least called more often, or at least forced us to set aside whatever silence sprang up between us while Dad was dying, and find our way back to each other, find our way back to being a family again. Because she was my mother. Had she not been, I would have been someone unimaginably different. And so how could I not have loved her all along, if I had any time for my own self? How could there have been a day when we let each other doubt that, when I didn't go back, when I didn't call, when I let that silence linger on between us? I used to think it was because of the divorce. Because my parents ended up apart, there were gaps in our family, there were hairline fractures. But it was me who chose them. Me who let them last. I could have left them all behind, and now she was dead, and I realised I'd always imagined that there'd be more time. Of course I had. Who doesn't? There would be time to fix things and create togethernesses we'd never known while she was living. Except there wouldn't. Except there hadn't been.

After a minute I straighten up and walk away from the window and down the stairs and climb back out of the house. Push the window closed behind me. Take another russet from the tree and walk a little way into the birchwood. I feel like someone's watching me, but there is no sound, no sign of anyone. Only an avenue, dark, nameless, without end. As I walk further in among the trees, here and there I pass oak and holly, the ghost of an older forest that grew here long ago. Someone has crammed a sheep's skull in among the branches of an oak, its empty eye watching as if it knew I was going to come back. Two hundred yards down the track, a fox breaks cover from the green bracken, stops and sees me, then disappears into the wood once more. I turn around and look behind me, and for a moment I'm convinced I'm going to see Mum walking towards me.

I drive back to the flat and drink alone, and then Amy comes home and sees the gin bottle out on the kitchen table, and sits down next to me, and puts her head on my shoulder.

'You all right?' she asks.

'There was a woman on the roof of the flats above the station,' I tell her.

'I know, it was on the news.'

'I watched her. She was doing little jumps up and down like she was trying to psych herself up to something. And the policeman was leaning out of the window trying to talk her back in. And everyone was watching and recording on their phones.'

'She's done it before, they said. They shouldn't let her have that flat.'

'I suddenly felt as if I was her. I felt like I was up there on that roof and looking down and only feeling alive because of the drop waiting for me. And I felt that if I had been up there, I'd have jumped. I'd have jumped for sure, much better than the embarrassment of going back in.'

'OK.' She takes my hand and closes both of hers around it. I know I'm drunk and talking nonsense now. I know that I should go to bed and sleep.

'I didn't go into the office in the end. I drove south instead.

I went back to the place where I used to live with Dad and Mum, and they weren't there, and it was totally empty. No one living there or anything. I actually broke in and looked around, there was a window open. And I felt so awful once I was inside. Because I don't know why this got into my head, but I think I genuinely thought I'd find them waiting. But they're not. They're dead.'

Amy rubs her thumb across the back of my hand. The thought occurs to me that skin on skin is love. It speaks more eloquently than anything else, and any other language is too finely nuanced to be really understood. At the start of the summer, this girl beside me might have died, I might have lost her when she hit her head and her blood was scattered over that strange room where we were staying. Now it's the rest of the world that seems to have gone, and she's still mine.

'We have to get out of here,' I say. 'I can't be here any more, in this city. This isn't my life. I don't know where it is, but it's not here, and I have to get out – I'm sorry.'

'It's all right,' Amy says. 'Don't worry. We'll leave, then.'

For a moment I can almost see the course of this year laid out around me, like a view from the top of a hill. From the vantage of this moment, I'm astonished by the strange unmooring that's taken place, one thing after another cut away. It seems as if I've been carried very far from where I used to be, and I wonder when that started and where it will end. Not here, that's all I know right now; this is not my place. Time to move on and look for my real life. Because I didn't find it living with Juliet, and I never did find it back home at the farm. And I'm not going to find it here in the city, or lost in the past, or anywhere like that. My real life is waiting in some place I haven't found yet.

The day of the funeral breaks over us, heavy and inevitable, a wave scattering sandcastles, and we change into our mourning clothes and travel back to the farm to be with Chris again, and drink together again, and then we get into our cars and make the long journey to the crematorium. I remember the mourners at Dad's funeral, which was small, with only half his relatives and a few friends in attendance. Drink had cut him off from the world. This is different. A crowd of people are thronging outside the crematorium when we get there. We file in first and they all follow after. We were offered the chance to carry her in, but Chris didn't want to, he said it felt religious, and Mum had wanted a secular cremation. So we follow the coffin in, and I feel the old familiar sense of drowning, which is how grief always feels to me. When we get to the front row I want to sit down, but we stand and wait till everyone's come in. Some people around us seem to be trying not to cry, but I let it happen, and the tears run down my face, and the ceremony happens, and we listen to the music, and we listen to the readings, none of the words anyone says going in, till the moment I've been fearing comes, and an electrically operated curtain is drawn across the plinth where the coffin's resting, and I know I'll never see my mum again. Amy holds my hand.

I am thinking of the will she left behind. That she called to talk me through just a year ago. That she wrote in the knowledge neither Rachel nor I would be carrying on the life she had built up, that once she and Chris had both gone we'd sell the farm. I'm thinking of how easy it was then to reject that idea, and how important it seemed to me to maintain independence for myself. Maintain individuality. And how unimportant it seems to me now that Mum should have known that that wasn't what we wanted. We never needed to tell her at all. We could have let her go through life believing that things would carry on after she'd gone, and she might have been happier. We could have made our decisions now. And I am sure they would have been the same ones, but there would have been no need for her to know about them. We could have been kinder and said nothing at all. Then in the last year we might have been together, we might have been a family in the old-fashioned way. If any family is still that any more. The ceremony ends, the music plays. We file back out of the room in the knowledge that right now, as we shuffle together, as we hold each other, she has gone into the fire, she has gone for good.

'They don't do it while we're still here, do they?' asks Rachel, tears smudging the make-up on her face.

'I don't know,' I say. I watch Rachel as she presses the heels of her palms to her eyes, her body shaking as she cries, and I wish I could say something that would help. We get into the car and drive to the wake, and stand in silence, in awkward groups, as people come up to us to offer condolences and then step gently away again. I want to smile and thank them all for coming, but I find I can't, I don't have the energy. When everyone's gone, we go back to the farm, Amy driving with me in the passenger seat, Chris and Rachel getting a lift in another car. I look out of the window and think of nothing, head heavy, sleep tugging at the corners of my vision; I feel so tired now, I just want to sleep. This is the land of lost content, and I have wondered in the time since she died whether I was wrong, whether I want to be here, but I can't stir the feeling. I know I don't belong. I have to reject this inheritance, be a citizen of nowhere, even though it means in the years to come there will be less and less left of the life my mum lived. Chris will leave this place in time as well; one way or another our family will leave here, and then there'll be memories, a few sticks of furniture, and the furniture will mostly break with time, and the memories won't all be passed down. The way my grandchildren tell our stories will grow shorter and shorter, just a few sentences to say what became of us will one day very soon be enough. We see the house as we end the journey. I remember I never asked Mum if it was our family who built it. There's no one to answer that question now. Perhaps it will be somewhere in some old parish record. But that's beside the point; it's not the fact I'm after, it's the story. It's the tales I left it too late to ask her for that I'm thinking of as I let myself into this childhood home, the old rooms that hide their secrets just under the surface, burying memory, saying nothing.

Once we sat and read about Narnia here. And about Middle Earth, and the Faraway Tree, all the escapes from this world we lived in, while out on the hills the lambs grew up, apart from the ones who sickened and died and had to be disposed of. Shepherding taught you strange things about love. You couldn't devote too much attention to the lambs, for fear of infecting them with something that might kill them. People could be carrying all kinds of viruses that might be fatal to a lamb if it caught them. It was important to keep a safe distance. And you couldn't let yourself see what city people saw in lambs either, because you had to witness so many of them dying. The ones who keeled over and rotted in the fields, that needed to be burned or buried; the ones that went away to the butcher. I had gone to the livestock market in Hereford often enough, ever since I was young; I knew what became of them. You couldn't feel too much for the lambs you raised or you'd get your heart broken. I had been amazed when Mum and Chris started keeping dogs as pets, really, because it seemed like a softening that might hurt them. But it wasn't the whole story that shepherding taught you to close your heart up. When I was younger, I had bottle-fed lambs whose mothers had died; I had worked with Chris and Mum to put ropes round a sheep that had fallen into a ravine to lift it out again to safety. The truth was that you worked to stop yourself getting too attached to the animals in your care, but it meant nothing. Everything was still felt just as deeply. You just learned to turn your face away from what you were feeling. Pretend your heart was different from everyone else's, when really your heart beat just the same.

After we've drunk ourselves into a stupor, after we've staggered upstairs to bed, after we've slept through half the next morning then come downstairs to find Chris has been up for hours and all of the washing-up's already done, and he's out in the fields, and we've missed the chance to help him, we start to pack our bags and get ready to leave, then sit around drinking coffee till Chris comes back for his lunch. When he comes in he sees us and smiles, but a veil seems to have come down on what's left of this family, shrouding our sadness, preventing us from sharing our feelings with each other, or not knowing how. We eat some toast together, and not knowing what to say, we speak mostly of the weather.

'I'll understand if you need to come here a little less now,' Chris says all of a sudden. We look at him, not quite knowing what he means.

'Why?' I ask.

'Now your mother's not here. I'll understand it.'

'Don't be silly, Dad,' Rachel says.

'Maybe not you, sure,' Chris ploughs on. 'But Ed, if it feels strange. I'd understand it.'

'Is that what you want?' I ask. I don't want to sound confrontational, but I simply don't understand what he's saying.

'God, no,' Chris says. 'I just wanted you to know.'

Amy steps in and rescues me, because she sees I'm on the brink of crying.

'We'll still be here,' she says. 'You're still here, aren't you?'

Chris smiles, and seems relieved, eyes suddenly bright. 'That's good,' he says. 'This is still your home.'

'Yes,' Rachel says, and for a moment none of us look at each other.

'You'll be glad to have me out here,' Chris says, getting up from the table to clear away the plates. 'People need to get away from things sometimes. You'll be glad to have this place to escape to.'

I say to myself that I must make sure he's proved right about that; I must ensure the rhythms of my life don't change, and I keep coming back here. It will be harder now, it will be a stranger journey, but my stepfather still needs us to visit just the same. I look round the farm. The Welsh have a word for this feeling, *hiraeth*, but there's no word in English. And that's strange, really, when you think about it. Because what country could be more haunted, more crowded by the remnants and the echoes of lost worlds than rain-soaked England? How could a feeling be more English than this one? It is a failure of our language, a failure of our culture, not to know how to speak of the things left behind.

We come back to the city and I start to feel that the place is making me sick. The feeling of having been unmoored in the midst of life gets steadily worse, and I observe the process of one day turning into another with a growing bafflement, because nothing seems to have changed at all, though the landscape inside me feels unrecognisable.

We start to look for somewhere we can move to, spend the evenings on Zoopla and Rightmove, searching for ways of escaping the city. I find it's the only sure way of taking my mind away from what's happened, a kind of dream therapy. Project yourself into the lives in these photos, the bright colours, impossibly tidy kitchens; imagine that's you, not this life, not this feeling of dislocation. And not the life behind you either, the farm, the things that are gone, the people who died and the places where their lives happened, but the future, the unwritten, where you might step outside of where you come from and find out who you really are. We book some viewings. Strange to search for a new place in the midst of grief, and feeling distracted while trying to make what ought to be one of the most important decisions, and completely unable to focus. But this is how life always seems to happen to me. The future can never just be created on its own. The ebb of one part of life turning into the past is what always seems to give birth to the future, so that every decision ends up being a reaction to something, not a thing in itself; every new choice is born of a kind of grief.

We travel out into the home counties looking at flats and houses, till a day comes when we see one we can afford, and call up the estate agent, and plan our escape. Then once we know the place is ours, I worry we've rushed, that we've done the wrong thing. The flat we're leaving doesn't mean a great deal to me, it's something Amy and I are sharing while we wait to begin, but it is one more stage in this casting adrift that has overtaken me in the course of this year, so I worry about what I'm losing now as the day of our leaving approaches.

After you leave them behind, I've found that for a time some places become impossible to revisit. After I finished school, that was what happened to me. It disturbed me to walk down the street past my school as it filled me with thoughts of things that had ended. I stopped going back. When I visited Mum and Chris I'd just drive straight to them, and stay on the farm. I didn't go anywhere else, because everywhere else was a lost world, and the indifference of those places to the memories I kept of them unsettled me. But it wasn't like that for ever. I walked back down the street past my school a year or so ago, going round old places while visiting the farm, and though I felt some apprehension on the way there, wondering what dragons' teeth I had sown when I left, I found when I walked along that street that somehow the ghosts had faded, and the place wasn't haunted any more. Time has a curvature like the earth has curvature, and over time things pass out of sight.

I start to pack the flat up into boxes. Everything we own tucked away into boxes and turned into bulk, into ballast. I look at it all and feel it weighing me down. A few days later I have to go into town, and I'm waiting for a train on an Underground platform when I see Juliet looking at me through the crowd. She's waiting for the same train as I am, and she's seen me standing by the yellow line, and held back, I suppose, in case I wouldn't want to speak to her. I smile when our eyes meet, walk through the crowd, and we embrace awkwardly, like distant relations.

'Hi,' she says.

'Hello.'

'How are you?'

'You know.'

'I'm so sorry. I was so upset when I heard. How are your family?'

'Yeah, you know.' I wonder what people are supposed to say in these situations. 'How are you, though? Are you doing OK?'

'Oh, I'm fine. Carrying on.'

'Yeah.' We're both wondering now, I guess, whether we should ask each other about our partners, about Amy and whoever has moved into Juliet's flat.

'Where are you living at the moment?' she asks instead.

'Actually, we're moving house quite soon.'

'Oh, right? Where are you moving to?'

'Out to freedom, actually, out of the city.'

'Really?' She seems surprised by this. 'You don't need to be here for work?'

'I don't know,' I say. 'I guess we'll find out.'

She smiles at this, and shrugs. 'I guess so. I hope we'll still bump into each other now and then when you come to town.'

'Yeah, that would be good.'

'It would be nice to stay friends.'

'We ought to go for a drink sometime.'

'Wouldn't she mind that?'

'Who?'

'Your girlfriend. Is her name Amy?'

'That's it. No, I don't think she'd mind.'

Juliet seems uneasy now. 'OK. Well, maybe we should, then. I'd better get this train.'

'Me too.'

'Will you give my love to all your family?'

'I will. Thank you.'

'And are you going to be all right?'

I find this question difficult to answer. What does she mean? Not in the long run I won't be, no; in the long run, I'm going to end up dead, as we all are. But what does all right amount to in the meantime?

'I'll be fine,' I say. Then the train pulls in, and we get on at different doors, and I guess unless we meet by chance at some mutual friend's wedding sometime, we'll probably not see each other again. Strange how quickly life can change.

I go to my meeting and my boss says he could move me to the company that owns his business, and I could do the same work I already do for them, and make a bit more money. There's a vacancy opened up there, and he knows a lot is changing in my life, and the work might suit me, and could be done remotely most of the time. He could take on a kid to do what I've done, and he'd be doing his boss a favour because he'd be sending them someone good. It's one of those strange, kind-hearted interactions that happen now and then, when you're reminded that the people around you are watching how you're doing, and do want to help you, and do want to make sure you're OK. I always find such concern for my well-being slightly disquieting, but I tell him I'll take the job, and thank him for it. I ask him what I'll have to do there, and he's not certain. More advertorial, certainly. But they sell a lot more stuff than us, he says, they own a lot of different companies. So it'll be all sorts of things, but it's all the same work really. And perhaps I should run a mile from that. But if you can earn enough to live, and leave your work behind at the end of the day, that's not so bad, is it? I head home feeling calm about the future, because I know quite soon there'll be more money coming in.

Amy is on the sofa, watching TV. 'How was it?' she asks me.

'They offered me some work. Good work,' I say.

'That's good. Well done.'

'I saw Juliet on the Underground.'

'Oh really?' Amy shifts on the sofa, turns her body to face me. 'Was that OK?'

'It was fine. I'd felt bad for not getting in touch with her, actually. She got on well with my mum. She sent me a text when Mum died, but I didn't get back to her. I thought she might be upset by it all; I probably should have called.'

'Why didn't you?'

'I don't know. It all felt like the past.'

Amy turns the TV down.

'Did it feel strange to see her?'

'No, it was fine. There's nothing to talk about, it's fine.'

'You sure?' She looks at me. She always knows when I haven't finished talking. Usually better than I do. There is something very finely tuned between us, so we can hear each other when we need to speak.

'I've been feeling bad about the way all that ended,' I say.

'Why?'

'Because I thought it was something to do with her. And it wasn't her, really. I just wasn't happy.'

'And how are you feeling now?' she asks.

'Strange.'

'Why strange?'

'Because I shouldn't be happy, should I? I ought to be grieving. But everything that's happening now is my life. Everything that happened to me before this year, I feel like it was someone else's.'

Amy doesn't say anything to that. She smiles at me, as if she knows better than I do that there's something else I meant to say, and that wasn't quite it, I haven't quite said it. I look at her. I feel as if I'm waking from a dream. It was something else, something to do with love. Whatever that means. That was at the heart of it.

'I was thinking we should try and book a holiday this winter,' she says.

'Yeah?'

'Somewhere hot.' It feels impossible, so soon after getting back from the funeral and as we plan our stepping out of London, to be thinking about going away somewhere again. But Amy has learned to look further ahead than I have.

'Where do you want to go?' I say.

'I don't mind really. Just anywhere hot.'

'I'd like to see Turkey. Turkey and Greece have the best food.'

She checks the weather app on her phone. 'Not hot enough. Sixteen degrees on average in November. What about Bali?'

'I'd rather not fly that far.'

'Where, then?'

I try and remember the advertising I've been subjected to in the last year, seeking to dredge up a place, a name. 'The Azores, maybe? They're off Portugal, I think.'

She checks. 'Still too cold. But what about the Canary Islands?'

We look them up, read about them, look at pictures. All hotels look the same online. The same empty chairs, anonymous spaces. Why are there never any pictures of people? Who wants to stay in an empty hotel? Still, we look them all up.

'I don't know whether we'll be able to afford it,' I say after a while, not wanting to burst the bubble but knowing it has to be said. 'With the house move.'

'I know,' she says. 'I just thought it might be nice to look it all up and see what we'd need. Let's just save the pages maybe,' she continues, 'and come back to this in another month, and see how we're feeling then about money.'

And I say yes, though I know we're not going to find the money we'd need in the next month. But I say yes, because it's good to dream about something.

When I was twenty or twenty-one, I had this feeling that I was swimming in the shallows of the world, and there was a current pulling at me that would carry me into the way the world worked before long, into holidays and tax bills and weekends off and mortgages and pension funds and planning for decrepitude, and that for a moment I had an opportunity not to be caught in that tide, if I just had the intelligence to see some different direction, some different way of living, and strike out on my own into new water, and live clear of the current that took hold of most people's lives and wore them down. But somehow I never found a way. I dreamed of living away from this ordinary world, but the current caught me, and now here we are, and we make do, we fit our vast dreams into these circumscribed rhythms, and we look up holidays online, and make sure we have things to look forward to. But I can still remember the feeling that there must be other ways. There must have been different directions, if only I'd had the wit to see them in time before the current caught me.

Two months pass after the funeral before the call comes. I'm drinking coffee when it happens, staring out the window and thinking about going to the shops for milk because I've just used up the last of what was in the fridge, when I feel the vibration in my pocket, take out my phone to see Chris's name on the screen, and answer, and hear what I'd wondered might be coming.

'Ed, hi.'

'How are you, Chris?'

'I'm fine.'

'You sure? You don't have to be.'

'No, I'm fine. I wanted to talk to you about something, though. You and Rachel, maybe.'

'OK.'

'I won't be too mysterious. I think that I should sell.'

'OK.'

'It's not mine, is it? I just lived here. And keeping it going for you doesn't make sense. You and Rachel aren't going to want it.' He pauses here, lets a silence open up. Even now, at the very last moment, even now he wants to be wrong.

'No, I'm afraid we're not,' I say.

'I thought not. I think you're probably right about that. But it leaves me with a bit of a puzzle.' He pauses again, sounding a little emotional now. 'Of course I could keep it on for your mother. In memory of her. But it seems a little perverse somehow. And I'm knocking seventy, and I don't want to work this hard for ever.'

'No.'

'I could sell it, and take my pension, and buy a place that was easy to keep up, and that would be just fine with me, as long as you two didn't feel let down.'

'Why would we feel let down by that?'

'If you thought it was letting down your mother.'

'Of course not. Of course we wouldn't think that, Chris. We'd want you to be happy.'

'Sure.' Again, he stops speaking. 'Very modern idea, that. Very unhealthy.'

'Happiness?'

'Always running after it. I don't know why people do that, really. It will come and go. It seems a bit perverse to go in search of happiness this year, you know?'

'Of course. I'm sorry.'

'No, sorry; it's coming out wrong. And I appreciate the sentiment. I just don't know whether I understand it.'

'No.'

'Whenever anyone asks me whether I'm happy, I want to cry, really. I don't know how it would ever be possible just to say yes. Which is not to say that I'm an unusually unhappy person.'

'No, you're not.'

'I actually think that I'm quite a happy person. But I also have nights when – well, you know the kind.'

'Yes,' I say, 'I do.'

'But I do appreciate the sentiment; I'm sorry. I don't know why I'm responding so strangely.'

'Should Rachel and I come over sometime soon, so we can all talk about it?'

'I thought that might be good, don't you? Then we could have a dinner and have a few drinks. Tell old stories. You should bring Amy.'

'That would be nice.'

'All right, then. When would work for you?'

'Can I check diaries with Amy and text you?'

'Of course. I'll call Rachel in the meantime.'

Then he said goodbye and rang off, and I sat thinking of him, staring out the window. Thinking how barbaric it was that we had left him alone in that place, how like a cage it must have been for him, what it must have been like there over these last two months for him to have come to this decision so quickly. We should have stayed while he reached this point, at least. I feel ashamed at the thought of him sleeping there alone on that hill where you hear nothing, where the buzzards circle overhead, on that hill where everything is always slowly rotting away. I open my phone again, and text Rachel.

Chris called you?

There's a moment's wait, and then the ellipses of her reply

are pulsing on the screen, and I think of her on the other side of town, sitting like me, staring at her phone like I am.

Yeah. When can you go?
I can probably do this weekend?
OK.
If that works for you?
That's fine for me.

So we go. Amy accompanies me, and Rachel travels with us in the car this time, sitting next to Ivan in the back, a journey we haven't made together in a long while. The sat nav takes us out over Hammersmith flyover, and as we crest the road and start to descend out of the city and into the wide world, the sun strikes all three of us, lighting us up. For a moment the fantasy takes hold in me that this might be a launching-off point into anywhere, into memory, other worlds, into the past. Then the road glides down to ground level again, and we're motoring, the speed limit gradually releasing us, a leash getting longer as we go. We drive for most of Saturday morning, and get to the farm, and Chris has made lunch for us. Just bread rolls and tins of tomato soup. He never did much of the cooking. He stands in the doorway as we get out of the car, and I see that he's burst into tears, and find that I've started crying as well. This man who has been there virtually all of my life. This man who has shaped me as much as anyone else has. Alone now out here, with no one to help him. I wouldn't wish this on him. Wouldn't wish it on anyone. He holds out his hand to me. I give him a hug. We all go inside and Rachel goes straight to the kitchen without asking, makes a pot of tea, and we all see the soup waiting for us in a pan on the hob and imagine the night that Chris must have had, knowing we were coming, wondering what to do. The place looks clean, and I guess that he's hoovered. I guess he's worked all morning so that we can sit down in this place with it feeling uncluttered, and work out what we're going to do with it.

'Thank you so much for coming,' he says, tears still on his face. He wipes at his eyes and seems frustrated. I suppose he didn't want to cry.

'We're really glad to be here,' I say.

Rachel brings the tea through, and we talk about nothing for a little while, Amy doing most of the talking, because she can see that none of us knows what to say. Mum's not here now. She won't be again. We have to work out how to connect with each other now she is missing. And we will work that out, because we have to, for Chris's sake, and for our own, but we don't know yet, so Amy talks about photography, tutoring, the government, anything she can say to fill the air, and I feel grateful, and I guess that we all do, as we smile and nod and feel sheltered for a moment. Then once the pot's emptied and all the tea drunk, Chris leans forward and changes the subject, and it's like opening a door into the night and stepping out into a hailstorm.

'So I think we ought to put this place on the market.'

'OK,' Rachel says. 'I think that's a good plan.'

'But I don't want to sell it if that's not what you want.'

'No,' she says, 'don't think like that. What we want can come later. Right now we want this to be about you. If you don't want to be here any more, we want to sell it.'

'But it will be gone for ever then. You won't get it back.'

'No,' she says, 'we know that. And we won't want it later. We don't think you're selling it from under us.'

'I'm sorry if we made it feel unwelcoming to you.'

'You never made us feel unwelcome. It's just not who we are, Dad, that's all, OK?'

After lunch we look at estate agents' websites together. There's one place that sells most of the houses round this way, so it makes sense just to call them and ask them to come round. Chris speaks to a young woman who arranges for someone to visit on Monday, make a valuation, offer some feedback. Then we call another agent and book them for the same day, so that Chris can have a second opinion.

'I was thinking it would make sense for you to have whatever money we get for it that I don't need,' Chris says.

'Don't be silly,' I say, 'we don't need it now. You should be keeping it for now.'

'But you having it now could help with inheritance tax, and you could buy a home,' Chris carries on.

'And you having it now would mean that you were all right, and we didn't have to worry about you and money.'

Once the estate agents are booked, Chris starts walking round the house, going into the kitchen then the living room to take them in, breathing deeply, clearly emotional. We follow him, not speaking. Rachel takes his hand. I suppose he's been building up to this for some time. I remember he said almost the first instinct he had when Mum first got ill was to go on Zoopla. This place was always going to be too difficult to manage once their strength had gone. And there, in the back yard, the place where my grandfather landed when he fell, the weeds that grow up differently round the flagstones.

This place was always going to be too deep in memory for one person to weather it all on their own. There must be a sense of release to having started, I guess, as I watch Chris watching the garden. It must feel like shrugging off a heavy weight.

'You two ought to think about what you'd like to keep, maybe.' I look around the room at the things that were once the carapace of my childhood.

'Really?'

'I won't need somewhere as big as this. If there are things you want, you should pick them out.'

It's like a fresh grief, to think of taking things back with me. A new breaking up of the world I used to know. But at the same time, I can see that it's inevitable. He is right that we should let some of this go. I stand and stare at all of it. It's just such a big thought, it's hard to take in. There is an old chest by me that Mum used to say had once come from India, carrying my great-grandparents' luggage with them when they travelled to England at the outbreak of the First World War. There is a plate my family have kept fresh fruit on for as long as I've been alive, that came to this house from the woods in West Sussex with us, a decorative ceramic plate, dark and heavy, patterned with broad strokes of rich colour, reds and browns. There is a tall bookcase of old pine where Mum's cookbooks are still stored, all the favourite cookbooks falling apart. Delia Smith. *The Complete Vegetarian*. All of this was part of her once, part of me, part of my becoming someone. How much of it should I be carrying with me into the future? I look around me. I can't take it in.

'Perhaps that's something to work out later,' I say in the end. 'It'll be a while before you sell the farm, I think.'

Chris laughs. 'You've got that right. Farms can take years. It might be years before I can leave here.'

'If it's hard to be here, you could always rent it out to someone till it's sold, and live somewhere else?'

'No, it's all right. I think that would be stranger.' He turns around to look at us. 'There was something else I wanted to talk about with you while you were all here.' I nod, though my stomach drops, because it seems suddenly obvious. I feel certain I know what's coming. 'We ought to talk about scattering her ashes.' It's what I thought he was going to say. I can see Rachel flinching as the thought hits her. I fight the urge to turn away.

'Of course,' I say. 'Do you want to scatter them here?'

'I think that's what she'd have liked, don't you?'

'Unless you wanted to take them with you.'

Chris shakes his head. 'I'm not likely to forget her, am I? But this was her home, this is where she ought to end up. It's just slightly difficult, because once she goes—'

'It'll get harder to come visit her,' Rachel says. Chris nods, saying nothing.

'Not really, though,' I say. 'Not really.'

'Why not?'

'Because it's this valley, isn't it? This whole valley was what she loved. We can just come here, and that would be enough. We don't need to go traipsing through the garden.'

Chris nods at this, and almost seems to be smiling. 'Yes,' he says, 'I guess that's right.'

'Where are they now – they're here now, are they?' Rachel asks, seeming suddenly agitated. I suppose the thought of Mum actually being in the house with us in some way is freaking her out.

'Yes, over there.' Chris points into the corner, and there on the table where Mum used to do her sewing is a little urn I hadn't noticed until now. It's not conspicuous, half in shadow by the sewing machine, in front of the curtain by the French window. The world seems to stop for a moment while we look at it. None of us seem able to breathe.

'Fuck,' says Rachel. We keep on staring.

'Not today, though,' Chris says, 'not just yet. We don't need to scatter them till we go.'

'Sure,' I say.

'Unless you want to.'

'I don't think we'll ever want to. We should do it when we go.'

'Can we go outside for a bit?' Rachel says. 'I feel like I'm going to fall over or something.'

We go outside. I look up at the house. I think of the generations that it's been home to. Mum and Chris, who were happy here. My grandparents, to whom it was a place of grief. Up there on the roof, my grandfather climbed one day and must have looked at the view, which must be very beautiful from so high up, then ended his life and fell back down again. Because he had not had a proper life. Because his mother had been an invalid here, mad and bedbound, in need of constant nursing. And that was what became of him. A parent to his mother. Who had been nursed before that by her mother-in-law. Who had lived here all her life long, raised her child, passed the place on to him. All those lives poured into this one place. All that continuity about to be broken.

Let it break. It seems to me like good news after all that hardship. Let it all go. This place isn't who I am. It's somewhere I came from. I stand staring at it, and Amy takes my hand. She hasn't spoken for a long time. She looks at me now.

'You OK?' she asks me.

'Yes,' I say. 'I'm fine.' And we stand together in the garden.

All of us eat together that night, cooking together with music on loud, George Michael and Sting and Rickie Lee Jones because that's what Mum used to like to listen to. We play their music from Mum's old CDs, not on our phones, a way of having her here with us. None of us speaks about the urn in the sitting room, because after the shock of seeing it for the first time, I don't think any of us thinks of it as her. Mum was always a storyteller, and home always seemed to me to be in the stories, not in this house, not in the world at all, really. So it might be in the stories that we'll find her, if she's anywhere to be found. I remember when I was very young Mum used to say when I was falling asleep, 'I'll meet you in your dreams by the trees in the top field. Walk up to the top field and I'll be there.' Perhaps it's in those stories that she's still waiting.

All of us go to bed too late, then wake hungover the next morning. Chris looks tired, but there is a calm to him that I didn't see when we got here the day before. As if he's breathed out, let go of something.

'Thank you,' he says to us.

'Are you going to be all right?'

'I'll be all right,' he tells us. And I almost believe him. And I hope in time it will be true. After breakfast we pack the car, and then get ready to drive away. The next time I see the farm, I guess there will be a 'For Sale' sign in the driveway. I try to imagine what that will feel like. I suppose it will feel neither good nor bad, but just like letting go. Chris embraces each of us before we get in the car.

'Drive safe, won't you?'

'We'll call when we get home,' I say.

Then we get in the car and drive away.

Amy and I pack boxes, book a removal van, order a sofa for the new house online that's due to arrive in time for Christmas. Then comes moving day. The bell rings in the flat and I go to the door and the van's outside, waiting for our life to be loaded into it, everything we own wrapped up and muffled and sealed inside boxes, ready to disappear into the exhaust fumes and speed of the motorway, bliss of speed like forgetting that sidles along motorways. Three men tramp up and down the stairs to our flat all morning, and slowly the place clears, stripped of personality, of memory, and I realise that for as long as these things are in boxes, the rubble we've used to shore ourselves up in this little eyrie at the edge of the indifferent city, we have no home at all, nowhere and nothing to belong to. Because it's not quite in places. That's not the heart of belonging. It's not in things either, but they are part of it somehow; take away everything you have gathered and called your own and you're left unmoored and damaged staring at the empty living room, the filthy carpet. On my hands and knees I clean black mould from the walls that must have been giving us fever dreams all the time we've been here. I pour bleach straight on to the walls and scrub, and my head aches, and I daren't think of what I'm breathing in and what the mould and bleach are doing to my lungs. Then the back of the van is closed and all the objects we love enough to take with us to the next place are packed away and out of sight and don't give off any meaning any more. They're only a stacked van, shut up and leaving, driving away from us into the future. It dawns on me that every removal van you see is loaded with the same dense and potent meaning I can see in the retreating form of our van, what I think of as our van because our lives are crammed inside it – every one of them is always filled up with the lives of people, all the hopes of people, all the dreams they have that aren't going to come true.

After the van has gone we hoover the rooms and check the flat one last time, and the place feels haunted and absent, as if it has already forgotten us. Perhaps it's us that have been haunting the place all along. We load the house plants and Ivan last of all into the car and then head west, through the grim streets and industrial units, past the scaffolders and run-down pubs, through the angry traffic and over the tram lines till we get to the open roads and accelerate, away from the nightmare of our youth spent trapped in this place, away from the cramped compromise of living in the city, towards a future we haven't yet written.

We get to the new house after an hour's drive and find the removal men waiting in a layby, eating fish and chips from the shop across the way. We open up the house and they start to take the boxes of our life inside and stack them in the rooms. I join in, carrying the boxes through the front door while Amy takes Ivan out into the garden. It should feel like a beginning, these boxes filling up the house, but there's a sense of loss to it as well, I find. To love is to want to keep everything, not to miss anything, to live in grief at the thought of someday saying goodbye, until everything, every action, becomes a farewell. After the van has been emptied and the three men who got us to this new place have gone, we spend two days unboxing our possessions.

The house has seven rooms. The first when you come in through the small hallway is the living room, which faces north. There is a wood-burning stove in the hearth and bookcases built into the alcoves on either side of the chimney. Through a door at the back of the room you enter the dining room, and beyond that is the kitchen and the bathroom and the garden. The front of the house was built in 1880, but the bathroom is an extension, added only thirty or forty years ago. The garden is a bare vegetable patch where I won't grow anything because the dog would only dig it up again. I will sow grass seed and plant apple trees there instead, a russet and a James Grieve, and have an orchard of my own.

In the dining room, the staircase to the first floor is boxed off by wooden panels that date from the time of the house's construction. Climb them, twisting once as you go, and you will find three more rooms: the main bedroom at the front of the house where the traffic whispers past; the spare bedroom at the back of the house; and then another, strange room that narrows towards the back window like the prow of a ship and which I will turn into a study. From that window there is a view of hills stretching fifteen, twenty miles away, into the blue of distance. An olive tree in the next garden rising up above the vines that shelter the neighbours' patio. Telegraph wires looping away from view to join up the dots of the world. It is a far cry from the place we've left, the living room, one bedroom, kitchen and bathroom and the back stairs down to the garden and the garden shed. By coming to this place, changing the landscape around me, I feel almost as if I will become a different person.

After the removal van has gone, and the house is secure, and the dog's fed and watered, Amy gets back in the car with me. I've told her about my superstition, about always going back one last time to check the house we've left. We strap Ivan into the back of the car and drive back into the city, into the suburb where we used to live, up the road that's already forgotten us. I get out of the car and take the house key from my pocket, and Amy and I walk up to the front door that used to be ours. I start to put the key in the lock to open the door, and then check myself. Take the key back out. Turn back to Amy.

'We didn't leave anything, did we?'

'No,' she says. 'We didn't.'

'I might just post the key, then,' I say. She looks at me quizzically, wondering why I've changed my mind.

'Yeah?'

'We don't need to go back in, do we? We could just go home instead.'

So I post the key through the letterbox, and we walk away, because people are made out of stories, the ones that led to them and the ones they tell, and I don't have to live looking over my shoulder. I could try and tell a story about what happens next, see what that changes.

Next morning we wake up in the new house, everything beautiful and strange, everything a chaos of unpacked boxes, and we eat breakfast, then walk Ivan in the big park that separates our new village from the nearest town. We walk down gravel roads away from our house, past the church and the village hall and the working men's club, then over the cricket green till we come to the mouth of the park. My mum's not here in the world any more. But we're still here for a little while longer. Ivan runs away from us into the oak woods, and we follow him, down holloways that have carried people for almost a thousand years through this place to their squatters' homes or to work at the gravel pits that used to be beyond our cottage, that have now been built over by the council and turned into flats. Magpies chatter in an alder tree; two rooks are trying to get at their young. We come to the first of the streams that tiger-stripe the park, and cross the footbridge, the water running under. As we pass out of the tree cover into an open field, a deer bolts, sudden and startling, from the hedgerows, dashing past us towards the next stand of oak. Ivan hares after her before we can stop him, pitched headlong in a race he'll never win, vanishing away from us as we both call his name. We hurry after him along the path that bisects the field, two more visitors drawn through this place, caught in currents that will become our lives.

Acknowledgements

I would like to thank Suzanne Bridson, Kate Parker, Kirsty Dunseath, Kate Samano, Bobby Mostyn-Owen and everyone at Transworld who supported this work; Caroline Michel and the team at Peters, Fraser and Dunlop; my family, who I have borrowed from to tell this story; Lamorna Ash, George Duncan-Jones, Aidan Grounds, Beth Lawson, George Spender, Jonathan Webb, Laura Williams and her colleagues at Greene and Heaton, Lydia Wilson, and Charlie Young.

I wish the dedicatee of this novel, Sophie Christopher, was here to read it. Her death in 2019 was a huge blow to everyone whose life was made richer and happier by knowing her. She was the most brilliant colleague I have had the privilege of working with, and the most steadfast friend through an extraordinarily difficult period in my life. I count myself incredibly fortunate that books afforded me the opportunity to meet her. I choose to remember her by the unbelievably characteristic last thing she tweeted:

'Joy!'

Barney Norris has been the recipient of the International Theatre Institute's Award for Excellence, the Critics' Circle Award for Most Promising Playwright, a South Bank Sky Arts Times Breakthrough Award, an *Evening Standard* Progress 1000 Award, a Betty Trask Award and the Northern Ireland One Book Award. His work has been translated into eight languages. He is a Fellow of the Royal Society of Literature, teaches Creative Writing at the University of Oxford, where he is the Martin Esslin Playwright in Residence at Keble College, and regularly reviews fiction for the *Guardian*.